LIZZY LEGEND

LIZZY LEGEND

MATTHEW ROSS SMITH

ALADDIN
NEW YORK   LONDON   TORONTO   SYDNEY   NEW DELHI

FOR CHRISTINE MCNAMEE SMITH

ALADDIN
An imprint of Simon & Schuster Children's Publishing Division
1230 Avenue of the Americas, New York, New York 10020
First Aladdin hardcover edition January 2019
Text copyright © 2019 by Matthew Ross Smith
Jacket illustration copyright © 2019 by Oriol Vidal
All rights reserved, including the right of reproduction in whole or in part in any form.
ALADDIN and related logo are registered trademarks of Simon & Schuster, Inc.
For information about special discounts for bulk purchases,
please contact Simon & Schuster Special Sales at 1-866-506-1949
or business@simonandschuster.com.
The Simon & Schuster Speakers Bureau can bring authors to your live event.
For more information or to book an event contact the
Simon & Schuster Speakers Bureau at 1-866-248-3049
or visit our website at www.simonspeakers.com.
Book designed by Steve Scott
The text of this book was set in Jansen.
Manufactured in the United States of America 1218 FFG
2 4 6 8 10 9 7 5 3 1
Library of Congress Cataloging-in-Publication Data
Names: Smith, Matthew Ross, author.
Title: Lizzy Legend / by Matthew Ross Smith.
Description: First Aladdin hardcover edition. | New York : Aladdin, 2019. | Summary:
Unhappy at not being allowed to play on the boys' basketball team, Lizzy Trudeau,
thirteen, wishes to never miss another shot and soon finds herself playing in the NBA
against her hero, the greatest player of all time.
Identifiers: LCCN 2018015201 (print) | LCCN 2018023946 (eBook) |
ISBN 9781534420267 (eBook) | ISBN 9781534420243 (hc)
Subjects: | CYAC: Basketball—Fiction. | Ability—Fiction. | Wishes—Fiction. |
Middle schools—Fiction. | Schools—Fiction. | Sex role—Fiction. |
Fathers and daughters—Fiction.
Classification: LCC PZ7.1.S6447 (eBook) | LCC PZ7.1.S6447 Liz 2019 (print) |
DDC [Fic]—dc23
LC record available at https://lccn.loc.gov/2018015201

1st Quarter

They said it'd never happen, that I was crazy to even dream it. But there I was under the bright lights at the Mack Center, surrounded by twenty thousand screaming fans, millions more watching at home. And hunched beside me, so close I could see the vein flickering in his temple, the hole where his diamond earring would go, the individual sweat droplets forming on his shiny forehead: the most famous athlete in the world, the guy on my freaking cereal box—Sidney Rayne.

"You okay?" I asked him. "How you holdin' up?"

He chomped his gum, smirking.

"I'm worried about you, man. You look nervous. You always this sweaty?"

He peeked up at the scoreboard.

They were up one.

5.7 seconds left.

"I let you have that last one," I said.

"Oh yeah?"

"More fun when the pressure's on." I diagrammed the final play on my palm, like we did at the playground. "So here's me," I said. "Right here. That's you. What's gonna happen is I'm gonna catch the ball, right over here, I'm gonna start—"

"Surprise me," he said.

"You sure?"

He winked. "More fun that way."

It was actually hard to hear him. The crowd was chanting my name.

LIZ-ZY LE-GEND (clap clap clap-clap-clap).

LIZ-ZY LE-GEND (clap clap clap-clap-clap).

"Listen," I said, leaning closer now, shoulder to shoulder, "in case I don't get another chance, I just wanna say—"

"Save it, rook."

"Nah, man, please, just let me say this." I was surprised to find myself getting choked up. "I had your poster on my wall growing up—you know, the one with your legs pulled way up high, looks like you're flying? I used to look up every night before bed and I'd think: *Man, Rayne's a punk. If I could just get one shot at him . . .*"

He laughed.

"Took me a while," I said, reknotting my braid, "longer than I expected. But here I am, and here you are. And I just wanna say—"

"Don't say nothin', rook. Just show me what you got."

He was right. There was nothin' left to say. What happened next, we both knew, would outlive us both. It was a defining moment. The kind every baller lives for.

I caught the ball just outside the arc. I started right, got him leaning . . . then "drew the curtain." I pulled the ball hard across my body, the famous Trudeaux crossover.

Later, Sid.

Three. I pulled up at the foul line.

Two. I lifted the rock.

One. A picture-perfect release, wrist tipped down like the head of a swan.

The ball hit the front of the rim, skipped forward, kissed the backboard, hit the front of the rim again, toilet-bowled around twice, sank 99 percent of the way in, then, somehow, at the last instant . . . spun out.

I stood there, palming my knees, stunned.

2

A second later, I was back at the playground in Ardwyn. The rocking, sold-out arena was now an abandoned factory with all the windows knocked out. The gleaming hardwood was now cracked, weedy cement. My only fan was a Buddha-shaped black boy in an unzipped winter coat, making a wood-chip angel beneath the monkey bars.

"We win?" he called, flapping lazily.

"Nah," I said. "Lost by one."

Toby sat up. It looked more like he'd *squashed* an angel. "There's something wrong with you," he said, squinting. "You know that, right?"

He shuffled over, sleepy-eyed, schoolbag on his shoulder. He had to keep his legs a certain distance apart or his baggy jeans would fall down. "I mean, are you *that* competitive? You can't even let *yourself* win?"

"I wasn't playing against myself."

"Oh, you were playing against Rayne again. Right. Forgot."

Wood chips were sticking out of his flat-top. He pinched one out like a Jenga tile and flicked it at me. I spun the ball on my finger—my *middle* finger—and looked over at the brick row houses on Dayton Road. Each had a little cement stoop and a weathered plastic awning.

"I'm just gonna shoot a few more," I said. "Go ahead. I'll catch up."

"Dude, haven't you been out here since *sunrise*?"

"Yeah."

"For the love of god, *why*?"

"Because Dad won't let me out before then."

Toby frowned. He flicked another wood chip at me and waddled off toward school, holding his breath as he passed beneath the sneakers strung along the power lines like dead birds.

EIGHTH-GRADE BASKETBALL TRYOUTS

Jim Gulch—Ardwyn Middle School Boys' Basketball Coach
You know what I remember most about that day, for some reason? The first thing that comes to mind? Her *sneakers*. I don't even remember what it was about them. They were, like, bright or something? Like blindingly bright? I remember joking that I needed sunglasses to look at them. I guess she got a new pair for tryouts.

Lizzy Trudeaux
Oh, god. [Sighs.] Nah, they weren't new. Dad had enough to worry about. I couldn't ask him for a new pair. I just couldn't.

Molly Church—Head Cheerleader/Identical Twin
I'll be honest. It was kinda weird.

Megan Church—Head Cheerleader/Identical Twin
Totally weird.

Molly Church—Head Cheerleader/Identical Twin
I mean, we'd never even *talked* to Lizzy.

Megan Church—Head Cheerleader/Identical Twin
She's scary.

Molly Church—Head Cheerleader/Identical Twin
Not scary. Just, like, *intense*.

Megan Church—Head Cheerleader/Identical Twin
Yeah. One day I saw her doing push-ups in the
stairwell.

Molly Church—Head Cheerleader/Identical Twin
So this one day in study hall we were painting our
nails and she comes up, all curious, and just starts,
like, *staring*.

Megan Church—Head Cheerleader/Identical Twin
Watching us like we were zoo animals or
something.

Molly Church—Head Cheerleader/Identical Twin
And so, trying to be nice, I'm like, "Hiiiii, Lizzy. Do
you want us to paint your nails?"

Megan Church—Head Cheerleader/Identical Twin
She thought this was funny.

Molly Church—Head Cheerleader/Identical Twin
God, she's so *weird*.

Megan Church—Head Cheerleader/Identical Twin
And then—we couldn't believe it—she went
up and took a bottle of Wite-Out right off Mr.
Zaleski's desk and started painting her *sneakers*,
those disgusting sneakers with duct tape on
them, the same way: dab it on, brush, blow,
repeat.

Toby Sykes—Trudeaux's Best Friend
Yeah. So the big day finally comes and Lizzy shows
up in these painted white sneakers.

William Richards—Eighth-Grade Basketball Player
Like she didn't already stand out enough.

Toby Sykes—Trudeaux's Best Friend
Imagine this long line of boys and just this one—

Lizzy Trudeaux

[Raises eyebrows.]

Toby Sykes—Trudeaux's Best Friend

Like I said, this whole line of *basketball players*, and one with these painted—

Jim Gulch—Ardwyn Middle School Boys' Basketball Coach

[Blows whistle.] "Everyone on the baseline! *Now!*"

Lizzy Trudeaux

The first hour we didn't even touch a ball. We just ran. And ran. And ran.

Jim Gulch—Ardwyn Middle School Boys' Basketball Coach

[Blows whistle.] "Again!"

Toby Sykes—Trudeaux's Best Friend

Oh, god. I'm winded just *thinking* about it.

Jim Gulch—Ardwyn Middle School Boys' Basketball Coach

[Blows whistle. Clicks stopwatch.] "Again!"

William Richards—Eighth-Grade Basketball Player

We were all bent over, gasping.

Jack Schulte—Eighth-Grade Basketball Player
Sean Dormond was curled up in the fetal position.

Sean Dormond—Eighth-Grade Basketball Player
Jack was puking in the trash can. I looked over—

Jim Gulch—Ardwyn Middle School Boys' Basketball Coach
Lizzy wasn't even breathing hard.

Jack Schulte—Eighth-Grade Basketball Player
She was just standing there.

William Richards—Eighth-Grade Basketball Player
She was rolling her neck like, *Wait, did we start yet?*

Lizzy Trudeaux
Coach Gulch had this cheap wire-bound notebook. I remember after the last sprint he looked down at his stopwatch, then at me, then at the watch again, then shook his head and scribbled something in the notebook.

Jack Schulte—Eighth-Grade Basketball Player
The best player—besides Lizzy—was Tank.

Toby Sykes—Trudeaux's Best Friend
Dude was huuuuuge. Like six six, two hundred fifty pounds in eighth grade.

Megan Church—Head Cheerleader/Identical Twin

He got his arm stuck in a Pringles can one time.
Remember that?

Molly Church—Head Cheerleader/Identical Twin

Yeah, they had to cut it off.

Megan Church—Head Cheerleader/Identical Twin

The Pringles can. Not his arm.

Toby Sykes—Trudeaux's Best Friend

Tank and Lizzy had a little history, too.

Sean Dormond—Eighth-Grade Basketball Player

Yeah. Back in first or second grade, there was this
legendary fight at the playground. It all started
when—

Molly Church—Head Cheerleader/Identical Twin

Oh, I remember that! Lizzy knocked out Tank's
front teeth!

Megan Church—Head Cheerleader/Identical Twin

Yeah, on the basketball court. She did this, like,
running jump punch—*bam!*

Molly Church—Head Cheerleader/Identical Twin

And then, wait—didn't she, like, *pick up* the teeth?

Megan Church—Head Cheerleader/Identical Twin

Yeah, she stepped over him, with the whole school watching, and she's like—

Molly Church—Head Cheerleader/Identical Twin

"You mind if I borrow these?"

Megan Church—Head Cheerleader/Identical Twin

And that night she cashed them in with the Tooth Fairy!

Lizzy Trudeaux

[Frowns.] I didn't pick up the teeth. That's disgusting. But he *did* deserve it. And I'd do it again.

Toby Sykes—Trudeaux's Best Friend

No, no, no. It wasn't on the basketball court. It was over by the swings. Tank said something about her dad. Or was it her mom? Well, anyway, it doesn't matter. The point is that Lizzy and Tank already have this long history, right, and now they're going at each other in tryouts. Tank starts off strong. He's killing everyone. He's just so freaking *big*. The skinniest kid in the whole school, Josh Gowen, is trying to guard him.

Lizzy Trudeaux

Josh is like one of those inflatable tube men at used car dealerships.

13

Toby Sykes—Trudeaux's Best Friend

Yeah, Josh is flailing. He just keeps getting "tanked on" over and over. Finally, Lizzy's like, "Yo, Josh, switch." And Josh is like, "But you're a . . . guard." Of course meaning, *But you're a . . .* girl. Lizzy frowns and chucks Josh out of the way—

Lizzy Trudeaux

This is actually one of my favorite moves. It takes a little setup, but it works almost every time against a bigger player. He's got me pinned behind him. I spread my feet wide and fight to hold my ground. After a few bumps, he lowers his left shoulder, and that's the signal—that's how I know he's about to charge. So I sidestep.

Jim Gulch—Ardwyn Middle School Boys' Basketball Coach

Oh yeah, I remember that. Tank fell right on the ball. It made this loud *oof* noise. And the whole gym went quiet. It was hard to tell if the air had come out of the ball or his lungs or both. He rolled over, furious, face red as a—

Lizzy Trudeaux

I took the ball and dribbled down the other end and swished another three.

Toby Sykes—Trudeaux's Best Friend

Then she looked back and blew him a kiss. I was dyin', man.

Lizzy Trudeaux

Coach Gulch smirked and scribbled again in his notebook.

3

When the final roster was posted outside the locker room, Toby bumped me out of the way with his big butt and checked the list first. Halfway down, he shrieked like his finger was stuck in an electrical socket.

"What?" I said. "I thought you *wanted* to get cut."

"I *did*! He put me on the team!"

"Relax, Drama Boy. I'm sure you can get yourself kicked off."

"Yeah. You're right."

It made more sense when I noticed the asterisk, aka Mark of Shame, beside his name. Down the bottom, in small print, it said: *Team Manager.

I took a deep breath and ran my finger down the list.

Once, twice, three times.

"That's funny," I said.

"What?"

"Nothing."

"You're on there, right?"

"No."

"Maybe they put you right on the high school team. Didn't your dad do that? Play for the high school team when he was in middle school?"

To be totally honest? I still wasn't worried. I'd been featured on ESPN.com the previous summer. I was *definitely* the best point guard, boy or girl, in the district. Everyone knew it. It had to be a mistake. I went to Coach Gulch's office. "Coach?"

"Oh hey, Lizzy. Come on in."

Gulch's office was a janitor's closet that'd been "repurposed." It still reeked of dirty mops and bleach. Hundreds of manila envelopes were stacked up to the ceiling on both sides of his desk. Every time Gulch finished a notebook, he sealed it in an envelope, signed across the flap, and mailed it to himself, thereby copyrighting, he claimed, all the original notes and plays within. The problem was that he had a terrible memory, so he couldn't remember the plays, and he couldn't open the envelopes without spoiling the copyright—what was known as a "Gulch-22," a riddle that couldn't be solved.

"Heck of a show you put on out there," he said, peeking up over his supermarket-bought glasses. "*Really* impressive. Reminded me of your old man. And I don't say that lightly."

"Thanks, Coach."

Gulch leaned back and mounted his size-sixteen Reeboks on his desk, accidentally kicking over a can of Dr Pepper. "Son of a . . ." If nothing else, he certainly *talked* like a real coach. He mopped up the soda with an ungraded Scantron test. He was the school's health teacher, but everyone knew he just played movies all the time so he could draw up new plays. "What can I do for ya?"

"I saw you posted the final roster," I said.

"This about Sykes?"

"*Toby?*"

"Yeah, he's a goof. But every team needs one. Keep things light. And someone to fill up the water jug. You know."

"It's not about Toby."

"No? What's up?"

"It's just . . . I think you forgot to put my name on the list."

Gulch dropped his glasses on the desk and rubbed his eyes with the base of his palms. "Listen . . . you know I can't . . . I just thought it'd be fun if . . ."

I glared.

"Come on," he said. "I can't *actually* put you on the team. You understand. Your tryouts are next week. I was just letting you—"

"Tell me I'm not good enough," I said.

"Huh?"

"Tell me I'm not good enough and that's why I'm not on the team, and I'll go."

"Listen," he said again, "I'm *sorry*, okay? My hands are tied on this one. If it were up to me, I'd say put the best five on the court. Period. But it's not up to me. League rules. Boys can't play with girls, and girls can't play with boys. No exceptions."

The bell for the next period rang.

He stood, searching for something under all his envelopes.

"Coach," I said. "I'm the best player in the school. You know it."

"No one's disputing that."

"And besides, you should want a girl on your team."

He found his keys. Smiled.

Was he even listening?

I stepped forward. "I said you should *want* a girl on your team."

"I'm sorry, Lizzy. I have class."

"These boys are *soft*."

"I'm sorry, Lizzy, I just can't . . ."

When I finally got to the playground after school, I wiped my eyes with my sleeve and looked around. It was the same dreary place I'd practiced a thousand times, but I swear for a second I had no idea where I was. The voices started up in my head.

You seen that Lizzy Trudeaux play?

Oh yeah, man. Caught a game last week. She's great. . . .

I heard that!

Yeah. Really amazing. Maybe the best I've ever seen. . . .

Really?

I'm serious! You gotta see her! She's incredible . . .

. . . for a girl.

4

The drug dealers were lurking at the edge of the playground—the normal shift change was at sunset—but I didn't care.

I kept shooting, a lone ponytailed silhouette beneath the flickering light. Same routine every time. Four dribbles. Bend the knees. Deep breath. *Swish.*

"Easy," Dad said, appearing out of nowhere. "It's not the ball's fault."

He was in his short-sleeved blue gas station shirt. Hands in pockets. "Gulch called me," he said, rocking up on his toes. "You wanna talk about it?"

People said Dad was always soft-spoken, but I wondered. Didn't he look so joyful with all his teammates in those old black-and-white photos? So full of life, with his long hair and sideburns, waving a towel over his head? Holding up the state championship trophy?

Now he was different. You know the effort it takes to call upstairs to someone? That was the effort it took for Dad to speak at a normal volume.

Four dribbles. Bend the knees. Deep breath. Swish.

I blinked and the ball was back in my hands. They used to

call him the Wizard, because of his first name, a family name that he hated, Ozzie.

The Wizard of—you get it.

He went by his middle name, Rick.

Four dribbles. Bend the knees. Deep breath. Swish.

"That one was a little off," he said, catching it before it hit the ground.

Billy Fritz, the cashier at the 7-Eleven, once told me that Dad used to catch *his own* made shots before they hit the ground. People in town were always doing that. Dad's greatness was like a precious ember everyone in Ardwyn had to keep blowing on or it would go out.

"I swished it," I said.

"Yeah, but not a *pure swish*."

"A what?"

"A pure swish. You do it right, the ball passes right through like there's no net at all. Totally silent. Try again."

I shot.

Swish.

"Nope, still heard it."

I shot.

Swish.

"Nope. But closer. Keep tryin'."

I shot.

Swish.

He pinned the ball on his hip. "Listen, I gotta go. Five more and that's it. You hear me? There's a French bread pizza in the freezer. And, hey, don't forget to turn the oven off this time, okay?"

"I thought maybe the house would be worth more if I burned it down."

"Not funny."

"Oh right, we don't have insurance, either."

Dad pressed his lips. *You okay, Lizzy Bean? Because if you're not, god help me, you know I'll go to that school and raise hell.*

I squinted. *Yeah, Dad. I'm good.*

He snapped me the ball and limped away, head down, breath fogging in the cold. I began my routine again, eager to keep trying for this mythical—what had he called it?—pure swish. But then a thought came to me. I paused before shooting. "Hey, Dad."

He turned back.

Swish.

"Thanks for listenin'."

woke up at four instead of four forty-five the next morning. I broke Dad's sunrise rule and began my normal workout in the dark. *You say I can't have this?* I thought, sweeping the court from end to end with a big industrial-size broom. *Well, watch this. I'm just gonna work harder.*

I swept in long straight lines, all the way up, then all the way back. I carried all the broken glass to the Dumpster using a soggy Big Mac box as a dustpan. I crawled across the cracked cement, plucking the weeds that had sprouted up overnight. I scraped up a wad of gum stuck to the three-point line.

That day, a special occasion, there was a drug needle on the far sideline. I slid my hands into the husks of Dad's old, oily work gloves so I didn't get pricked. I slid the needle into a plastic Pepsi bottle, carefully, like it was an antique ship-in-a-bottle in some rich guy's office or something. I twisted the cap extra tight, and—

What's that thing our hippie guidance counselor told us about? The invisible scoreboard where the gods keep track of all the good and bad things you do when no one's looking?

Oh right—*karma*.

I shot the needle-in-a-bottle into the Dumpster, holding my finish high like Dad taught me, wrist tipped down like the head of a swan.

Two points.

6

And now that the dance floor was cleared, so to speak, I could *really* get to work.

I zigzagged between little orange cones. *Keep your head up. Keep your head up. Keep your head up.* I tied a rope around my waist and dragged a twenty-pound tire up the full length of the court. Up and back, up and back, up and back. I did that thirty times, imagining that Sidney Rayne was chasing me, trying to steal the ball.

Next, I stood at midcourt and circled my tattered ball around my body. Ginger was bright and tacky when I first rescued her from the discount bin at Walmart, but now she was saddle tan and smooth as a peach.

I tied on Dad's rusty ankle weights and rose up on my toes until my calves burned. By now, lights were blinking on along Dayton Road. *Working class. Up with the sun.* I did wall sits until my thighs twitched. I ran suicides until I puked in the grass.

Then I shot jumpers.

After all that—just a normal morning for me—it was seven thirty. Reaching down for Ginger, dripping sweat, I saw Toby waddling toward the court.

"You puked again?" he said, hauling up his pants.

I shrugged.

"Ah," he said. "A lady never pukes and tells."

He scooped up Ginger and stumbled around the court, dribbling once for every three steps. "Three . . . two . . . *one* . . ." His shot missed everything, even the backboard. The ball rolled over by the monkey bars. "Annnnnd they still win," he said, flashing those goofy-colored braces I joked he'd never get off. "They were up by forty!"

"Convenient," I said.

"Well, it's the only time I get in the game. I'm just trying to make it as realistic as possible."

I smirked. "I gotta rinse off. I'll meet you."

For some reason, that day, as I passed beneath the sneakers strung along the power lines, I looked back. It was just after sunrise, and for a half second the abandoned factory shimmered like one of those ancient castles you see on TV—you know, with the stone towers and the ivy swirling up its walls? But then I blinked and everything became its dreary self again. The ivy sank into the walls and became ghetto ivy. *Spray paint.*

That day after school, I was in a really bad mood. Toby and Tank and all the other boys had their first day of practice. The girls' tryouts weren't until the following Monday. I'd just left school and was walking home. I was doing this thing—maybe you've done it?—where I kicked the same pebble over and over. Every time I kicked it as hard and straight as I could. It wasn't quite as good as shooting free throws, therapy-wise, but it helped. A little.

As I neared the playground, I felt a familiar buzzing in my pocket.

I gnashed my teeth and tried to ignore it. The debt collectors had been calling me nonstop. Sometimes four or five times per day. It didn't matter that I was thirteen, apparently. I was next of kin, so they could harass me day and night.

"JUST STOP!" I answered. "OKAY? JUST STOP CALLING. I TOLD YOU. HE DOESN'T HAVE—"

It wasn't a debt collector.

No.

It was *worse*.

It was one of those robocalls.

"*Con-grat-u-la-tions,*" the mechanical voice said. "*You have been pre-sel-ected for—*"

I laughed.

It was all I could do.

"*Con-grat-u-la-tions,*" the mechanical voice said again. "*You have been pre-selected for—*"

"Sorry," I said. "I'm a little busy. I have to—"

And just before I hung up, I heard:

"*One free wish.*"

I narrowed my eyes.

"Say what?"

"*To re-deem your wish, press one. For more op-tions, press—*"

I pressed one.

"*Thank you. Please hold.*"

I waited.

And waited.

Elevator music played.

Smooth jazz.

And then:

"*Hell-o. This call may be re-cor-ded for qual-ity assur-ance. Please say your name af-ter the beep.*"

Beep.

"Um, Lizzy?"

"*Hell-o, Um-Lizzy?*"

It patched in my human voice for my name.

"*It is nice to speak with you to-day, Um-Lizzy?*"

My eyes darted around.

A white van was parked on the corner.

Was this some kind of prank?

Could Toby have pulled this off?

28

"Please state your wish af-ter the beep."

"Wish?"

"Please state your wish af-ter the beep."

"I'm confused."

"Please state your wish af-ter the beep."

This was weird, man. I probably should've just hung up. But in the same way you might as well flip a penny into the fountain at the mall when you walk by, I said the first thing that came into my mind—my secret fantasy: "I want to never miss another basketball shot for the rest of my life."

"Thank you, Um-Lizzy? Your wish has been re-cor-ded. Let us re-view. Your wish is: 'I want to never miss another basketball shot for the rest of my life.' *Is this cor-rect? If so, press one. If—"*

I pressed one.

"Thank you. Good-bye."

8

Well, that *was weird*, I thought, staring down at my phone.
But I didn't dwell on it for long.

I had five hundred more jump shots to get up before dark.

I carried my ball around the broken merry-go-round, ducked beneath the rusty monkey bars (where the outline of Toby's wood-chip angel from the week before was still faintly visible), and onto the basketball court. I stomped on a rolling cigarette butt, carried it to the Dumpster, and made my way back to the ghosted-out foul line.

Same ritual as always.

Four dribbles. Bend the knees. Deep breath . . .

Just as I shot, a gust of wind blasted in from the right.

The ball drifted left . . . but then it did something impossible.

It changed direction. The ball curved back into the wind like a heat-seeking missile and darted down through the rim.

I laughed.

You ball outside long enough, you'll see some crazy things.

Gust number one blows the ball left.

Gust number two blows it back.

Then, suddenly, like someone in a control room somewhere

had pushed a button, the downpour started. I'd never seen anything like it. The raindrops were hatching on the court like a plague of spiders. Lightning flashed across the sky. I closed my eyes and began my routine.

Four dribbles. Bend the knees. Deep breath . . .

I closed my eyes and shot. The ball, passing through the rain, sounded like a radio dial cutting through heavy static.

And then . . .

Somehow . . .

I heard it.

It was the squeak of a sneaker on freshly waxed hardwood.

It was the horn blaring when you check into the game.

It was the shriek of a referee's whistle.

The crunch of frozen grass in the winter.

The soft scrape of sidewalk chalk in the summer.

The turning of a heavy, old-fashioned key.

A single string plucked on a violin.

The radiator clanking in my room.

A car door lock popping up.

My mother's voice.

It was all of those things at once, and many more.

Had you been there, standing under the basket, you know what you would've heard?

Nothing.

A pure swish.

2nd Quarter

9

On September 25, 2009, my mother, Nora Collins Trudeaux, was jogging along Niles Road very early in the morning. She was training for an Ironman, the competition where you swim 2.4 miles, bike 112 miles, and run 26.2 miles, all in a row. She was hit from behind by a Toyota 4Runner driven by an overnight security guard named Jack Perkins who fell asleep on his way home from work. Dad and I were both in the hospital room when she died. I was asleep on one of the chairs we'd dragged in from the hallway. When I shut my eyes, she was breathing. When I opened them, she wasn't. I had a dream about ninjas.

There was a funeral.

A burial.

A reception.

There was cake.

Dad made me go see a therapist for a few months afterward. I resisted, of course, but looking back I'm glad that I went. I always felt better—actually physically lighter—when I left Dr. Kelly's office. She was divorced. She had lots of framed academic degrees on her wall, and also a painting of a sailboat in a storm. The boat was tipped *way* up on its side; the man was leaning *way* back, almost parallel to the choppy water. It was real somber: all blues and grays and blacks. Dr. Kelly said: "You like that painting?"

I shrugged.

"You've been staring at it for the past twenty minutes. Must be *something*."

I shrugged again.

Dr. Kelly leaned forward. She was the first woman I ever saw wearing a tie. She lifted it off her leg, rubbed the silk between her fingers, then set it back down again. "What do you think when you see that painting, Lizzy? I mean—how does the experience of looking at it make you *feel*?"

"I don't know."

"There's no right or wrong answer."

"I know. I just . . . I don't really feel anything."

"Nothing?"

"I don't know. It's just a stupid painting."

She smirked. I liked Dr. Kelly. She asked lots of mushy questions, but I didn't hold it against her—that was her *job*. "I'm going to tell you something that helps me when I'm feeling sad, okay? Maybe it will be helpful to you, and maybe it won't. But I'm just going to say it and you can store it away for later. You see those dark patches on the surface of the water? You know what those are?"

"Oil?"

"Good guess. But no."

"Fish?"

"Even better, but still no. They're *wind*."

I squinted.

"Experienced sailors know to scan the water for those dark patches. But sometimes they gust out of nowhere—"

"It's, like, one of those things," I said. "From Language Arts class. A metaphor."

"That's exactly right," she said. "The reason I like this painting—the reason I have it here—is because it reminds me of something important. It reminds me that there will always be those dark patches in life, those gusts, and no matter how good a sailor you are, or how fast your boat is, you can't outrun them. You can't go around them. You have to go *through* them. You see what I'm saying, Lizzy? Lizzy?"

I'd drifted off into one of my daydreams again. I was remembering a time Mom and I were sitting on the stoop, watching some older boys play half ball in the street. Half ball's the one where you cut a tennis ball in half and hit it with a broomstick. We were sitting there watching, and a scuffle broke out; I don't know why; someone pushed someone. Mom hopped up, but the fight fizzled. She sat. "You know how to throw a punch, Lizzy?"

I was tonguing the smooth gap where my front teeth used to be. "Yeah."

She turned her body and held up both palms.

I narrowed my eyes and smashed her right palm.

Her hand closed around my fist. Her hands were shockingly strong. "No. You do that and you'll break your wrist." She tapped the groove between my middle and pointer knuckles. "You lead from here, from the inside of the hand. Got it?"

She raised her mitts again.

This time, the smack was even louder.

She sighed. "You and that Sykes boy have been watching too many movies. Keep it short."

I punched again. This time a more controlled strike.

"Good. But hit through it. Like you're following through on your shot."

I hit through the target.

"Good."

Just then, the half ball rolled over to Mom's feet. She scooped it up and turned it over it like she'd found a penny and was trying to decide if it was lucky or not. "Your grandfather was a boxer," she said. "A featherweight. You know that, right?"

"Back in Ireland?"

She nodded.

"He was tough?"

"Oh, he was the biggest softie I ever knew. He used to carry bugs outside and let them go. Drove Mom nuts. She'd yell: 'It's just gonna come back in, John!' And he'd mutter"—I loved when Mom put on her Irish brogue—"he'd mutter, 'Well dat's his choice.' Dad was a champion mutterer. I don't think he ever opened his mouth in his life, except to sip his tea. He showed me what I just showed you, when I was your age. He said, in his way, real soft, 'Now listen, Nor. When ya feel scared—in dat first rush—yer impulse'll be ta run—but don't. No. Ya go forward. Ya cut off what's comin' at ya, ya knock it off balance. Ya knock it off balance, ya create an opening—that's what it's all about. Ya go *forward*.'" Mom whipped the half ball back to the boys in the street. The power of her arm startled them. They gaped, limp-armed.

*She added the standard disclaimer that fighting should always be my last resort.

**Throwing a punch was just a general life skill, like those patches all the other girls my age were getting on their Brownie sashes.

"But you used to get in fights all the time," I said.

"Not all the time."

"Matt Murphy told me that you knocked his dad out cold once."

She swept her hair from her face and laughed. "I did. And he deserved it. But things were different back then. The boys were a lot rougher. They're all Mr. Softees now." That's what she called Dad when they were teasing each other—Mr. Softee, like the ice cream truck. Sometimes, she hummed the music just to get a rise out of him.

"Dad says I have your temper," I said.

She pinched my chin roughly, tilted my face up, and peered down into the secret room behind my eyes. "That's true," she said. "But you're still more like your father, Lizzy. More than you know."

10

T he Monday after the spooky robocall, Coach Gulch called me into his office. "Have a seat," he said.

"*Where?*"

"Move some of those envelopes. There's a chair under there somewhere."

In addition to about seventy-five thousand manila envelopes, Gulch also had one of those old-fashioned projectors, the kind with the two big reels. He flipped a switch, and the reels clunked into motion. It reminded me of train wheels making that first, heavy turn. A ghost blinked awake on the far wall. "You recognize this game?"

Of course I did. It was the Pennsylvania state finals. There was Dad. Number twenty-four. He had those goofy sideburns. The high socks with the red stripes on them.

"We'd lost to Spring Valley in the final the year before," Gulch said. "God, look at those shorts. You can see our thighs. It's borderline indecent."

I watched the ghosts moving on the wall, cursed to repeat their same actions for all eternity.

"The day before the game, Valley's star player, Paul Smith, was quoted in the paper saying he was going to hold your dad to single digits."

"Smith played for Denver."

"And Utah. And Seattle. And Detroit. Had a nice pro career. Your dad *destroyed* him. Sixty-two points. After the game, Smith said what everyone said after they played us: 'That was the greatest basketball player I've ever seen.'"

"I already know all this, Coach."

Just before the final play, when Dad did his famous cross-over move, pulling the ball sharply across his body—"drawing the curtain," they called it—freeing himself to make the winning shot—Gulch clicked off the projector. Dust motes swirled up. Gulch waved them away, coughing. "Listen, I made some calls. Explained the situation. And good news: You can play."

I didn't say anything.

"Did you hear me? I said you can *play*. With *us*. They granted you a waiver. You can play, starting today." He rubbed his hairy hands. "God, Lizzy, these boys have no idea what's about to hit 'em."

"I don't know, Coach."

"Are you serious?"

Part of me was overjoyed.

I could play!

On the boys' team!

But another part was annoyed that I'd had to deal with this at all.

"Maybe I'll just play for the girls' team," I said. "Coach Varisanno's a good coach. She played D-3."

"You're not hearing me. You're a *Trudeaux*. You're going to play for *me*. I mean, for us."

"I don't know. I need to think about it."

"What's there to think about?" he said. "It's simple. To get better, you need to play against the best competition possible, *right*?"

"Maybe I'll just go play for the Bells, then."

The Bells were the pro team in Philly.

Gulch did one of those half laughs where you expect the other person to fill in the other half.

I didn't laugh.

"You know," he said, leaning back, "first time I saw you shoot, you were shorter than this desk here. You used to run out on the court during time-outs and shoot. The crowd always liked watching you better than watching the actual games. Couldn't blame 'em. I used to watch too. We all did. To get the ball up to the rim, you had to get a running start and heave it from your hip. But it *always* went in. Or seemed to. I remember thinking one time, *Look out, she might go pro one day!* But then I laughed. *Yeah. Like* that *would ever happen. . . .*"

I leaned forward.

Instead of kicking over his projector, like I wanted to, I said, "Okay, Coach, I'm in."

11

ARDWYN MIDDLE SCHOOL

BOYS' BASKETBALL

OFFICIAL TEAM CONTRACT

As handed down to the founder of basketball, James Naismith, in the year 1891 AD, on a ~~stone tablet~~ coach's whiteboard, as he stood atop a ~~mountain~~ ladder, nailing a peach basket to the wall.

Thou shalt not *whine*.

Thou shalt not *cry*.

Thou shalt not *cheat*.

Thou shalt not *reach*.

Thou shalt not *loaf* (on defense).

Thou shalt not *covet* (the ball).

Thou shalt not *question* (thy coach).

Thou shalt not *quit* (ever).

Thou shalt not throw a behind-the-back pass when a chest pass would do just freaking fine.

And, of course . . .

Thou shalt not record, sell, or distribute any of Coach Gulch's copyrighted plays if thou dost not have express written permission—violators subject to five months in detention and/or five hundred suicides with no water breaks.

Read closely and sign if you agree.

Name (printed): _____

Name (signed): _____

Date: _____

12

Thank god for Toby. He always knew how to make me laugh, which kept me from being a total, brooding, self-serious ass.

He came up to me before my first practice. "Hey. Be honest. Does this uniform make me look fat?"

He had a basketball stuffed in his XXL practice jersey, making him look pregnant, and two more in the back of his shorts, giving him what we called a "bubble butt."

"You've got a lovely figure," I said.

He peeked over his shoulder. "Really? You think?"

A whistle blew.

"Gather 'round!" Gulch said. "Sykes, quit messing around!"

Toby birthed the basketball and cradled it.

Gulch frowned. He had a rolled-up baton of papers in his hand—our team contracts that we'd need to sign or he wouldn't let us play. "Now listen up," he said. "Good news. As you see, Lizzy's joining us. You all know what she can do. The rest of the league's about to find out."

Tank Marciano raised his hand.

I braced. You know how they say your vision gets worse from sitting too close to the TV? That's how I felt being around Tank. Like my IQ was dropping just being near him.

"Coach," he said in his caveman voice. "I forgot my sports bra in my locker; can I go get it?"

"Sure," Gulch said. "Go ahead. But if you do, don't come back, and see if you can find your brain while you're down there."

Tank stared with his mouth open.

"Now then," Gulch said. "There is one *actual* uniform issue. And that's the number twenty-four. Lizzy—"

"*I'm* twenty-four!" Tank yelled.

"I know this is important," Gulch said, "so we'll decide this *democratically*." He was always a little too pleased with himself when he used big words. He tried to spin the ball on his finger. It fell right off. "We'll settle this with a game of PIG."

PIG, of course, is a shooting game where you have to make the same shots your opponent makes, or else you get a letter. If you spell P-I-G, you lose. (You can also play HORSE or ELEPHANT or HIPPOPOTAMUS if you have the time.)

Tank and I rock-paper-scissored to see who would shoot first. I threw paper and he threw rock, meaning I should've won—*paper covers rock*—but he just smashed through my paper with his caveman fist. He wasn't much for games of skill or strategy.

Speaking of which . . . PIG wasn't the best game for him. He carried the ball to the corner and shot a knuckle ball, a hideous thing, no rotation at all. Somehow it grazed the corner of the backboard and banked in. *A corner bank!* You watch basketball enough, maybe you'll see that once a year. You can't *get* any luckier.

He celebrated like he'd clubbed something to death.

I caught the ball before it hit the ground and skipped out to the same spot. How many times had I drained this exact shot? A thousand? Ten thousand? I took one dribble, pulled up to shoot, but then—

I stopped.

Toby tilted his head. His flat-top slanted.

Coach Gulch squinted. He sort of wheezed through his whistle.

I'd never been one to hesitate. Or doubt myself.

Everyone was staring.

It wasn't doubt. It was the opposite. It was *certainty*. I knew that even if I closed my eyes and shot a wild, falling-over hook shot, the ball was going to go in. And that, strangely, made me hesitate. It was one thing to shoot alone in the rain. But in front of the team, I felt weirdly, I don't know, exposed. "You can have it," I mumbled.

"Play the game," Gulch said.

"No," I said. "He can have it."

"Play the damn game!"

"The team's the most important thing, Coach. I don't care about a stupid number. I just want to win."

Later, walking home, Toby said: "What the heck was *that* all about?"

"What?"

"You backed down from Fred Flintstone. Then you went the whole practice and didn't even shoot once."

"Yeah, but I had like thirty assists. Our team still won."

"Are you trying to prove a point or something? Because I'm all for it. I'm *all* for proving stuff. I'm in. I just don't understand what the point is."

"I can't tell you."

He was genuinely hurt by that. I knew because he wasn't a good enough actor to fake it.

"I have to *show* you," I said. "Meet me at the court at six tomorrow."

"*Six?* Nooooooo way. It's gonna be, like, thirty degrees!"

"Fine. Six *fifteen*. Bundle up."

13

Toby appeared at the top of the hill just after dawn. For some reason I thought of one of those *Just Married* cars, dragging a bunch of clattering junk behind it. Except his would've said *Just Woke Up*. His jacket was unzipped, his sneakers were untied, and he had a frosted Pop-Tart hanging from his mouth.

I shot the ball from the foul line. *Pure swish.*

"Wow," he deadpanned. "Never seen that before."

I stepped back to the three-point line. *Pure swish.*

He yawned. His breath plumed in the early-morning cold.

Half-court. *Pure swish.*

That one made him raise an eyebrow. It wasn't just that it went in. It was the *way* it went in. The way the ball seemed to *accelerate* through the hoop.

I carried the ball to the far corner of the court, about ninety-five feet away, and lofted up a sky hook shot.

The ball flew through the overcast sky.

It was up there so long it could've evolved.

It could've grown wings and flown away.

But it just kept tracking toward the hoop.

Closer . . .

Closer . . .

Pure swish.

Toby stared like his brain had turned to Pop-Tart mush.

I swished the same ninety-five-foot hook shot again.

And again.

And again.

"Let me see that ball," he said. He shook it at his ear. "It have magnets in it or something?" A popular theory among the conspiracy theorists these days.

"You try," I said.

He shot a free throw. His normal form. A two-handed push shot.

Air ball.

I carried the ball to half-court and turned my back to the basket. One-handed, over the head. *Pure swish.*

"You could always shoot," he said. "But not like *this*."

I told him everything. The robocall. The wish. The first shot in the rain.

"I just can't *believe* it," he said, rubbing his cold hands.

"Well, it's real, man. So you'd better start—"

"No. I mean . . . I just can't believe you didn't wish for more wishes. I mean, *come on*. How do you *not* wish for more wishes? You totally blew it!"

"I was kinda put on the spot—"

"Well, next time that happens, don't be so selfish. You could have totally hooked me up!"

"Actually . . ." I stopped.

"What?"

"After the call, I got this text—"

"Lemme see."

I showed him the weird follow-up text I'd gotten the next day.

[RESTRICTED NUMBER]

Thank you.

Please keep this for your records.

Wish #39765488335251 has been granted.

Term Reply X – 01

"What's X-minus-one?" I asked.

"Maybe it's computer code—isn't that all zeroes and ones?"
He squinted. "Or maybe it means you still have one wish. Like
in a video game, you know how it says your lives left, like x01?
Let's try to text—"

I snatched the phone back. "*Don't.*"

"Jeez. Relax. I'm just—"

"You can't tell anyone," I said. "No matter what. Promise?"

He turned an imaginary key at his lips . . . then bugged his
eyes.

"What?" I said.

"I . . . swallowed . . . the . . . key."

I shook my head. "Idiot."

14

Our first game was against Springfield. They were the defending league champs. They had a freshman forward, Reggie Burton, who supposedly was already getting college scholarship letters.

We bumped fists before the tip and did little side stretches as we waited for the clock operator to figure out how to reset the game clock. The gym smelled like boiled hot dogs and dust. The stands were 95 percent empty. A sparrow had gotten inside somehow and was hopping around. The janitor, Grumpy John, was chasing it with a bucket.

Finally, the clock was set and the potbellied ref came forward. He pointed. "Red this way. Brown this way." We were red. They were brown.

It seems silly to say, but I think I was more nervous before this game than all the much bigger ones that followed. Maybe it was because—for some reason—Dad wasn't there. Or maybe because I hadn't played a game yet since . . . you know.

The ref tossed up the ball.

Tank tipped it to his left.

Billy Castaldo, our starting small forward, caught it there.

On the far side, I broke for the hoop.

Just as Gulch had drawn it up.

Billy zipped me the ball.

And, just like that, three seconds into my boys' basketball career, I was cruising in for an open layup. Instinct took over. I took two dribbles. Right foot. Left foot. But just as I was about to lay the ball off the backboard, I froze. Instead of shooting, I just landed with the ball. The ref blew his whistle, wheeled his arms. Traveling.

The boys on the Springfield bench were elbowing one another, laughing.

I looked down. I was still clutching the ball.

The ref signaled a delay of game warning. Or rather, he tried to, but didn't know the signal for it, so he just pointed at his wrist and rolled his eyes.

Coach Gulch stuck his fingers into the corners of his mouth and half whistled/half spit. He lifted his shoulders. *You okay?*

I waved him off and jogged back on defense.

"Got something sticky on your hands?" Reggie Burton joked.

I considered saying something back, but instead I just waited until he got the ball and immediately stole it from him. *Yeah*, I thought. *I don't know what it is. The ball just keeps sticking to them.*

I fired the ball ahead to Tank for an easy layup.

The next time down, I started hard right, so Burton took a big step . . . then I threaded a bounce pass right through his legs to Sean Dormond for another easy layup.

Maybe this point guard thing isn't so bad after all.

We won, 52–40. They don't keep stats in middle school

other than points and fouls, so, according to the official book, I had no impact on the game whatsoever.

Unofficially, of course, I controlled the game. I *owned* it.

You're probably wondering why, once again, I didn't shoot the ball. It must seem, from the outside looking in, like I was holding a winning lottery ticket and was too afraid to cash it.

The truth is, I *was* afraid, and it *was* affecting my play, but not in the normal way. I think I knew, even then, that once I *did* shoot, when I revealed this magic power, nothing in my life would ever be the same. And then the one sacred place I'd always been able to control things, the basketball court, would be just like every other crappy place in the world.

15

After that first win against Springfield, I went right to the Stop-N-Pump. I saw Dad through the glass as I walked up. He was down on his knees, fixing a wheel on an overturned mop bucket, wearing his sweat-stained baseball cap (the cheap free-giveaway kind with a McDonald's logo on it). I pulled open the door. *Ding*.

"How much you win by?" he said without looking up.

"Twelve," I said.

"That's it?"

"Our starters sat the whole fourth."

"How many your man have?" Dad always did that—asked how many my *opponent* had instead of how many *I* had.

"Two."

He spun the repaired wheel and stood, stiffly, pushing up off his knees. "Well, that gives you something to work on for the next game."

I asked Dad about his injury once—*How did it happen? What did it feel like? Where exactly on the court were you?*—but he just grumbled, "Drop it, okay?"

After his injury, Dad had moved home to Ardwyn and gotten

a job at the local auto shop. He wasn't a natural there like on the basketball court, but, in a weird way, that was exciting. He worked at it. He borrowed books from the public library and studied. He was never their best mechanic, but he was their most reliable. He was one of those steady role players every team needs. One year, the shop even printed him a cheap little certificate that said TEAM MVP. They didn't put it in a frame or anything. They just gave it to him. It had oil-smudged fingerprints all over it. I never would've known about it if I hadn't gone snooping for our electricity bills. The printer must've been low on ink, so his name was ghosted out, but I could still read it: RICK TRUDEAUX, TEAM MVP. He worked there for seven years, and though things weren't perfect, they were . . . okay. We survived the worst that life could throw at us in those years and kept moving forward. We had each other. We were okay.

Then the auto shop closed. "Tax issues."

The owner was thrown in jail.

Dad scrambled to find a job, and that was how he ended up working the overnight at the Stop-N-Pump. He couldn't afford to wait around for the perfect job, he said. He'd taken out a loan for night classes years earlier, and the interest was piling up on that, plus all our other bills—food, utilities, the mortgage, etc.

Don't worry about me, he said. *I'm fine. When's your next game?*

I pushed him to open his own shop—*Why not?*—but he said it was too much of a hassle, too much paperwork.

How was practice? he asked. *When's your next game? What'd you learn at school?*

Another few months passed. That was when he got those bags under his eyes. And that was when I realized that time moves differently for adults. When you stop imagining the next thing in front of you, it all sort of blurs together, and it's easy to get stuck.

16

Dad limped back behind the register. "Sorry," he said. "Maria went into labor, and I had to cover."

"Don't apologize, Dad."

"I'm not apologizing. I'm explaining."

His voice was as cold and thin as the mist that came out of the beverage fridge. I grabbed a yellow Gatorade and chugged three-quarters of it. He looked annoyed.

"What?" I said. "Do you have to pay for these?"

"No. I mean, yeah. But it's fine. Some kid came in after school. He put like ten candy bars in his schoolbag, right in front of me, and just walked out."

"Do you have to pay for *that*?"

"No. But it's just like . . . I'm standing right here, you know? *I'm right here.*" He slipped his thumbs inside his fingers—the way someone who didn't know how to punch would make a fist—and cracked his knuckles.

I hated when he did that.

"You eat?" he asked.

"Yeah."

"Liar. Take a frozen pizza."

"I told you, I ate. They fed us after the game. I'm fine."

"Take one."

"Nah. I'm good. I have some homework, though. I'll see you at home." I shouldered out the door—*ding*—before he could say anything else.

Still wearing my game jersey beneath my sweats, I ran suicides at the playground until the light went out. I staggered home, limping on fresh blisters. I ate a half sleeve of saltines and washed them down with a glass of Ardwyn tap (always refreshingly cold in the winter). I ate a half jar of applesauce for dessert, rinsed off in the shower, and collapsed into bed. I was too tired to dress myself, so I just lay there in my towel. I was exhausted, but I couldn't sleep. I didn't have any data left, so I just stared at the weird text on my phone until the letters and numbers all blurred together.

17

Dad had to work on Thanksgiving, so I had dinner with my second family—Toby's family, the Sykeses. Around three thirty, I put on my winter coat and jogged across our one-way street, across the desolate basketball court, up the hill, through a hole in a rusty fence, around the abandoned factory, and over to Bryn Auden.

Though it was less than a half mile away, everything was different up there. The houses all had big yards and three-car garages. Mr. Sykes's BMW was parked at an angle in the drive-way. I entered the four-digit passcode and ducked under the rising garage door. I pushed the button on the inside, immediately sending it back down. I imagined the house opening its mouth to say something, then changing its mind.

The garage smelled of gasoline. The lawn mower had its own parking spot.

Inside, the living room walls were scarlet red, with matching furniture. The hardwood floors gleamed. The ceilings were high—I couldn't jump up and slap the door frames like at our house. Family photos crowded the walls—the three of them at Martha's Vineyard, by Big Ben in London, by the Coliseum in Rome, by the Statue of Liberty in New York, and so on. I

used to joke that they just had a photo booth in the basement and they changed out the backgrounds. It wasn't one of my best jokes, but it made me feel a little better because Dad and I never went anywhere.

I followed the smell of roasting turkey into the kitchen. There, Toby's mom, Karen, was pouring milk over a bowl of steaming potatoes. It reminded me of our science teacher at school mixing chemicals, except she wasn't wearing a see-through plastic apron, just a red one that said WHAT'S COOKIN', GOOD LOOKIN'? You know when you buy a bag of ice and sometimes the cubes are clumped together? That's what her wedding ring looked like. She'd just picked up the mixer when I said, "Hey, Mrs. S."

She flew back against the fridge. It sounded like a bird hitting a window.

She found this hilarious. I have so many happy memories of being in Toby's house, and so many of them are in that kitchen, cracking up with his mom.

She still had her hand over her mouth. "Lizzy, you scared me!"

"Everything scares you, Mrs. S."

"Not *everything*."

Pretty much.

Karen's hugs were the best part about her. She squeezed you *super* tight, long enough to make it feel genuine, not mechanical like the assembly-line hugs at school. "You're lucky you weren't a robber," she said, "or I would've mixed you to death!"

I didn't know what to say to that.

Luckily, she was the adult, so she had to talk.

"They have your dad working today? On *Thanksgiving*?"

I shrugged. "People need gas."

"It's a sin. We'll make him a plate."

"Thanks."

All this time she was *still* hugging me. She finally let me go. "The boys are downstairs."

"Football?" I said.

She rolled her eyes. "You know Frank."

The Sykeses' basement was a shrine to Philadelphia sports. Mr. Sykes—Frank—was an obsessive collector. The first thing you saw going down the steps was a huge, framed photo of the Palestra, the legendary arena in Philadelphia where the local college basketball teams—The Big Five—had been battling on winter nights for generations. He also had a pair of boxing gloves autographed by Joe Frazier, a hockey stick used during the 1974 Stanley Cup finals, a creepy-looking white goalie mask, a 1980 World Series baseball, a Super Bowl–used football, and about a thousand other things. He was like a pharaoh who'd decided to get entombed with *everyone else's* treasures.

As I came down the steps Mr. Sykes was yelling at their huge, new, flat-screen TV. The volume was so loud I practically had to wade through it. "Run it!" Mr. Sykes was yelling. "Run the ball!" He was wearing his standard rich-guy uniform: a button-up white shirt with the sleeves rolled up, gold watch, and boat shoes with no socks. He always smelled like he'd just stepped out of a barber's chair—talcum powder and aftershave.

Toby was across from him, on the recliner. He was spun

upside down—head on the footrest, like a giant bug caught in a spider's web. He was holding his phone out, broadcasting a special upside-down episode of *The Toby Sykes Show!* live on Instagram. "*Another* reason why football is dumb," he was saying, "is that—"

Somebody fumbled.

Mr. Sykes shot up. "Get on it! Get on the—oh hey, Lizzy. Get on the ball!"

"Exciting game?" I said to Toby.

He ended his broadcast with a fart noise and spun right side up. "Whoa. Head rush."

Mr. Sykes went behind the bar (never taking his eyes off the game) and opened the mini fridge. "Sprite, Dr Pepper, Coke, root beer, or ginger ale?"

"Dr Pepper," I said.

Mr. Sykes flipped me the soda can like he was lateraling a football, then flopped back on the leather couch. "Ah, come *on!*" he yelled at the TV. "Are you blind, ref?"

Toby rolled his eyes.

I smirked.

Mr. Sykes had made a fortune in junk bonds. To be honest, I still have no idea what that means. But they always had at least five different kinds of soda in their mini fridge and, as I mentioned, a parking spot for their lawn mower.

When a commercial came on, Mr. Sykes said, "Heard you been runnin' circles 'round those boys, huh?"

I shrugged.

"*Good.* You deserve it. I mean that. I'm leaving for work—

you're there on the court. I get home—you're there on the court. They probably deliver your mail there." He nodded over at Toby. "And what's this one doing? He's up in his room all day, broadcasting to the six losers who—"

"Seven."

"Huh?"

"I had *seven* viewers just now, for your information. Seven. Not six. That's a seventeen percent ratings spike."

An uncomfortable silence filled the basement.

You know, except for the blaring TV.

"I'm just playin'," Mr. Sykes said, leaning back, smiling, arms spread like a king. "By the time you're through, son, Oprah's gonna be callin' *you*, askin' you for a loan!"

Toby beamed. "And I'm gonna be like, 'Who is this? Stop callin' here!'"

They both laughed; I was laughing too, though at the same time I think I was a little jealous. Dad never said things like that about me.

He never said anything at all.

wo hours later, after stuffing ourselves full of delicious turkey and mashed potatoes and string beans and cranberry sauce and pumpkin pie with homemade whipped cream, Toby and I climbed the stairs to his room. I sat in my normal seat: the tall, cloth-backed chair marked DIRECTOR. "How did your parents end up together anyway?"

"The man, as you may've noticed, doesn't take no for an answer." He ran his finger across his Blu-ray collection. "*Rocky*?"

"No. Please. God, no. Not again."

"*Creed*?"

"No."

"Fine. We'll just sit here and stare at each other."

"Fine."

We did that for about ten seconds, then he said: "Abracadabra fart brains froggy froggy moose cream choo-choo train."

"Excuse me?"

"You ever just wanna say something that's *never* been said before? I mean, something totally original?"

"No."

"Try it."

I shut my eyes. "Twinkle twinkle couch crumbs photo blender grasshopper wood chips Chewbacca."

"Feels good, right?"

"It kinda does, actually."

"Karen's therapist charges her, like, three hundred bucks an hour for that."

He fell back onto his queen-size bed, rolled over, and screamed into a pillow. He did that for about five seconds, then ditched the pillow and said very calmly: "I think that car horns should be a person's deepest, darkest secret. You could control it by how hard you push. So if you just tap it, it whispers, 'I killed a man.' But if you really hold it, it yells, 'I KILLED A MAN! I KILLED A MAN!' You know? Then people would only honk when absolutely necessary."

I tipped my head back and stared up at the ceiling. It was trippy in there with his red lava lamp clotting and unclotting.

"What do you think old people daydream about?" he said. "I mean, do you think they still imagine themselves doing *new* things, like what they could still *become*, or do you think, like, you reach a certain age when you start daydreaming *backward* . . . you know, like, remaking the classics?"

"Why don't you ask Nana?"

"Can't."

"Why?"

"Because it's awkward. It's like saying, 'Hey, Nana, you're gonna *die* soon—what's *that* like?'"

"So?"

"So it's *weird*."

"What? Death?"

Toby pulled his knees to his chest and rolled from side to side. "Yeah. But not any weirder than life, I guess." He shot up. "Question."

"Shoot." He was the shooter this time; I was the rebounder. We took turns.

"Heaven," he said.

"Yeah?"

"How does it, like, *work*?"

"What do you mean?"

"Like, if I flew up there now and saw Grandpa Stan, would he still be all old and wrinkly, like *we* knew him? Or would he be young—you know, the age that *he* wants to be? And what about *kids*? Remember Becky Hammond? Does she get to grow up in heaven or is it, like, just because she choked on a grape in kindergarten, now she's stuck wanting to go to Chuck E. Cheese for all eternity?"

Toby's mind was like those green bottles of sparkling water his mom always drank—lots and lots of bubbles rising to the surface all at once.

I picked up the book we'd co-illustrated in second grade, *The Adventures of White Bread and Graham Cracker*.

"That's a classic right there," Toby said. "You remember what White Bread says to Graham Cracker at the end, when they defeat Captain Crunch and return back to Doughville to live snackily ever after? She says, 'You're my best friend in the whoooole world, Graham Cracker! I loaf you!'"

I cringed. "Pretty lame, man. Pretty lame."

He shrugged. "I thought it was sweet."

WHITE BREAD & GRAHAM CRACKER

Toby Sykes—Trudeaux's Best Friend
You remember how we met, right?

Lizzy Trudeaux
[Laughs.] Like you'd let me forget.

Toby Sykes—Trudeaux's Best Friend
See, the thing you all don't know about Lizzy
Trudeaux is . . . I *saved* her. Without me, she never
would've become Lizzy Legend.

Lizzy Trudeaux
Please.

Toby Sykes—Trudeaux's Best Friend
I did! It was—what? Second grade?

Lizzy Trudeaux
First.

Toby Sykes—Trudeaux's Best Friend
Lizzy was the new kid. The class bully—Tank—
already hated her 'cuz she'd knocked his teeth out
on the first day. He'd been plotting his—

Lizzy Trudeaux

"Plotting" seems like a strong word. This is Tank.

Toby Sykes—Trudeaux's Best Friend

True. True. So he was . . . gonna get her back. Let's say that. He'd been waiting for his chance. So one day we're playing football at recess. Lizzy's quarterback, of course, I'm offensive line, *of course*, and Tank blitzes . . .

Lizzy Trudeaux

It was on my blind side.

Toby Sykes—Trudeaux's Best Friend

She didn't see him coming at all.

William Richards—Bystander

I saw the whole thing happening. I was like, "NOOOOOOOO—"

Sean Dormond—Bystander

At the last second, Toby threw himself in front of Tank. It was crazy.

Toby Sykes—Trudeaux's Best Friend

[Shrugs.] I saw it on TV once.

Sean Dormond—Bystander

Tank *crushed* him.

William Richards—Bystander

There was this horrible squishing sound, like an artery bursting.

Sean Dormond—Bystander

The game stopped. Toby's rolling around on the grass, holding his heart.

Lizzy Trudeaux

I'm standing over him. "Are you dead? Are you dead?"

Sean Dormond—Bystander

And then he's like, real soft—

Toby Sykes—Trudeaux's Best Friend

Thank . . . god . . . you . . . were . . . there.

Lizzy Trudeaux

We have no idea what he's talking about. Is he talking to himself?

William Richards—Bystander

Then he unzips his jacket.

Sean Dormond—Bystander
He unzips his jacket.

Lizzy Trudeaux
And I see it.

Sean Dormond—Bystander
A Twinkie.

Lizzy Trudeaux
He had a Twinkie in his jacket pocket.

Sean Dormond—Bystander
It had absorbed the force of the hit like a
bulletproof vest.

William Richards—Bystander
Splat!

Sean Dormond—Bystander
[Laughs.] Cream was all over his new shirt.

Lizzy Trudeaux
He's trying to catch his breath, like—

Toby Sykes—Trudeaux's Best Friend
It's . . . not . . . funny! I . . . was . . . going . . . to . . .
eat . . . that!

Lizzy Trudeaux

It was so funny. [Thinks.] I guess Toby *did* kind of save me.

Toby Sykes—Trudeaux's Best Friend

[Beaming.] Yeah. And we've been best friends ever since.

oach Gulch was extra stressed at practice the next day. His whole body was breaking out in hives. The game against our big rival, Darby, was coming up. "Is that a *question*, Tank, an actual question, or are you just holding both hands above your head like you're a bear again?"

"I'm a bear! Rarrrrrrrrr!"

Coach Gulch pinched the bridge of his nose like he had a migraine. "I swear that growth spurt damaged your brain."

I'd decided today was the day. So long as I didn't take any preposterous, impossible shots—shots that I normally wouldn't expect myself to make—then who could question me if they all went in? Right?

We began scrimmaging. The first time down I passed the ball to Toby, who had to play because a few of the boys were out sick that day. It went through his hands and knocked the wind out of him. The other team picked it up, ran a three-on-one fast break (I was the one, of course), and scored.

Okay, enough of that.

The next time down, I put my fist up, calling for our standard play, "motion." The two forwards down-screened and the guards popped out to the wings. The boy guarding me, Sean Dormond, was sagging off a good two feet. I hadn't shot the ball all season, so I think he (and everyone) forgot that I still could. I pulled up. I shot. The ball rocketed through the hoop.

Coach Gulch nearly swallowed his whistle. "Heck yeah! Let 'er rip!"

I let 'er rip.

Swish.

Swish.

Swish.

Pure swishes, all.

"*Cripes*," Sean Dormond said. "You could do this the whole time?"

I didn't say a word. I just kept shooting.

Just like there are the Five Stages of Grief that we learned about in Language Arts class, there are, I believe, the Five Stages of Being on Fire (that the person guarding you goes through):

Denial. *Okay, you made a few, big deal.*

Curiosity. *All right, that was a tough shot. Something may be going on here.*

Acceptance. *You, sir/madam, are on fire. Happens. Nothing I can do . . .*

Elation. *You still haven't missed!!! Holy %*#@, this is crazy!!!!*

Delirium. *This is beyond me. My tiny human brain can't comprehend what is happening right now. I am a dog trying to understand the internet. My tail is wagging. My tongue is hanging out of my mouth. I'm slobbering all over the court. Words words words words words words words.*

. . .

I lost count, but I think I made about forty in a row. When the last one went in, practically trailing smoke, everyone piled on, celebrating.

"LIZ-ZY! LIZ-ZY! LIZ-ZY!"

Even though there were eleven bodies piled on top of me—all of us like one conjoined, multilimbed floor monster—I felt no pain.

I felt like I'd finally stepped into the outline of who I was supposed to be—into a silk-lined dream tailored just for me—and, oh, it fit *just right*.

20

The game was *at* Darby, a fifteen-minute bus ride away. Buses have always made me feel nauseous—especially school buses with that diesel exhaust/hospital smell—so I was leaning my forehead against the cold rectangular window, trying not to puke.

Toby was picking at the dark green seat covering beside me. "What do you think this seat's made of?" he said. "Dead iguanas?" He picked harder. "What's the difference between an alligator and a crocodile anyway? Do you ever look at a rhino and just think, like, wait, that's, like . . . a dinosaur?"

My headphones were on, so I pretended like I didn't hear him. I liked to build a cocoon around myself before games. Lizzy Trudeaux—who was a fairly nice person—went into the cocoon. Someone different came out.

"It could be dried boogers," Toby said, sniffing his fingers. "Here, taste and tell me."

I smacked his hand away. "Quit it, man."

"What, you're nervous? I've never seen you nervous."

"I'm not nervous. I'm *sick*."

"*Bus* sick?"

"Leave me alone."

"What are you listening to?"

"Don't worry about it."

"Those headphones big enough? You look like you should be landing airplanes in those things." He pretended he was waving glowing red batons, landing planes.

I pressed my forehead harder against the cold window.

Toby reached across me to open the window—you know the kind where you compress the two hinges?—but that was just a fake out. When I lifted my arms, he reached down and yanked the black cord attached to my headphones.

He stared at the loose cord for a second. "Wait, you've got your headphones plugged into your *pocket*?"

"We can't all afford—"

"Oh, please. Don't play the poor card. You're just *weird*."

He was right, of course—the headphones were to keep sound *out*. I told you about my cocoon. And if that was weird, *fine*. Whatever. Nothing mattered except getting ready for the game.

I wasn't allowed in the locker room with the boys, so I changed alone in the girls' bathroom. The tiled floor was ice-cold, even through my socks. It only took me about eight seconds to get changed because I'd slept in my uniform the night before.

When I came out of the bathroom, Coach Gulch and the boys were streaming out of the locker room. Gulch was carrying a spiral-bound notebook, like always. He was glaring over at his mortal enemy: Darby's head coach, Pat Brothers. He crooked his meaty finger, summoning me. "Hope you got some of that magic left from yesterday," he said. "This is a big one."

"That was just the beginning, Coach."

"Good. Don't hold back today, hear me?"

21

How many people were in the gym that day? Twenty-five? Thirty? The stands were like a huge brown continent dotted only with major cities. One fan here, one there, two there, mostly open space in between. Dad was up in the far corner, alone, like always. He was Juneau, Alaska.

I kept staring up at the ceiling as we cycled through our pregame layups. Darby's gym was famously cramped; the ceiling was so low you *had* to shoot line drives. One of the metal-encased lights was permanently burned out, so there was a dark patch between the three-point line and half-court that was known as the Darby Triangle. If you crossed through that area, legend had it, you would vanish.

Darby also used their gym as their cafeteria, so the floor was super sticky in some spots, where soda had spilled, and ice-rink slippery in all others. I kept palming the dust from the bottoms of my sneakers. That might actually be what I remember most about middle school basketball—constantly palming dust from the bottom of my sneakers so I didn't slide all over the place. Oh, and the old scratchy jerseys with the numbers peeling off. I remember those, too.

"Now, listen up," Gulch said in the pregame huddle. "Listen

up. This isn't personal, okay? Despite what you may have heard, I have *not* been holding a personal grudge against the Coward Pat Brothers since he broke my nose on March 2, 1979. This is about *you guys*, okay? Not me. So go out there and have fun. That's the important thing, right? Have fun. So let's have fun. *So* much fun. And what else? What did we talk about? *Execute.* Execution. Let's execute, right? Also, last thing, remember: the gods forbid us from looking back. They say, if you look back at that game on February 4, 1980, when the Coward Pat Brothers nearly yanked your arm out of its socket when you went up for a rebound, you will be turned into a pillar of salt. So let's not get turned into pillars of salt out there, okay, guys?"

We all looked around at one another until Toby—god bless him—said: "Great plan, Coach."

uys," I said. "I'm still feeling it. Just get me the ball and this'll be fun."

"Right," Gulch said. "Like I said, just pass the ball to Lizzy and get the heck out of the way!"

Now, *there* was a game plan.

The horn sounded.

"All right!" Gulch yelled. "Here we go! Everyone, hands in!"

We piled up our hands (Toby called it the Ouija Board Moment). "One . . . two . . . three . . . DE-FENSE!"

Darby didn't have any star players like Reggie Burton. But they were all tough—kids from Darby were always tough. They all had the same military-style haircut and wispy black mustaches. The ref came forward and tossed the ball up—I can still see it spinning—and, *blink*, somehow the ball was in my hands. I took a few left-hand dribbles, head up, surveying the other players as they settled into the far end of the court. I pulled up for a deep three-pointer. It was a line drive, skimming just below the metal light casings. The ball rocketed through the rim with so much momentum it ricocheted off the back wall and hit one of the Darby players in the neck. He went down.

3–0.

I stole the inbounds pass, dribbled out to the far corner, and hit another line drive.

6–0.

On the next possession, I rebounded a Darby miss, pushed the ball, found a pocket in the retreating defense (imagine nine paper boats floating lazily down a river, and one weaving aggressively between them), and pure-swished another three. *9–0.*

Before I could inflict any more damage, Darby's coach, Pat Brothers, walked out on the court, holding his hands over his head in the shape of a sideways *T. Time-out.*

He stared at me, bewildered, like, *Who the heck* is *this girl?*

By the end of the first quarter, it was 36–7. I'd scored all thirty-six points. I was twelve of twelve from deep. The gym was abuzz, somewhere between Stage Four (Elation) and Stage Five (Delirium). (The Five Stages apply to fans, too.) Students were running out into the hallway during time-outs, grabbing teachers, janitors, anyone they saw, "You have to see this! It's amazing! She's the best player I've ever seen!"

Midway through the second quarter, I was up to forty-five points. Darby had already burned all their time-outs trying to devise a way to stop me, but I kept carving through them like I'd weaved through those little orange cones at the park. My mind was hyperalert. I was one step ahead. I anticipated where the open space would be, like Sidney Rayne.

The crowd mock-booed when I passed to Tank for a wide-open layup, the first time anyone on our team but me had shot the ball. "Boooooo!"

Jogging back on defense, laughing, I thought of Coach Paul Westphal's famous quote: "Basketball's simple. Three rules. One: if you're open, shoot it. Two: if someone else is more open, pass him the ball and let him shoot it. And three: have fun."

·Normally, I agreed with that, but not *this* game. This was *my* game. I decided right then I wasn't gonna pass anymore, no matter what. On the playground, we called those types of players ball hogs, and everyone knew the basketball gods frowned on ball hogs. But this was different. I'd been given this gift *by* the gods, right? They obviously *wanted* me to use it.

With eight seconds left in the first half, I had sixty-three points, already the league record. Coach Gulch put his finger up and yelled, "One shot! Last shot!"

Guess who was gonna take it?

I took the inbounds pass, knifed between two Darby defenders, squeezed between the sideline and a third, spun back past a fourth, shimmied my shoulders and blew past the fifth (the crowd loved that one), and released the ball as time expired.

For the first time all day, there was a sound other than pure outer-space silence as the ball passed through the rim. As I came down, my right foot landed on a defender's foot. My ankle turned over.

Crack!

The gym went silent. Hands over mouths. I writhed on the ground, holding my right ankle. I rolled over and punched the court. *No. No. No. This can't be happening.*

Toby rushed off the bench. His eyes were huge. "Lizzy, Lizzy, you okay?"

Dad bolted down from the stands, leaping three levels at a time. He squeezed through the halo of players around me. Only it wasn't Dad—it was the Wizard.

He didn't wait for a doctor or an ambulance. He swept me up and carried me right out to the icy parking lot. The sweat immediately froze to my body. "So this one time," he said, gliding like we were on one of those moving ramps at the airport, "this one time when you were about five, you had this assignment at school where you had to draw a picture of what you wanted to be when you grew up. You remember that?"

Pain bolted up my leg.

"The other kids all thought about it, the teacher told me, tapping their crayons on their lips, you know, like stupid kids. But not you. Not Lizzy. You just picked up the crayon, face all scrunched up, same way you do your homework now. A minute later, you raised your hand and said, 'Done!' You remember what you drew?"

"A basketball player?"

He laughed. "Nope. A *zookeeper*. You drew a zoo, all the animals in their cages. You said you wanted to be a zookeeper."

"*Really?*"

"Yeah. And then you said, 'But I'm gonna let them all go. Zoos are animal jail!'"

For the few seconds he was telling that story, casting his spell, I forgot he was carrying me through an icy parking lot. But then pain shot up my leg again.

"It's not . . . that . . . bad," I said, wincing. "It's just a little . . . sprain. I can play."

"I know," Dad said. "I know. We'll just have the doctor take a quick look."

For about two seconds, after he'd lowered me into the passenger side of his Chevy, but before he'd gotten in the driver's side, I was alone in the car. A half sob escaped, but I swallowed it. I wiped my tears with the back of my hand and bit down on the inside of my cheek. Blood pooled under my tongue.

23

We sat in the emergency room for two hours, waiting while more urgent cases jumped us in line. Heart attacks. Strokes. Sawed-off fingers. Who knew the world was so dangerous? *My entire basketball career is hanging in the balance*, I thought. *What could be more urgent?* And yet we waited. And waited. And waited.

As if things couldn't get any worse, it got so late that Dad had to call out of work. I *hated* making him call out of work. Hated, hated, hated it. The debt collectors had been calling even more lately, and I was seriously starting to worry. Could we lose our house? Where would we go? How does it work? Do they just dump all your stuff on the sidewalk, change the locks, and say "Good luck"? Would we have to go to a homeless shelter? Would we have to share a bed?

It seemed unfair that all Dad wanted to do was work, and all I wanted to do was play basketball, and yet . . . *that* was too extravagant? *That* was living beyond our means? In the richest country in the history of the world? We couldn't afford to live in our little row house in Ardwyn, where we wore gloves in the winter instead of turning on the heat? I answered the call once and said to the debt collector, "You know he's trying, right?

He's trying his best? Can you just lay off? Give him a little time to get back on his feet?" And you know what she said? She said in this tired, small voice, "I'm sorry, honey, I'm just doing my job."

Honey.

That pissed me off.

But it was true, I guess.

She was just doing *her* job.

Another hour passed. Dad brought me water in a white paper cone. "You know what *I* wanted to be when I grew up?"

"Um, a basketball player?"

"No. *God, no.*"

"Astronaut? Fireman?" I cycled through all the things little boys were supposed to want to be. "Policeman? *President?*"

"I actually wanted to be a *sheep shearer.* We went on a field trip to this sheep farm in first grade. They took us all the way out there, like an hour away."

"And?"

"It was pretty lame. It was just a bunch of sheep."

I laughed. "What did you *expect?*"

"I don't know. But then they brought us into this barn and there was this older guy in there, this bald guy, shearing the sheep. He went right down the line, with these big electric clippers, giving them all buzz cuts. The sheep didn't mind at all. They looked like they were kind of enjoying it. The wool fell right off. They almost seemed *relieved.* And I thought, *Wow, that's this guy's* job. *He just wakes up and shears sheep all day. That's so* cool. *No one bothers him. I wish I could do that.*"

"Wow, Dad. Dream big."

"Says the zookeeper with no animals."

I sipped my water. It tasted like the paper cup.

Another hour passed. My foot started to throb. And *finally*, I was taken back to wait for X-rays. The young doctor came in pouring a king-size bag of Skittles into his mouth. "Oh, *hey*," he mumbled, thrusting the candy behind his back. "How we feeling?"

"Been better," I said.

"Let's just take a quick look."

"Do they teach you to say that in doctor school?"

"They do, actually."

He pressed on my foot. "That hurt?"

Yes. God. Yes. "No."

"We had a construction worker in with the same thing yesterday," he said. "Guy was crying like a baby."

He took X-rays. We waited another half hour. Then he came back. "See these two specks?" he said, aiming a Snickers bar up at the X-rays. "Those are little bits of bone that you tore off with the ligaments." He was going on about how cool it looked—"It's hard to do that, actually!"—when I cut him off.

My foot looked like a loaf of bread with purple toes. "How long am I out? Our next game is Friday. . . ."

"Oh no, no, you won't be back for that. You ripped the ligaments right off the bone. The good news is there's no fracture. You'll be in a cast for a few weeks, then a few more weeks of PT and you'll be good as new."

Great, I thought, *physical therapy. How much does* that *cost?*

24

Back home, frozen peas piled atop my ankle like sandbags, delirious with pain and exhaustion—as if things couldn't get any worse—my Sidney Rayne poster began trash-talking me.

"Hey, man, don't you guys ever turn the heat on? I'm *freezing* up here."

"Yeah, well, sorry. I don't pay the bills."

"Who does?"

"*No one.* Stop bitching. Put on your warm-ups if you're cold."

"I'm kinda stuck in midair here. . . ."

The floorboards creaked in the hallway. Dad was hovering outside my door. I could see his shadow. I imagined him reaching his hand up to knock, but then lowering it. Limping away.

My breath fogged when I sighed.

Sidney was right.

It was *freezing*.

"Keep your head up, rook. This is just a little setback. Keep your eye on the prize. I'll be waitin' for ya."

"It's just not fair, you know? I was just getting started."

"It doesn't matter how you start, rook. It matters how you finish."

"Did you *really* just say that?"

"What do you want from me? I'm a poster."

"Oh. Right."

Sidney flew closer. Or seemed to. "Hey, rook. Can I ask you somethin'?"

"Shoot."

"It's something I've always wondered. But I'm kinda afraid to ask."

Sidney Rayne? Afraid? "Go ahead, man. It's just the two of us."

"Do I . . . make it?"

"Like, are you successful? Do you reach your goals? Do you become as good as you can be, reach your full potential? Is that what you mean?"

"No. I mean, like . . . do I make this *dunk*? I feel like I'm not gonna make it. The basket's still, like, super far away. And I just keep thinkin': This is gonna be really embarrassing if I don't make it."

I smiled. "You really feel that way?"

"Sometimes," he admitted.

"Just believe in yourself, man. If you don't, who will, right?"

"Now who sounds like the poster?"

25

The rest of December inched by like a slow-moving freight train. I was on one side of the tracks, behind a flashing red stop sign. The rest of my life—my destiny—was on the other side. I caught little glimpses of it, little flashes of light, between the train cars. But mostly I just waited. Christmas passed. New Year's.

The middle school team was still decent without me—they still had Tank—but the other teams quickly figured out how to stop him. They hacked him any time he caught the ball, knowing he was a 30 percent free-throw shooter. Coach Gulch kicked chairs and tore out what was left of his hair, but there was nothing he could do. Tank couldn't shoot free throws, and he didn't have the patience or persistence to learn. The team finished 12–7 and lost to Darby in the second round of the playoffs.

Season over.

At the same time, the closest pro team, the Philadelphia Bells, was having one of the worst seasons in franchise history. By early March, they were already mathematically eliminated from the playoffs.

I won't lie: It was a dark time for me. I couldn't sleep. I

couldn't concentrate at school. I could still shoot at the playground, but I never missed, so that got old. One day, I stood at the side of the court and heaved the ball as far as I could toward the abandoned factory. It soared into the distance but then boomeranged back and went in.

Toby laughed. "Ha! Look at that, folks! She's on fire! She can't miss!"

"Shut up."

So instead of shooting, I spent hours circling the ball around my body, working on my ball handling. The freight train kept inching by.

Finally, in mid-March, they sawed my cast off with what looked like an electric pizza cutter. The skin underneath was wilted and flaky. I had to rub special lotion on it five times a day. Toby's aunt was a physical therapist, so luckily we didn't have to pay for that. I went to therapy every day after school. She had me doing all kinds of weird exercises, like putting my foot flat on a sloped block of wood. Every day, my range of motion improved. By early April, I was more or less back to full speed. I had a little soreness at first, but that went away. I resumed my early-morning training. The next thing in front of me, I thought, was summer ball.

But then one Friday afternoon, something changed. The tree branches in the park had little water crystals on them. It was finally warm enough to shoot outside in short sleeves. Toby—who had gotten a part in the community theater's spring production of *Peter Pan*—came squishing down the hill at dusk, still in his costume from rehearsals.

"What are you?" I said. "A pirate?"

"I am"—he lifted his chin proudly—"Unnamed Lost Boy Number Four."

"Any lines?"

"*Two*, in fact. The first is: 'Gee golly, Peter!' The second is: 'Please don't go, Miss Wendy!' But I think I can work in a few more. It's loose."

"Wow. Next stop, Hollywood."

"I've actually got a small part for *you*, if you're interested."

"In a *play*? Ha. No thanks."

"No. I was thinking we'd do a little one-time performance, like the old days."

Toby and I used to make up little one-act plays in his basement. There was only one rule: You could never play the same character twice. It was fun, but those days were long gone. I was a teenager now. I didn't have free time anymore.

"When?" I said skeptically.

"Tomorrow."

"Can't."

"It's *Saturday*. We don't have school."

"Yeah, but I finally convinced Gulch to give me the key to the gym and—"

"Stop. For all your crap I've put up with over the years you *owe* me this. It'll only take a few hours, and you'll thank me afterward. Trust me, okay? Meet me at the train station at nine a.m. And bring your ball."

He skipped off in his Lost Boy costume, fingers plugged in his ears, singing, "La-la-la-la-la-la-la-la."

26

This had better be good," I told him the next morning, legs dangling from the grimy train platform, ball under my arm. I was wearing my red Ardwyn Middle School basketball sweats and my duct-taped sneakers. The Wite-Out on them had cracked so it sort of looked like they were hatching. Toby wouldn't sit because he was wearing a pin-striped business suit. His suitcase was monogrammed FSS—his father's initials. "It's beyond good," he said. "It's my most cunning plan ever."

"Are we traveling back in time to when people used the word 'cunning'?"

"Just follow my lead, and when the time comes, do your thing."

I stared up the track. "What are you, like, a lawyer or something?"

"*Sort of.*"

"Well, whatever," I said. "But if you think I'm gonna play your secretary, they'll bury you in that suit."

He grinned, the colored braces making him look ever more like a kid playing dress-up with Daddy's clothes and suitcase.

I still had no idea where we were going, but to cover myself I'd texted Dad saying I was going to Toby's house, and he'd no doubt done the same in reverse with his parents.

"So here's the deal," he said as we took our seats on the train. "Bad news. You've recently been diagnosed with Helsinki syndrome."

"Helsinki—?"

"It's a city in northern Europe and also, if anyone asks, a very rare, incurable disease."

"You just made up a disease?"

"I would *never* do such a thing!"

"Yeah right."

"Google it."

I had to laugh.

He'd made up a fake Wikipedia page for it.

"Just follow my lead," he said again. "Whatever happens, go with it."

Stop after stop flickered by until, nearly an hour later, the Philly skyline came into view. We got off at Suburban Station and, after winding through some urine-drenched tunnels, we switched onto the subway. We came up aboveground right next to the Mack Center, the famous home of the Philadelphia Bells.

I'll admit: I wasn't feeling good about any of this. I'd have much rather have been back at the gym in Ardwyn, zigzagging between little orange cones. For every hour of practice I missed, I knew I'd have to pay back double.

We circled the arena until we came to the dark-glassed employees-only entrance. Toby knocked and knocked and knocked—the same way you just keep letting a phone ring and ring—until finally a freckle-faced man in a Bells golf shirt answered. He smelled like Irish Spring soap. "Can I help you?"

"Hi," Toby said crisply. "We're here from the Grant-A-Wish Foundation."

"Grant-a-what?"

"Wish. You know, the charity that grants the final wishes of sick children?"

Toby clicked open his briefcase and produced the documentation—their logo at the top and everything.

The guy looked over us, scanning the empty parking lot.

"Well, can we *come in*?" Toby said. "Or do you want us to stand out here all day while my friend's platelets continue to, uh—"

"Come in! Please! I'm so sorry! What're your names?"

"I'm Archimedes," Toby said—his go-to fake name, his favorite mathematician—"and this is my sister . . . Beatrice."

"Come in; please, come in. I'm Mike. I'm over in marketing. You're lucky it's a game day or else . . . you know what?" His finger shot up. "Hang here a tick." He speed-walked down the hallway, taking the extra-long steps of a person trying to dislodge a wedgie without taking their hands out of their pockets.

I shoved Toby. "Come on, man. This is crazy. Let's go."

"Are you feeling weak?"

"I'm feeling like I'm going to break your face if we don't leave this building right—"

But seconds later, Mike came back with—I couldn't believe my eyes—the legendary Philadelphia Bells coach. He was wearing a wrinkled black suit, the same one I'd seen him wearing on TV the night before, with a pink flowered tie. The suit he always said he wanted to be buried in. His funeral suit. He famously never slept after losses. The championship ring on his right hand glistened like a single brass knuckle. "Jimmy Mack," he said, scowling. "Who the heck are you?"

his is Archimedes," Mike from Marketing said, "and his sister, Beatrice. Beatrice is"—he whispered behind his hand—"*very sick*. But she's a big Bells fan, and it was her wish to come down and, uh . . . what was your wish again?"

"Tour the building," Toby said in his lawyer suit. "*Full* tour."

"Right," Mike said. "Would you, uh, mind showing them around, Coach?" He offered the question like a slab of raw meat to a tiger.

Coach Mack dipped his hand into his jacket pocket and lifted out his famous cigar. *A bubblegum cigar.* Bright pink. Still wrapped. He ran it beneath his nose.

I stared down, ashamed. That was when I noticed he was wearing black dress shoes with no socks. Toby noticed too. He couldn't help himself. "New socks, Coach?"

"Yeah," Coach Mack said, not missing a beat. "They match my gloves. You like 'em?" He sized me up like a draft prospect. I imagined his brain was processing me in black and white, like an X-ray. Seeing right through me.

Toby started recording with his phone. "You mind, Coach?"

"What the heck do I care?"

The locker room wasn't the fancy wonderland I expected,

with fake waterfalls and flat-screen TVs in every locker. When Coach Mack flicked on the lights he yelled: "Scram, rodents! Back in your holes!" It was dark and smelled like wet pizza boxes. The carpet squished in the spots where the pipes were dripping overhead. He led us past all the lockers, explaining what was wrong with all his players. "Stiff. Stiff. Gimp. Stiff. No left hand. Prima donna. Stiff. Stiff. *Big* stiff. Choke artist. Whiner. Crybaby. Has-been. Stiff."

"Tough year?" Toby said.

"Kid, we couldn't beat the Little Sisters of the Poor."

Even though the locker room was a dump, I was still in awe.

"Come on," Coach Mack said, running that pink cigar beneath his nose again. "Stinks in here. Let's go to church."

oach Mack knelt at the edge of the gleaming court, mumbled a silent prayer, made a sign of the cross, and struggled to his feet again. "Don't be shy," he said, nodding at my ball. "That's what they built it for. Let's see what you got."

Toby grinned.

And now I understood his plan.

"Coach," he said. "I gotta tell you something. My name isn't really Archimed—"

"Archimedes of Syracuse," Coach Mack said. "One of the all-time greats. Mathematician. Astronomer. You know how he died? This is good. I love this. Second Punic War. Roman soldier busts into his tent. Soldier says: 'Yo pops, let's go!' Archimedes says, 'Hold up, I'm finishin' this *equation*.' Soldier says, 'Let's go, pops. *Now*.' Archimedes lifts his finger like, 'Just a few more minutes, pal. I'm almost done.' Soldier unsheathes his sword and stabs Archimedes in the gut. Archimedes bleeds out all over his papers. Now, *that's* the way to go out. Play hard till the final horn!"

Toby and I both stared, dumbfounded.

"Sister Margaret," he explained. "St. Ann's School. Seventh-grade Latin class. Still got my notes written right here." He showed us his ruler-scarred knuckles.

Toby said: "That's, uh . . . amazing. But seriously, Coach, that's not my name. She's not sick. I'm really sorry, but it's the only way we could get you to see."

The purple veins in Coach Mack's face were beginning to glow like lightbulb filaments. "See *what*?"

Toby turned to me.

I closed my eyes and took a deep pull of the cool church air. *It's messed up how you got here, but that doesn't matter now. Just shoot.*

I shot.

From half-court.

The ball sped through the hoop.

Pure swish.

"Ha," Coach Mack said, limping back toward the tunnel, "it *would* go in. Listen, I'm from Philly. I appreciate a good con much as the next guy . . . but you kids gotta go. Don't make me call—"

"*Coach*," I said. I'd almost forgotten what my own voice sounded like.

Coach Mack stopped. Turned.

"Just watch," I said. "Please."

Toby chased down the ball and heaved it back.

I pure-swished another.

Coach Mack stepped forward. He was—I'll never forget this—biting down on his championship ring. "This one of them reality TV shows?"

I pure-swished another.

"Let me see that." He weighed the ball on the scale of his palm. Satisfied, he snapped me a chest pass.

I pure-swished another.

"Okay, kid. You got my attention."

"She doesn't miss," Toby called from under the far basket, still recording. "*Ever.*"

"Shut up!" Coach Mack yelled. Then, to me, calmly: "Shoot at the other basket."

I stepped across the half-court line, pivoted, and pure-swished another.

"You know what we used to call that when I was comin' up?" he said.

"A pure swish."

He laughed. "How you know that?"

"My dad taught me."

"Who's your dad?"

I told him.

"Well, heck. Now at least this makes a *little* sense."

"You know my dad?"

"Saw him at a summer camp once. Followed him in the papers, too—we all did. Didn't need much coachin', as I recall."

While Toby was uploading the video to YouTube, Coach Mack limped toward the tunnel again. I thought he was leaving, but instead he grabbed a chair from the bench and planted it at midcourt, directly beneath the ArenaVision. "Go ahead," he said. "I'm gonna sit here till you miss."

For the first time since we'd arrived—maybe for the first time since my injury—I felt like myself again. I said, "You don't have that long, Coach."

29

When I got home Dad was asleep on the couch. He was still wearing his Stop-N-Pump shirt and his black sweatpants, the ones with the frayed elastic bands at the ankles. I tiptoed across the living room, hoping not to wake him, but his wizard powers alerted him to my presence. Eyes still closed, he said: "How was it?"

I froze, midstep, like a burglar in a cartoon. "What?"

"Did you forget your lie already?"

"Huh?"

"Your text said you were going to Toby's."

"I know."

"You know how I know you're lying? I know when I ask you a question and you ask me a question back."

"What?" *Ugh, his stupid wizard powers.* "No I don't."

He laughed. "Yes you do. Now spill it."

"Fine. But promise me something?"

"What?"

"Promise me that you won't get mad."

Back when I was in second grade, just after Mom died, he used to read me *A Wrinkle in Time* every night before bed—you know, the story about the girl who goes on an adventure across the universe to save her father from evil space blobs? I didn't especially love the story, but it was my favorite book by default because it was the only one I could find that had a kick-ass girl as the main character. We had an unspoken system: When Dad finished the last line, he just started immediately on the first again, so it was like this perfect never-ending story loop. That night, in the gap between the last and the first page, I said, "Dad, promise me you'll never get captured by evil space blobs." And he said, "Why?" And I said, "So I won't have to come and rescue you." And he said, "What, are you too busy?" And I said, "*Yeah*. Actually, I *am*." And, closing the book, holding his place with his finger, he said, "You wouldn't rescue me?" And I said, "I *would*, but I'd *prefer* not to." And he said: "But wouldn't that be a fun adventure?" And I said, "*No.*" I'd never flown in a spaceship, but I assumed it was just like riding a smelly bus across the universe, so it'd be boring and I'd be spacesick. Plus, there was no gravity, so shooting a basketball would be impossible. Tucking me in, he said, "I'm sorry, I can't promise that." I remember balling my fists and getting so mad—*just promise that you won't get abducted by evil space blobs!*— but, unlike most parents, he wouldn't promise what he couldn't control just to appease me. He was stubborn that way—still was, obviously. "Sorry," he said. "I can't promise that."

A game show was playing on the TV, muted. The contestants, dressed in the greens and browns and oranges of the 1970s, were celebrating.

I closed my eyes. *Just tell him.* I sighed. "So, I just met Jimmy Mack."

He leaned forward. "*The* Jimmy Mack?"

I nodded. "Toby set up this visit down in Philly. We took the train. He"—shame washed over me—"he set up this thing where they thought I had Helsinki syndrome."

"Hel-*what?*"

I showed him the Wikipedia page on my phone.

Helsinki syndrome:

A rare, incurable disease of the upper butt.

"That's . . . ," Dad said, shaking his head, "just brilliant."

Back when *he* was in middle school, Dad and his buddies used to take the train to Philly and sneak into Bells games all the time. Anything went as long as you got inside. "I mean, that's horrible," he said. "But, you know, kinda brilliant."

"Yeah," I said. "So they brought us through the locker rooms—"

Dad laughed.

"And out onto the court."

"You were on the court with Jimmy Mack? Today?"

"Crazy, right?"

"That's incredible. Did you shake his hand? Like a vise grip, right? He used to squeeze a squash ball a thousand times a day. A thousand times each hand. You couldn't pry the ball away from him if you had a pack of horses."

"Pack of horses?"

"It's an expression."

"Is it?"

He shifted on the couch. "So, what happened?"

"This is the don't-get-mad part. I think . . . I think they might try to sign me."

"Ha. Good thing you warned me. The Bells want to sign you. I'm furious."

"I'm serious, Dad."

"Uh-huh."

I knew there was only one way to make him believe.

"Come over to the playground with me," I said.

"Now?"

After I'd made about twenty in a row, including a few full-courters, I told him about the robocall.

"It's some kind of . . . miracle?" he said.

"I don't know."

He understood one thing right away, like I did. Maybe it was being from Ardwyn: If you had a winning lottery ticket you'd better bury it deep in your pocket, keep your head down, and walk a little faster. "You can't tell anyone," he said.

"I know. I told Toby. He's . . . basically no one. You know what I mean."

Out of nervous habit, the way a normal person would've chewed their nails, Dad spun the ball on his finger. He rolled the spinning ball up and down his fingers, keeping it going with an occasional slap. "You know what?" he said, steeling his jaw. "*Take* it."

"Huh?"

"I said, *take* it. When has anyone ever given us anything? This shot? This power? It's *yours* now. Anyone asks, I don't know . . . just tell them you worked harder than everyone else. You figured out the jump shot, solved it like a math problem."

"But I *did* work harder than everyone else, Dad."

"I know. I know." The ball was still spinning on his finger. He slapped it, fanning the flame. I loved seeing this side of him. Everything had always come so easy to him he'd never had to fight. But I knew he had it in him. It made me feel like we were a team. "But here's the important thing," he said. "*Enjoy it, okay?*"

I almost threw up. Was he really giving me the most-important-thing-is-to-have-fun speech? Now? Was he *getting* this? Was he grasping what I was capable of?

He came to his senses. "What the heck am I saying? Of course you'll enjoy it. You'll enjoy it when you're kicking those boys' butts out there."

Damn right.

30

The Bells GM, Doug Braman, aka Stick-Up-His-Butt Braman, called later that afternoon. I'd left our home phone number with Coach Mack. Dad answered the kitchen phone and held the receiver between us.

Braman sounded tired. There were stories in the paper every morning about how he was going to be fired immediately after the season. "So we saw the video," he said. "It was . . . unusual. We're wondering if Beatrice might come down for another visit."

I smirked. They still thought my name was Beatrice. Beatrice Trudeaux.

"You mean *Elizabeth*?" Dad said. "Lizzy?"

I imagined Braman in his office, covering the phone, gesturing like: *Is this a joke, guys? Are you pranking me? This has to be a joke.* "I'm sorry," he said. "Lizzy. Coach Mack is a little hard of, um—he's old."

"Who's 'we'?" Dad asked.

"Pardon?"

"You said 'we.' *We* were wondering . . ."

"Oh. Right. Our scouting staff. And myself."

"So, like a tryout?"

"Not exactly. This is"—there was that word again—"unusual. Let's not call it anything. Let's take it slow. Is Lizzy available? Sorry"—he remembered I was thirteen—"are *you* available, sir? Both of you?"

"You mean now?"

"Yes."

Dad looked over at me.

I shrugged like, *What the heck, let's go.*

"We'll be there," Dad said.

"Great," Braman said. "And just to be clear, this is just, uh, a—I don't know what it is. Can you not tell anyone about this? Can you not share that link, or perhaps take down the vid—"

Dad frowned. "We're on our way, Doug." He hung up. "Ready?"

"Yeah. Just gimme a few minutes to do my nails."

"Ummm—"

"I'm kidding, Dad. Let's go. Can Toby come?"

"What is he, your agent?"

"Actually, he kind of—"

"Yeah, yeah. Call him up. Let's go."

31

So we went to Philly for the *second* time that day, this time with proper adult supervision. Dad, stubborn as ever, parked in the General Lot, even though all the VIP spots were open.

Coach Mack greeted us at the entrance. He'd ironed his funeral suit, possibly while still wearing it. He went down the line, crushing all our hands. He held on to Dad's hand a little longer. "The man, the myth," he said. "It's good to see ya."

"You too, Coach."

"Any chance we get a two-for-one deal? Father-daughter?"

"You're gonna have a hard enough time signing her," Dad said. "Plus, now you broke my hand, so I'm useless."

I shook my head. *Dad jokes . . .*

Braman, the GM, was in his late fifties. He was salty on top and doughy in the middle. He had on a charcoal-black suit with no tie and white basketball sneakers. "Doug Braman," he said. "You must be Lizzy. We saw your video."

"*My* video," Toby said.

"Right," Braman said, peeking at his watch. "So how about you put up a few shots?"

"My pleasure," I said. "Where you want me to shoot from?"

"Wherever you're comfortable."

"How about here?" I was ten feet behind the three-point line. *Deep*, as they say.

Braman peeked over at his scouts. "Sure," he said, smirking.

I took a ball off the rack. I squared up.

"What are you doing?" Braman said.

"You said to shoot."

"Yeah. But you're facing the wrong way."

I was facing the *other* hoop. *Waaaaaaay* deep. About sixty feet. "Am I?"

"You are."

"Oh, wow." I batted my eyelashes. "How silly of me. Gee, thanks, mister."

He was losing patience.

The scouts were covering their mouths. Hiding their laughter.

To be honest, I wasn't quite sure what I was doing. I was making it up as I went along—always my best self.

"Just shoot the ball," Braman said.

I turned back to the closer basket, still over thirty feet away.

I shot.

The ball rocketed through the hoop.

Pure swish.

I made the same shot.

Again.

And again.

And again.

And again.

And again.

No one was laughing anymore.

32

J ust then one of the Bells players, Alou Achebe, poked his head out of the tunnel. Achebe is the tallest player in pro basketball history. Seven seven. He gets his height from his mother, he says. She's six ten. His father is *only* six eight. He's from Sudan.

Now *my* mouth was hanging open. Alou could reach up and grab the rim without jumping. The basketball gods had given him this great gift, but, like always, comedians that they are, they'd counterbalanced it. He was also probably the weakest player in NBA history. He had, as Dad once observed, a whole arm full of wrists.

"Alou," Braman said. "We've got a rising young star here. Meet Lizzy Trudeaux."

I extended my hand, but Alou ignored it. Instead, he leaned all the way down and draped his long arms around me. It was like hugging a giant coatrack.

"Pleasure to meet you," he said. His voice was deep, his accent subtle.

Braman asked if he'd mind playing a little defense—"just for fun."

"Sure," Alou said. "But only a little."

Coach Mack scoffed. That could've been the team's official motto that year. *Come see the Bells. We'll play defense . . . but only a little.*

Alou windmilled his arms to get loose. He had on light brown corduroy pants, brown slip-on shoes (size twenty-seven), and a cream-colored button-up shirt. All his clothes were custom-made, of course. "One-on-one?" he said to me.

I smiled. "Bring it."

He reached down and plucked the ball from my hip, rolled it back like an apple.

"Ball in," he said.

I was just behind the foul line. He was in the lane, arms half raised like he was wading into cold water.

"Game to three?" I said.

He smiled. "Sure, sure."

I took two steps back, dribbling the ball between my legs each time, and shot.

He didn't even bother lifting his arms.

Pure swish.

He smiled. "Nice shot. Nice shot."

He carried the ball out to the foul line and turned.

"Oh no," I said, circling outside him. "Winner's out."

"Make it, take it," Toby called.

"Of course," Alou said, smiling. "Of course."

I started with the same move: two backward, between-the-legs dribbles, but this time I up-faked with my shoulders, causing him to lift his arms and hedge forward. While he was off balance, I made two hard dribbles to the left and pure-swished another.

The scouts exchanged looks.

Braman watched, arms crossed.

Alou rolled up his sleeves, one fold at a time. "You didn't tell me she could shoot like this," he said to Braman. Then, to me: "It reminds me of back home."

He explained how the rims back in Sudan never had nets on them, so the ball passed through in total silence. "You'll have to teach me that trick," he said.

We checked the ball again. I knew I needed to add at least one more move to the sequence this time. I made the same two moves then hesitated, causing him to lift slightly out of his stance, and made three more hard dribbles down to the baseline.

He lunged to block me.

Like I knew he would.

I waited for him to fly by then leaned back the other way, arm fully extended. I flipped it up—a finger roll. The ball floated up and up and up. A half second later, a shadow blurred from the baseline. The ball bounced into the stands.

Crap.

Somehow he'd recovered and blocked it. Spiked it like a volleyball.

I was stunned, but I guess I shouldn't have been. It wasn't as if *my* superpower prevented other players from exercising *their* superpowers. Pro sports players are really just a bunch of humans with superpowers. You just forget because they're playing against one another, canceling one another out.

Toby retrieved the ball from the stands and heaved it back.

Relax, I thought. *You're up 2–0, and it's still your ball.*

We checked the ball, and right away I started dribbling backward. Alou stopped at the three-point line (there's an invisible fence there that emits a high-pitched frequency that only centers can hear), but I kept backing up. I was nearing half-court now, the unofficial out-of-bounds line for a one-on-one game. I had plenty of space to shoot.

And yet . . .

Did I want to win this way? Backing up?

No.

I charged, full speed, right at him. I had no idea what I was going to do. No plan.

My mind was totally blank. But here was the important thing: I was the aggressor. I was moving forward. My action would force him to react, and based on his reaction I'd know what to do.

He took a step back, and I glimpsed my opening.

I cut hard to the right. That caused him to take a big, awkward step to his left. While he was midstride, I crossed over and ducked between his legs, like a video game character passing through a wall.

I came out the other side and banked in a wide-open layup.

3–0.

Game.

Alou couldn't stop laughing.

I carried the ball over to where Dad and Toby were standing.

Toby flashed me a quick, eyes-wide thumbs-up.

Dad pulled me in beside him. *A wizard-like move, if there ever was one.*

Braman still had his arms crossed atop his soggy stomach. He moved his lips, but no words came out. Finally, he forced one out, round as an egg. *"How?"*

"Oh, come *on*," Toby said, now reclined on the Bells' bench, ankles crossed, hands behind his head like he owned the place. "Just get her a *uniform* already."

"Wait," Braman said. "Who the heck are *you?*"

"That's Archimedes," Coach Mack said. "He's got a disease that makes him say dumb crap all the time."

"I'm perfectly healthy, thanks," Toby said, sitting up. "In fact, I'm her *agent*, so you'll need to run the contract by me first."

Braman closed his eyes and pinched the bridge of his nose. This was getting more ridiculous by the minute. "Excuse us, please."

The scouts huddled, talking into their hands like secret service agents. (As scouts do.) "We'll need to see a little more," Braman said. "See how this . . . plays out."

"Now or never," Dad said. "This video's already going bacterial."

"You mean *viral?*"

"Call it what you want. We've already got a tryout set up with New York tomorrow, Boston on Monday."

BS, but they didn't know it.

The scouts huddled again.

"Ten-day contract," Braman said. "We're willing—I can't believe I'm saying this—we're willing to offer a ten-day contract. But we need approval from upstairs."

117

The Bells owner, Hal Kurtz, had to approve any new contracts. He was out of the country on business, Braman explained, "so it may take a week or so."

"But there's only two weeks left in the season," I said.

"I know," Braman said, exhausted. "And thank god."

Looking back, I wonder if he signed me as a last-ditch attempt to save his job, or because he just didn't give a crap anymore.

Whatever the reason, *it was happening*.

It was really happening.

Halftime

3rd Quarter

THE CONTRACT

Hal Kurtz—Bells Owner

Do I remember when Braman first called me with the Trudeaux thing? Sure I do. I was on my yacht down in St. Martin. No, Jamaica. No, the Dominican Republic. No, St. Martin. No, Bermuda. Anyway, it was nice out. My wife and I were on the yacht. The little one. The big one was in for repairs. So anyway, I'm out on the deck and my hands are all covered in sunscreen, so I have to answer my phone with my nose, and I say: "Doug, this had better be good."

Doug Braman—Bells General Manager

It took a while to get Mr. Kurtz on the line. He was in an important business meeting, as I recall.

Hal Kurtz—Bells Owner

My wife was wearing one of those big floppy hats. She said: "What'd *he* want?" I said: "He wants me to sign a thirteen-year-old girl." We both laughed our heads off. Even the dogs were laughing in their little orange life vests. *Howling*.

Doug Braman—Bells General Manager

He thought I was kidding at first. But then I sent him the video.

ad was admiring the skyscrapers as the bus came out of the Lincoln Tunnel, into New York City, but I barely noticed them. I had my big headphones on, the ones meant to keep sound *out*. Toby's face flickered in my mind as we crossed over Broadway—I imagined him bowing before a roaring audience, roses showering down—but I chased that thought away.

My first pro game, on national TV, was just a few hours away.

I had to focus.

Shootaround was at 9:00 a.m. A pro shootaround is basically a study hall—mostly, you just have to be there. All the players were in sweats. Coach Mack limped onto the court and went over the scouting reports.

I didn't shoot, if you're wondering. It wasn't that I was scared. I knew that with my magic power I was better than all of them—maybe better than anyone who'd *ever* played. But still, it didn't feel right to be out there showing off, you know? What had I done to *earn* this magical ability? To share the court with these pros?

I'd answered a freaking phone.

It'd be different when the actual game started, I told myself, when the bright lights came on and it was time to *perform*, to fulfill my destiny, but until then I just sat on the bench and watched. (I'm pretty sure they all thought I was a ball girl.)

One notable thing did happen at that shootaround. Something even my biggest fans, who've seen all my YouTube videos hundreds of times, don't know.

While Dad was off somewhere calling out of work, Coach Mack came over and slumped beside me on the bench. He was still in his funeral suit with the pink flowered tie. He extended his heels onto the court, and I noticed that again he wasn't wearing any socks with his dress shoes. His lips were moving, but I was still wearing my big headphones, so I couldn't hear him. I uncovered one ear. "Huh?"

I thought he'd just come over to bust my chops, or to rest, but then he leaned forward and rubbed the back of his neck. "Listen, kid. There ain't no good way to say this. Bad news. I can't play ya."

My chest tightened. *"What?"*

"Word just come down. Change a' plans."

The GM, he told me, had gotten cold feet.

"Braman knows he's gonna be lookin' for another job in two weeks. Doesn't want this hangin' over him. So looks like you're on the bench tonight. Sorry to say."

All I could think to say was, "But he *saw*, right?"

Coach Mack tilted his head up and closed his eyes. His eyelids were like rain-soaked paper that's dried out in the sun. "Listen," he said. "It ain't the worst thing. This all plays like I think it's gonna, it's gonna be *big*. Bigger than you know. We still got LA and Cleveland next week. This one don't mean nothin'. Keep your head up, kid. Your time's comin'.'"

I broke down and began bawling so hard Coach Mack didn't know what to do. Actually—come on, you know me—that was what I felt like on the *inside*. Outwardly, I just bit my lip and clenched my fists and mumbled, "I understand, Coach."

Dad came back and we followed my new teammates up the tunnel. Looking back over my shoulder at the arena—silent now, but soon to be filled with twenty thousand fans—I remembered one of the last things Mom ever told me, when I'd complained about a book having too many big words in it. She was always pushing me to read beyond my grade level—it was the only way to get better, she said, like playing against the older kids at the playground. Sitting at the foot of my bed, still dressed in her scrubs from work, she squeezed my hand. "It's not *supposed* to be easy, Lizzy. You know that, right?"

Her ghost faded as I crossed into the locker room.

t felt like that lazy atmosphere before a movie starts—dim and warm and a little bit magical. *Yes*, I thought, marveling at the wood-paneled lockers. *This is what a pro locker room's supposed to be.* Padded massage tables. Cold tubs. Hot tubs. A Great Pyramid of Ankle Tape. I carried my uniform down to the last stall and locked myself inside.

This was where the fantasy came apart again.

I cracked my elbow on the toilet-paper dispenser. My ancient shoelace snapped with a cloud of dust. The only thing that kept me from Incredible-Hulking the crap out of that stall was imagining Toby standing outside it.

Let's go, Clark Kent. Hustle up in there. The bad guys are getting away.

To which I responded: *Clark Kent didn't have to put on a freaking sports bra.*

To which he responded: *Not young Clark Kent . . . but old Clark Kent with man boobs. . . .*

I slid out of the stall. It wasn't too late. The moment could still be salvaged. This was a big one—the moment I would first see myself in a pro jersey with my name on it! I stepped in front of the mirror like it was an oncoming car.

It was bad, man. The uniform was *huge*. It looked like I was wearing a ball gown. I pulled the strings in my shorts like they were connected to those slatted blinds we had at the house, the ones that Dad always said he was going to clean but never did.

Speaking of Dad, he was leaning against the wall with his arms crossed. His ankles were crossed too. He must've transported there using his Wizard powers—I hadn't heard him. His already-thin voice was even thinner in the tiled bathroom. He said, in what may've been the dad comment of the century, "Looks a lil' big."

"Gee," I said. "Ya think?"

35

t was now 11:30 a.m. Ninety minutes until game time. My new teammates were scattered around the locker room, going through their various pregame rituals. Glen Grant, the shortest member of the team, was hanging upside down in his locker like a bat. Ray "Junkman" Anderson appeared to be doing some variation of the Hokey Pokey. Abe "The Hammer" Gillman was tapping each of his toes with a xylophone mallet.

The exception was seven-foot-seven Alou Achebe, who was sitting in a fold-out lawn chair in front of his locker doing the *New York Times* crossword puzzle. Reading glasses were perched on the tip of his nose, giving him a professor-like look. Bare feet spread wide, toes curling into the carpet, he was staring down at the crossword, tapping the eraser of a number-two pencil against his teeth. "Six letters," he said. "Third letter's a *u*. Between the engine and the gearbox."

"Clutch," Dad said right away.

"Clutch," Alou repeated. He filled in the letters, then finally looked up—the only time, of course, that Alou Achebe was *ever* looking up at me. He folded the newspaper and set it on his lap. He palmed his knees. "Nervous?"

"I feel like I'm wearing a costume," I muttered. Talking to anyone else, I would've played it cool, but somehow I felt comfortable around Alou. Everyone did. He had that special something you can't teach, like knowing where a rebound will come off or being able to catch a pass in traffic. But he had it for *people*. "How did *you* feel before your first game?" I asked.

He did me one better.

He went all the way back to his first day in *America*.

"First day," he said, still palming his knees, head back, smiling. "I was eighteen. I flew from Khartoum to London, London to DC. I was five foot nine when I boarded the plane, honest. I fell asleep over the ocean. I dreamed I was a giant and woke up like *this*. My heart was racing." He mimed a pounding heart, then a plane skidding across a runway. "I was here, man! *Here!* America! I raced up the tunnel and burst out, looking all around. The very first person I saw—I'm serious now—was a witch." He said it like *weech*. "I mean, a *witch* witch. Pointy black hat, broomstick. *No*, I thought. *No. No. No. I'm still dreaming. I'm flying. I'm over the ocean. I'm dreaming.* I rubbed my eyes. Next person I saw was a *clown*. Rainbow-colored hair, white face, red nose. Beside him—there was Elvis! Marilyn Monroe! Now I was freaking out. *I'm dreaming*, I thought. *I'm dreaming.* I kept pinching myself. I found a police officer. I tapped him on the shoulder. 'Officer,' I said. 'Officer, where am I? What's going on?' He turned around and his eyeball was hanging out of its socket! I ran. Everyone was staring like *I* was the freak. I stumbled outside, crashed into a taxi driver. 'Whoa,' he said. 'Whoa, big man. Whoa.' He laughed, then he said this word I'd never heard before: '*Halloween*. It's Halloween, man. Halloween. Relax!'"

I knew what Alou was saying—*this is all new to you, just relax, everything will be fine*—but it was hard. I felt like the planet was spinning wildly out of control and I was the only one who noticed. I broke a sacred game-day rule and turned on my phone.

L: hey

T: who dis

L: ha ha

L: wish u were here

T: where?

L: um

L: in NEW YORK

L: remember????

T: ur in ny???

T: ha

T: i know, just playin'

T: im streamin' it

T: break a leg!

L: first of all

L: u don't say that to

bball plyers

L: second

L: it doesn't matter

T: ????

L: [...]

T: listen man

T: don't overthink this

T: u got the role of a
   lifetime!

T: just PLAY it!

T: 🏀

T: 🐐

PHILADELPHIA V. NEW YORK

Paul Reagan—New York Head Coach

I'm not usually one to talk about "vibes" or "energy," but there's no other way to say it. There was a weird energy in the building that day. Weird vibes, man. I sensed it right when I walked in.

George Van Arden—New York Assistant Coach

We were all uptight before the game . . . but that was normal. It's hard to explain if you haven't coached. We were in first place. We'd already wrapped up the division. On paper, the game meant nothing . . . but that's exactly why it was stressful. When you're at that point, with the playoffs so close, you're just trying to get *through* a game like that. You just want it to be over as quick as possible without anything freaky happening.

Harry Hawkins—Bells Guard

I remember [Trudeaux] on the bus that morning, sitting there with her dad. She didn't say much. She just stared out the window with those big headphones on. Looking back, she didn't seem overwhelmed, like you'd think. Or even happy. Or sad. Or *anything*. She just stared out the window, man. It was hard to get a read on her.

Doug Braman—Bells General Manager

Everyone thinks that I ordered Jimmy not to play her that first game. That's not true. I don't know where that came from. Did I suggest, casually, that maybe he should *consider* the implications of playing her? Yes. But I stand by that. This was *huge*. This was a pivotal moment in the history of the *league*, let alone the franchise, for many reasons. I recognized that in the moment. Some other people didn't. Yet somehow I'm always the bad guy. I'm the villain. I was the one who *signed* her. People forget that.

Jimmy Mack—Bells Head Coach

Braman can say whatever he wants. He ordered me not to play her. Period. He said, "Jimmy, you put her in, so help me god I'll come down and fire you in the middle of the . . ." It was like he woke up with a hangover—*What'd I do?* His plan was to pin it on the owner, Kurtz. Spin it like a gimmick to pluck a few bucks from a last-place team. I told him to kiss my old, wrinkled [butt]. "You pick the players," I said, "I coach 'em. That's how this works." Funny thing is, I wasn't *plannin'* on playin' her. I told her that before the game. I didn't think she was ready, didn't wanna rush it. I was worried about her. [Bites down on ring.]

134

Spud Larkin—Famous Movie Director/New York Fan

I almost missed the game, man. I was *this* close to missin' it. I was sick. I had this bad head cold and a sore throat. My wife said, "You know you don't have to go to *every* game, right?" That hadn't occurred to me. I called around to see if anyone wanted the tickets. Everyone said, "Who they playin'? Who they playin'?" I said, "The Bells!" They said, "The *Bells*? Yeah. No thanks." [Laughs.] So I'm sitting there with $500 paper in my hands. Finally, I just decided to suck it up and go. My wife made me promise I wouldn't yell too much. I had to be on set the next week. I was just getting my voice back. I said, "Me? Yell?" She rolled her eyes.

Alou Achebe—Bells Center

I think it was something like 36–12 after the first quarter.

Harry Hawkins—Bells Guard

Man, Spud was running his mouth the whole game. They were up forty in the third, and he was *killin'* us. "Your game got more holes than your mama's drawers." "Your daddy's *unicycle* got more handles." Stuff like that. He told me his, and I quote, "itchy-butthole-havin' dog" dragged his butt up the sidewalk faster than I got up the court. It was rough, man. Funny, but rough.

Alou Achebe—Bells Center
As a player, you'd try to tune him out . . . but it's just impossible. Spud is Spud. He's like a force of nature. You can't shut him up.

Tim Ferguson—Head Referee
It got to that late-game stage where everyone was kind of on autopilot. Most of the fans had already left. I was standing there thinking about where I was going to eat after the game. Suddenly, out of the corner of my eye I saw someone shoot up off the bench. I kind of did a double take.

George Van Arden—New York Assistant Coach
I thought she was a ball girl. You know, like she was picking up the jacket of someone who'd just checked in. Never in a million years did I think *she* was checking in. It didn't register that she was wearing a jersey with her name on it. The jersey was, like, five sizes too big. She was swimming in it.

Emily Murray—Philadelphia Sports Columnist
She was wearing these filthy old sneakers with duct tape on them.

Paul Reagan—New York Head Coach
Jimmy walked out on the court and called a time-out. That pissed me off. I hate when he does that.

Plus, there was about twelve seconds left, and we were up forty. That's when I saw her. She was just kneeling there with her elbow on the scorer's table. I turned to my assistant and said, "What the heck is going on?"

Edgar Patrick—New York Center

I was out of the game by then. It was a blowout. I was down the end of the bench, joking around with the guys. Someone nudged me and was like, "Yo, man, check this out." I looked over and there was this *girl* coming on the court. I thought she was a fan. I thought that a fan had run onto the court. I always wondered why that didn't happen more. I mean, the fans are right there. So the game stopped.

Jimmy Mack—Bells Head Coach

[Runs pink bubblegum cigar under nose.] One of the best moments of my life. Seein' their faces.

Tim Ferguson—Head Referee

There was some confusion. I think there was, like, fourteen seconds left. I went over to Jimmy. I said, "Yo, Jimmy, what's the deal?"

Jimmy Mack—Bells Head Coach

Ferguson came over. He says, "What's up?" I says,

"I'm sorry, Timmy, I'm gettin' old, maybe I didn't hear it." "Hear *what*?" he says. "The horn. I didn't hear it. Didn't know the game was over." He says, "It ain't over." I says, "Oh, well, good. Then I'm puttin' my bleeping player in the game." Just like that. Well, maybe it wasn't *that* polite.

Tim Ferguson—Head Referee

Jimmy never made things easy. I went over and checked with the scorer. The rules are simple. All players have to be listed in the official scorebook to be eligible to play. The coaches have to initial the book before the game to approve it. It's a technical foul if you try to sub in a player that's not listed. Thing is—especially by that point of the season— sometimes you kind of cut corners. Nobody admits it, but it happens all the time. I just counted up the number of players on both sides before the game, circled that number at the bottom, and gave the book back. Happens all the time. I missed it. So now, thirteen seconds left, I look closer and, sure enough, her name is in the book. First time I ever saw it. Lizzy Trudeaux. Jimmy snuck it in there, just in case. Sneaky son of a . . . [Laughs.]

Paul Reagan—New York Head Coach

I don't remember what I said, but I remember not

being happy about it. I thought Mack was sticking his thumb in our eye. Like, I can't beat you, so here, I'll turn this into a circus. He would do that.

Toby Sykes—Trudeaux's Best Friend
I was streaming the game at home on my phone. I was going crazy when they put her in. I kept yelling, "Oh my god, Lizzy's on TV! Oh my god, Lizzy's on TV!" Even though, you know, it was on my phone. The whole thing was surreal.

Edgar Patrick—New York Center
It was surreal, man.

Jack Steele—New York Guard
I don't know how else to describe it except "surreal."

Emily Murray—Philadelphia Sports Columnist
You know what's funny? That famous moment when she first checked in? Almost everyone on press row missed it. There's this tradition where you write your game story while the game is still happening so all you have to do is plug in the final score and you can make deadline. So a lot of us on press row weren't even looking when it happened. [Laughs.] That's about right.

Tad Wexler—Bells TV Announcer

Oh yeah. We were caught off guard. That's an understatement. The team had sent out a twelve-word press release overnight, but it got buried—it was a Sunday morning—and the people who did see it figured it was a prank. [Bells color commentator Ovid Green] and I looked at each other like, "Are we in the Twilight Zone?"

Ovid Green—Bells Color Commentator

If you rewatch the broadcast, there's about a five-second pause when she came in when all you can hear is the rustling of papers. We were stunned, just stunned.

George Van Arden—New York Assistant Coach

If you knew what to look for, everything she would become was right there in that first moment. She had this, I don't know, this *presence* about her. This intensity. It was like she'd imagined this moment so many times in her head it was almost normal.

Tim Ferguson—Head Referee

To her credit, she was totally calm. Like any sub, checking in the game. You could tell she felt at home on the basketball court, *any* basketball court. I waved her in. "Let's go," I said. "Let's go. Let's play this thing out. There'll be time for answers later."

Emily Murray—Philadelphia Sports Columnist

Oh, Spud lost it. [Laughs.] He couldn't believe they were putting a girl in the game.

Spud Larkin—Famous Movie Director/ New York Fan

Listen. I want to be clear about this. I'm an equal-opportunity hater. You're wearing the other team's jersey, you're gonna get it. Period. I had nothing against the girl . . . except that she was wearing a Bells jersey. I was just having fun.

Harry Hawkins—Bells Guard

Spud started in on her right away. Nothing harsh, just stuff like, "This is your team, Philly? *This* is your team?"

Tad Wexler—Bells TV Announcer

There wasn't enough time to process the magnitude of the moment. It was just happening. Achebe inbounded the ball to her. I was so flustered I said her name wrong. I was reading it off the back of her jersey. I said, "And they inbound the ball to . . . Trubedeaux?"

Edgar Patrick—New York Center

Nobody knew what to do. A thirteen-year-old girl had just checked into the game. It was crazy. We were all standing up. Everyone left in the building was standing.

Paul Reagan—New York Head Coach

Scootie Sanders was in the game for us. Kinda fitting—a Philly guy. He was the one supposed to be guarding her.

Scootie Sanders—New York Guard

Coach Reagan started hollering, "Back off! Back off!" So I backed off. We all sorta drifted over to the sideline. Got out of the way. The clock was running down.

Jimmy Mack—Bells Head Coach

Oh, man. She didn't like that.

Alou Achebe—Bells Center

You could tell she didn't like that.

Bill "Chalk" Rasner—Nationally Syndicated Sportswriter

She did *not* like that.

Scootie Sanders—New York Guard

So I'm drifting to the sideline, and here she comes, right for me. I didn't know what to do. I just started running, like, the other way.

Joe Dugan—Bells Beat Writer

Maybe the first time in the history of basketball that the player with the ball was chasing the *defender.* [Laughs.]

Spud Larkin—Famous Movie Director/ New York Fan

It looked like Sanders had a little bee chasing him. He couldn't shake her. I started running down the sideline, flipping out.

Toby Sykes—Trudeaux's Best Friend

A lot of people didn't get that—her chasing him—but I got it right away. Lizzy is—how to put this?—she's *super* competitive. She hates losing, but someone *letting* her win? That's even worse. It pissed her off that they weren't guarding her.

Jimmy Mack—Bells Head Coach

I loved that. I'd a' done the same thing. There's time left on the clock, play the game.

Emily Murray—Philadelphia Sports Columnist

She finally picked up her dribble, and I thought— we all thought—okay, that's it. Now the clock will run out. There were only seven seconds left.

Tad Wexler—Bells TV Announcer

She picked up her dribble, and everyone kind of relaxed, including Sanders. He exhaled and started to turn away. Then . . .

George Van Arden—New York Assistant Coach

Someone told me that YouTube clip has, like, forty million views. The one where it's a close-up and you can see her mouthing something after she spikes the ball off his legs.

Edgar Patrick—New York Center

It looked like she was playin' dodgeball.

Scootie Sanders—New York Guard

[Shaking head.] That *hurt*, man. The ball flew,

like, ten rows up. And then, swear to god, she goes, "Guard me, punk." I said, *"Whaaaat?"* She said: "You heard me."

Jack Steele—New York Guard
Oh, god. Everyone on our bench lost it. Scootie was getting punked by this little girl. Spud was practically having a seizure. He was stomping up and down the sideline, chewing on his hat.

Scootie Sanders—New York Guard
[Rolls eyes.] So now I *had* to guard her.

Tad Wexler—Bells TV Announcer
Three seconds to go.

Bill "Chalk" Rasner—Nationally Syndicated Sportswriter
At first she couldn't get open. She started right, cut back left, kind of zigzagged. She finally caught the ball about forty feet out.

Toby Sykes—Trudeaux's Best Friend
It was just like she used to count down at the park. I was counting in my head. Three . . .

Tad Wexler—Bells TV Announcer
She went hard right. Sanders was there with her, step for step.

Toby Sykes—Trudeaux's Best Friend

Two . . .

Tad Wexler—Bells TV Announcer

She threw on the brakes, pulled up.

Toby Sykes—Trudeaux's Best Friend

One . . .

Tad Wexler—Bells TV Announcer

Sanders bit on the pump fake. He lunged forward. She leaned into him, absorbed the contact.

Tim Ferguson—Head Referee

My hand went up. Boom. It was clearly a foul. He got her pretty good.

Tad Wexler—Bells TV Announcer

Somehow, falling down, she flipped up this impossible, over-the-head, sidewinder shot. Like a hook shot crossed with a finger roll. The horn sounded a split second after she released it. The red light behind the basket lit up.

Edgar Patrick—New York Center

Right out of her hand, you could see it was . . . different. It had this crazy-fast backspin.

Jack Steele—New York Guard

It was like a video game. The ball, like, accelerated through the hoop. *Whoosh!*

Emily Murray—Philadelphia Sports Columnist

I've never heard a crowd make a noise like that, when the ball went in. Never before and never since. It was like when you step on a dog's foot and it yelps. That's why you sign up for this job. All the bad coffee, all the miles, all the greasy fast food, it's all for that moment, that sound.

Bill "Chalk" Rasner—Nationally Syndicated Sportswriter

My ears popped when the ball went through. Everyone's seemed to. I looked around, and everyone was tugging down on their ears, wide-eyed, in disbelief.

Alou Achebe—Bells Center

I reached down and helped her up. She was lying on her back, smirking. She said, "Did it go in?"

Bill "Chalk" Rasner—Nationally Syndicated Sportswriter

And then, if things couldn't get any more surreal, she had to shoot the free throw.

Tim Ferguson—Head Referee

By rule, even though there's no time on the clock, you still shoot the free throw. You stand out there on an island, all alone, and shoot it.

Paul Reagan—New York Head Coach

If she had any fear in her body at all, she didn't show it. She walked to the line and waited for the ball like she'd done it a million times.

Tim Ferguson—Head Referee

I stood under the basket and passed her the ball.

Toby Sykes—Trudeaux's Best Friend

I knew her routine by heart. Four dribbles. *Bang. Bang. Bang. Bang.* Deep breath. Bend the knees. But then . . . she didn't shoot.

Edgar Patrick—New York Center

She didn't shoot it.

Alou Achebe—Bells Center

She *looked* like she was gonna shoot it, but then she didn't.

Harry Hawkins—Bells Guard

She pinned the ball on her hip and turned her head.

Spud Larkin—Famous Movie Director/ New York Fan

She stared right at me, man.

Jack Steele—New York Guard

Spud was sayin' somethin', but when she looked over, he just froze, midsentence, mouth open.

George Van Arden—New York Assistant Coach

Forget everything that came after. In my mind, *that* was the most impressive thing she ever did. *That* was the miracle. She shut up Spud Larkin. [Laughs.]

Joe Dugan—Bells Beat Writer

We all kept waiting for her to shoot it. It was tense. I've never felt suspense like that at a basketball game. Any game. She just stood there with the ball on her hip, staring.

Tim Ferguson—Head Referee

You get ten seconds to shoot a free throw. Everyone knows that, but no one ever actually uses the time. I was doing a silent count, extending my arm, one, two, three, four, five. Just before I got to ten, she shot the ball. The thing was, she never looked back at the basket! She just kept staring at Spud.

Spud Larkin—Famous Movie Director/New York Fan

She never blinked, man. I swear to god. She. Never.
Blinked.

Alou Achebe—Bells Center

Everyone's heard of a no-look pass. But a no-look
shot?

Jack Steele—New York Guard

A no-look shot. [Shakes head.]

Emily Murray—Philadelphia Sports Columnist

And of course she drains it. A no-look shot. A four-
point play. She held her follow-through high to
punctuate the moment. The image that became her
logo—arm up, hand tipped down like the head of a
swan.

Joe Dugan—Bells Beat Writer

Her teammates rushed her off the court, into the
locker room. She hid on the bus, we later found out,
while all the other players showered. She basically
ran right out into the parking garage.

Tad Wexler—Bells TV Announcer

The final score was something like 126–89. And you
know what? It didn't matter. Not even a little bit.
The score didn't matter.

36

After some initial celebrating, it was surprisingly quiet on the bus ride home. The New Jersey Turnpike has that effect. I pressed my ponytail into the seat back and stared out over the bus driver's shoulder. I opened my mouth slightly, imagining I was swallowing up lines on the dark highway like Pac-Man pellets.

The taillights became swarming red ghosts.

The exit signs, new levels.

I must've drifted off. When I came to, Coach Mack was holding out two plastic-wrapped pink bubblegum cigars. "My wife used to buy me eighty-two cigars before every season," he said. "Eighty-two cigars for eighty-two games. One for every win. Used to smoke a whole lot of 'em too. Now she buys me gum."

"But we lost," I said.

"Yeah, but only by thirty-seven, thanks to you."

We both unwrapped the sugary cigars and clamped them between our teeth.

"Are you serious?" I asked. "When you talk about coaching until you . . . you know?"

"Until I *croak*? Ah, who knows. Fifty years I been at this. I don't know what else I'd do."

"Maybe you could go back to St. Ann's. Maybe they need a fifth- and sixth-grade coach."

"CYO ball?" He held out his cigar like he was admiring its glowing tip. "Now, *there's* an idea. Though I'd wanna coach the girls this time."

"How come?"

I expected him to say: *Fundamentals. Girls care about the fundamentals. They play the right way.* That's what everyone always says.

But instead he said: "They're tougher."

I smiled in the dark.

We passed Exit 7.

"Pure swish," Coach Mack said a minute later, gnawing at his cigar.

I looked away.

"Don't worry, kid, I ain't gonna quiz ya. The media'll do that plenty, trust me. They already got their stories written, just gotta get ya to fill in the words. They'll keep askin' till ya say it right."

As we crossed over the bridge, back home into Pennsylvania, a notification pinged on my phone. "TobySykes3000 is broadcasting live." He was in his bedroom, in a coat, tie, and pajama bottoms, doing a postgame show. "That's *my* best friend!" he was saying. "My best friend! Did you see when—" I clicked on his account and noticed that the video he'd posted from the secret tryout was now up to 167 views. By the time we were over the bridge, it had 274. A minute later, it had 489. Then 633.

And when I looked again the next morning, it had 3.6 million.

37

t's weird, going viral. You're laying there in bed, reading all these internet articles about yourself, you're trending on Twitter, you're the lead story on ESPN.com, but then you look up and it's still your same crappy room with the crappy peeling wallpaper. The same Sidney Rayne poster, the same trophies on the dresser. The same sound of Dad snoring on the couch as you tiptoe downstairs. The same discount-brand cereal boxes on top of the fridge. The same milk. The same desolate playground across the street with weeds climbing out of the cracks on the basketball court. The same—

It's like there's this lag.

That's the best way I can put it.

Loading . . .

Loading . . .

Loading . . .

But what's bizarre is that it's the *real world* that's rebooting.

Updating itself around you.

Every time you blink.

38

When Toby appeared at the playground the next morning, he looked taller somehow. He pretended to trip at the edge of the court and barrel-rolled toward me in slow motion, pausing for dramatic effect before each successive roll until he hit my shins. He was wearing an XXXL T-shirt that said THE TOBY SYKES SHOW!

"Morning," I said, and helped him up.

"Before you say anything else," he said, "I need to tell you something."

"Uh-oh."

"Nah, it's not bad. It's just, I woke up this morning . . . and my feet were transformed into these hideous *things*."

Oh yeah.

Forgot.

He was also wearing Rollerblades.

Which explained why he'd looked taller.

"You're a monster," I said.

He skated like Adrian in Dad's favorite movie, *Rocky*: choppy steps, arms out. "There's something different about *you*, too," he said, making a wobbly orbit around me.

"Oh yeah?"

"You look . . . tired. Were you, perhaps, out of town last night, in a big city to the north of us, and got back very late?"

"Me? Nah. I was home studying. I have a big math test on Monday."

"Studying. Weird. Because I saw a girl on TV last night that looked *just* like you."

"Did you now?"

"Mmmm-hmmm."

"How'd she do?"

"Who?"

"The girl on TV?"

"Well, actually, it was on my phone. But yeah, she rode the pine most of the game."

"Just like you."

"But she got in with like ten seconds left and made this *crazy* shot—a four-point play. I know you don't know much about basketball, but that's, like, pretty rare. That's like shooting a triple bogie in golf."

"People shoot triple bogies in golf all the time," I said. "That's *bad.*"

"You're ruining this moment with your obsessive need to be . . ." His eyes shifted onto something behind me. He pointed. "Hey, look."

39

A news van was illegally parked on the corner. The reporter was holding up a handheld mirror, doing his makeup. He spotted us and began speed-walking toward the court. From a distance, it sort of looked like he was carrying a participation trophy.

"Whoa, look!" I said. "That's Chad Stephens!"

"Who?"

"The dude from Channel Seven. *And now*"—I blew gun smoke from the tip of my finger—"*back to you, Dan*."

"Oh, right! I hate that guy! Come on, let's go mess with him!"

"Mess with him?"

The orange-faced reporter, Stephens, was about halfway to the court now. His participation trophy, I saw, was actually a Channel 7 microphone. He was tall, six four, handsome in a gin commercial kind of way. He seemed a little surprised that we were striding toward him with mirrored enthusiasm. "Lizzy!" he said, grinning like a child molester. "Lizzy! Chad Stephens! Channel Seven News!"

"Lizzy!" Toby shouted back. "Lizzy! Chad Stephens! Channel Seven News!"

Stephens came right for me, microphone extended, but Toby blocked him with his offensive lineman–size body.

I was surprised. It was borderline athletic.

"Lizzy!" Stephens said. "How do you feel about being the first *girl*—"

"LIZZY!" Toby said, jamming an imaginary microphone in *his* face. "HOW DO YOU FEEL ABOUT BEING THE FIRST GIRL—"

"What was going through your—"

"WHAT WAS GOING THROUGH YOUR—"

Stephens dropped his head and waited for the anger to recede. Then he tried again in a deeper, more professional, *60 Minutes*–like tone. "How—"

"HOW—"

"What's your—"

"WHAT'S YOUR—"

"When did you—"

"WHEN DID YOU—"

Stephens's cheek was quivering. It reminded me of the quick flash you see before a building implodes. "Shut up, you fat *freak*! I'm trying to do my *job* here, okay?"

Toby turned back to me and smiled. "You get that, Poncho?"

"Got it." (I was the cameraman.)

"Good. Our work here is done." Toby pointed. "Hey— what's that?"

We ran.

40

Well, *I* ran.

Toby skated.

Stephens chased for a minute but then either realized that (a) he was chasing a pair of thirteen-year-olds across a playground at 7:00 a.m., which was creepy even by his standards, or (b) his cameraman couldn't keep up, and if it wasn't going to be on camera, then what was the point?

We turned up the trash-filled alley behind my house and hid behind a Dumpster to catch our breath. (Well, for Toby to catch his breath. I was fine.)

"You wanna come to LA with us?" I said.

"Dude, I have school."

"Call it a field trip. I'll write you a permission slip."

The front wheel of his Rollerblade was still spinning. "Karen will want it notarized."

"I don't know what that means," I said, "but I'm sure my agent can handle it."

41

'll never forget the first time I saw the Bells' owner, Hal Kurtz. I peered out the private jet's egg-shaped window—and there he was. He was standing on the runway with his socialite wife, Helen. A floppy sun hat obscured her million-dollar face (literally, if the rumors were true). She was holding six leashes that were attached to six shivering puppies. Kurtz—all four feet nine inches of him—was in a chalk-white suit, hand raised like he was hailing a taxi. Instead of walking the fifteen feet to the steps, he was making the plane come to him. He waited until the plane steps were directly in front of him—"little more, little more, little more"—then climbed up into the cabin. He spotted me and offered his hand. "*E-liz-a-beth!* I just wanted to say how excited we are to have you as a part of our *family*." He clamped down with his other hand, creating an icy vise grip.

I wrenched my hand free and buried it under my leg. "Hi, Mr. Kurtz."

"Please. Please. My father was Mr. Kurtz. You can call me Uncle Hal. All the boys call me that, right, Alou?"

"Yeah, okay," Alou said. "Sure."

Kurtz's Fruit Roll-Ups–colored lips parted into a wet smile. His teeth had been knocked out by an elephant on a big game hunt in Botswana, supposedly, and his dentures were made of poached ivory. "If you need anything at all," he said, teeth glistening, "you just let me know."

"How 'bout a few beers?" Toby said.

Kurtz glared.

"*Root* beers, I mean. You got A&W?"

"I'm sure we'll have anything you might desire."

Toby leaned back and rolled his neck. "Great. Thanks, Hal." He cupped his hand at the side of his mouth. "You da maaaaaaan."

Kurtz trapezed back to his private section, using the tops of the seats as handholds. His wife followed with the puppies, each of them wearing—I kid you not—their own custom-made parachutes and pilot goggles. Mrs. Kurtz dragged them along, rattling a bottle of pills. "Come on," she said, "who wants one of mommy's special treats?"

Alou was laughing so hard at the parachute-wearing dogs he had to cover his face. He couldn't take it. "What a country," he said. "I love it!"

42

When we touched down in California, I had 416,000 followers on Instagram, more than double the two hundred thousand I'd had when we'd taken off. (I'd had thirty-seven just last week.)

"Ready for this?" Toby said, holding up his phone.

"Dude, are you recording *right now?*"

He grinned. "Oh yeah, we're live, people! Live *inside* the plane where *my* best friend, Lizzy Trudeaux, is about to—"

I punched his arm.

The phone dropped in the aisle.

He squealed and crawled after it. "Aaaaaand we'll be right back after this commercial break!"

I put on my big headphones, shouldered my schoolbag, and followed my new teammates down the corridor to the terminal. I couldn't believe it. It looked like our local newsman, Chad Stephens, had cloned himself a thousand times. Cameras were leveled at me from all angles.

I floated through the terminal.

"LIZZY! LIZZY! HOW DOES IT—"

The mob closed in around me.

"LIZZY! LIZZY! WHAT DO YOU—"

I felt like a suspect being rushed from a courtroom. After about a minute of push and pull, I planted my feet, dug in my heels, and yelled: *"STOP!"*

It was weird:

Everyone and everything around me stopped.

Dad stopped.

Toby stopped.

Alou stopped.

The other players stopped.

Coach Mack stopped.

The reporters stopped asking questions.

The plane out on the runway stopped turning.

The *planet* stopped, or so it seemed.

It just hung there in space.

No one had ever given a crap what Lizzy Trudeaux had to say.

But Lizzy Legend?

I decided to take a few questions, hoping the media would get what they needed and leave me alone.

"LIZZY! LIZZY! WHAT'S WITH YOUR SNEAKERS? ARE YOU MAKING SOME KIND OF POLITICAL STATEMENT?"

"Um, they're just my sneakers."

"BUT SURELY YOU CAN AFFORD A NEW PAIR NOW."

"Dude, I make the league minimum."

"And she happens to *like* her sneakers," Toby added.

"AND WHAT IS THAT SWEATSHIRT YOU'RE

162

WEARING? IS THAT NIKE? ADIDAS? HAVE YOU SIGNED ANY ENDORESMENT DEALS YET?"

Why were they so concerned with what I was *wearing?*

Where was I? The red carpet?

"Um, it's from Target," I said.

And another thing:

Would they have been asking a *male* player these questions? *I doubt it.*

Reading my mind, Toby said: "Does anyone have any *basketball* questions? For the *basketball player?*"

"IS IT TRUE YOU CAN'T MISS?"

"IS IT TRUE YOU SOLVED THE JUMP SHOT LIKE A MATH PROBLEM?"

"IS IT TRUE YOU WERE THE FIRST GIRL TO EVER PLAY—"

"WILL YOU BE STARTING TOMORROW?"

"I don't know," I said. "That's up to Coach Mack."

"CAN YOU COMMENT ON THE RUMOR THAT—"

"IS IT TRUE THAT THE OWNER—"

"ARE YOU DATING ANY—"

The reporters, all smashed together, started to look like a many-headed monster. And actually, when I saw them that way, as one big Press Monster, with cameras for eyes and bobbing microphones for hands, they weren't scary anymore.

It was just *ridiculous.*

"Don't worry about them," Dad said in the back of our bulletproof SUV, on the way to the hotel. "Just do all your talking on the court."

PHILADELPHIA VS. LA

Emily Murray—Philadelphia Sports Columnist
Leading up to the game, they kept her sheltered as best they could. I don't think she left the hotel room. They canceled the shootaround. It was just too crazy. She seemed pretty calm, actually, now that I think of it. Considering.

Tad Wexler—Bells TV Announcer
Tickets were selling for $2,500 on game day. Which I guess isn't a lot for LA people.

Jack Starr—Hollywood Actor
Oh yeah, baby. I was there. I wasn't gonna miss that one.

Cedric North—LA Guard
To be honest, it felt more like a pro wrestling match than a basketball game. Like it was all a big, scripted spectacle, you know? Except no one had given us a script.

Bart "Bulb" Edison—LA Head Coach
I said to the guys before the game: "Listen, I don't know what the heck's going on. I don't know any more than you do. But if they put a thirteen-year-old girl on the court . . . you know what to do."

Alou Achebe—Bells Center

All those flashbulbs before tip-off. Goose bumps.

Emily Murray—Philadelphia Sports Columnist

I was on press row. Just before tip-off, I said: "Watch. We'll know how this is gonna go in the first quarter. One way or the other, we'll know." My buddy laughed. "What?" he said. "You mean the *score*? What does *that* have to do with anything?"

Tad Wexler—Bells TV Announcer

LA won the opening tip. It was clear what they wanted to do. Whoever Lizzy was guarding, that's who was getting the ball. Cedric North posted her up on the first play. He had her by six inches and at least a hundred pounds. He backed her right down and scored the easiest two points you'll ever see in a pro game. He soared right over her. I looked over at my broadcast partner like, *Whoa boy. This could get ugly quickly.*

Ovid Green—Bells Color Commentator

The Bells inbounded immediately, and Lizzy rushed the ball up the court. North was waiting for her at the three-point line. But she never made it that far.

Bart "Bulb" Edison—LA Head Coach

She pulled up from about thirty-five feet. From *deep*.

Alou Achebe—Bells Center

I'd seen it a few times by now. But it was still unreal. The way the ball came out of her hand.

Buzz Moonheim—LA Radio Announcer

My ears popped when the ball went through. Or seemed to.

Tad Wexler—Bells TV Announcer

Second time down, LA gave the ball to North again. *Uh-oh*, I'm thinking. *Here we go again*. He posts her up. He backs her down just like before. She's got her feet spread real wide, and she's doing everything she can to hold her ground, but it's hopeless. It's like a gum wrapper against a firehose. North takes one last hard dribble, lowers his shoulder, and . . . *whoosh*. She sidesteps. North tumbles down and falls on the ball.

Toby Sykes—Trudeaux's Best Friend

I was behind the Bells bench with her dad. I said: "You teach her that one?" He swore he hadn't.

Alou Achebe—Bells Center

Lizzy was the only player I ever saw that had moves on *defense*.

Bart "Bulb" Edison—LA Head Coach

I felt bad for Cedric. I looked at him down the end of the bench with that oxygen mask, and I thought, *Man, this is gonna be all over* SportsCenter. And it was. Poor guy. He fell right on the ball. He couldn't get his wind back.

Emily Murray—Philadelphia Sports Columnist

So play finally resumed, and Lizzy rushed the ball up the court again. I couldn't believe it—they were *still* giving her space. It was like the sight of her, a girl, in that baggy uniform, those duct-taped sneakers, lulled them, made them forget. This time she pulled up from a little farther out, I'd say about forty feet. *Swish.*

Buzz Moonheim—LA Radio Announcer

A lot of shooters are what we call "streak-shooters." If they hit a few early, watch out. You see them start to kindle up and get hot. With Trudeaux, it was just a full-on blowtorch from the opening tip. She hit her first seven shots, all three-pointers. Jack Starr was down on his knees, bowing. I'd never seen anything like it.

Cedric North—LA Guard

I'll be honest, man. At first it was almost—what's

that word?—*emasculating*. I'd think I had her all locked up and—*bam*—she'd step back. She only needed the tiniest window to get her shot off. I'd never seen such a quick release.

Lizzy Trudeaux
I used to practice that in the mornings, at the playground. There was no one there to pass me the ball, so I'd throw the ball as hard as I could off the backboard, catch it, and release in one motion.

Tad Wexler—Bells TV Announcer
They were difficult shots . . . but not impossible. Not circus shots like the first one in New York. Every shot you could say to yourself, *Okay, wow, great shot there, but one a pro player can make.* It was the cumulative effect of them . . . *bam, bam, bam* . . . that was incredible.

Ovid Green—Bells Color Commentator
The Bells were up twelve after the first quarter. 42–30. She'd scored all their points.

Buzz Moonheim—LA Radio Announcer
The record for points in a quarter.

Emily Murray—Philadelphia Sports Columnist
She picked up right where she left off in the

second. She'd spend the first twenty seconds of the shot clock curling off screens, running laps around these giant pillars, running the defenders ragged. She was essentially sprinting nonstop for the entire game, but she never got tired. There'd be a time-out, and the LA players would be bent over, tugging on their shorts, gasping. I never once saw her out of breath.

Toby Sykes—Trudeaux's Best Friend

All those times she was late to school because she just *had* to run one more sprint. And then one more. And then one more.

Bill "Chalk" Rasner—Nationally Syndicated Sportswriter

I was there in '62, the night Wilt Chamberlain set the scoring record. One hundred points. He had fifty-nine at halftime. Trudeaux had *seventy-eight*. Twenty-six shots. Twenty-six makes. All three-pointers. Absolutely unbelievable.

Tad Wexler—Bells TV Announcer

We were starting to legitimately wonder if her arms were getting tired.

Bart "Bulb" Edison—LA Head Coach

I didn't know what to say at halftime. We were shell-shocked. We all just sat there, staring down at our feet. Finally, I just said, "This is bigger than us, man." What do you say?

@SillyBilly99xx—Detroit, Michigan
y'all seein' this right now????? #lizzylegend

@WookieAteMyHomework—San Diego, California
girl got GAME yo!!!!!! #lizzylegend

Toby Sykes—Trudeaux's Best Friend
I caught eyes with her as she was coming back out for the second half. She had this little flicker of mischief in her eyes, the one that meant, *Watch this.*

Lizzy Trudeaux
Yeah, a hundred. Wilt's record. I knew.

Ernie Jenkins—Sideline Reporter
I tried to grab her for an interview before the third quarter started, but she ducked me.

Emily Murray—Philadelphia Sports Columnist
Bam. Bam. Bam. Bam. She hits four more in a row to start the third.

Buzz Moonheim—LA Radio Announcer
They had three guys chasing her around the court! Three grown men! But she was quick.

Tad Wexler—Bells TV Announcer

And the thing everyone forgets, 'cuz of her shooting—

Buzz Moonheim—LA Radio Announcer

She had what the kids these days call a "sick handle."
Between the legs. Behind the back. Both hands. I
remember thinkin,' *Man, she could be a* point guard
if she wanted. Funny, 'cuz she had ninety points, but
that's what I thought.

@usoundlikeurfromLONDON—London, England

99 points!!! one more! one more! #lizzylegend

—SPONSORED TWEET—

@PAPAJacksPizza

Watching the game, bro? Nice! You know what would make your
life even NICER? Pizza!!! Order now!!! [Click to order]

@AkihikoBBall23—Osaka, Japan

any1 have live stream this match??? i missing it!!!!! help!!!!!!!
#lizzylegend

@MooBoy1234—Jaipur, India

i gochu bro [click for FREE LIVESTREAM!]

@give_IM_the_HEATER_ricky—Cleveland, Ohio

dude that link is a virus!!! butts spinning all around my desktop
DO NOT CLICK

Emily Murray—Philadelphia Sports Columnist
Everyone in the building was standing. I mean *everyone*. This was it. She was about to go over a hundred.

Jimmy Mack—Bells Head Coach
I think I was the only one in the building who actually *saw* it. Everyone else had their doohickeys in front a' their faces.

Ovid Green—Bells Color Commentator
Yeah, everyone had their phones out.

Tad Wexler—Bells TV Announcer
She was dribbling out front, weaving in and out of double teams like she'd been doing all night. She found a little opening and pulled up—

Alou Achebe—Bells Center
I couldn't believe it.

Ernie Jenkins—Sideline Reporter
She passed the ball. She jumped like she was gonna shoot and, in midair, like it'd just occurred to her, she fired this beautiful pass to Alou for an easy dunk.

Lizzy Trudeaux

[Smirks.]

Toby Sykes—Trudeaux's Best Friend

That's Lizzy, man. That's why she's always been so good. That's her thing.

Lizzy Trudeaux

It's like a crossover. First thing Dad ever taught me. Get 'em leaning one direction, go the other. Simple game.

Tad Wexler—Bells TV Announcer

And then of course she stole the inbounds pass and drained a three from the corner.

Ovid Green—Bells Color Commentator

That was it. That put her over. 102 points.

Cedric North—LA Guard

We was all just starin' up at the scoreboard like, *Is this* real?

Tad Wexler—Bells TV Announcer

Something changed after that. I mean, her shot was the same. The exact same every time. Same motion. Same result. Straight through like it was trailing flames. But *she* was different. I'm

173

not sure how to explain it. It was all just sort of mechanical. She wasn't laughing anymore.

Leonard Roosevelt—Bells Statistician
126 points. She didn't miss a single shot.

Bart "Bulb" Edison—LA Head Coach
And she didn't even *play* the fourth.

Leonard Roosevelt—Bells Statistician
Somebody stole the scorebook after the game. I left it on the scorer's table for like two minutes while I ran to the bathroom, and it was gone.

Emily Murray—Philadelphia Sports Columnist
They say that thing's worth, like, a million bucks. Wherever it is.

Ernie Jenkins—Sideline Reporter
You know you've reached a new level when your opponents—grown men, professional basketball players—are lining up for your autograph after the game.

Emily Murray—Philadelphia Sports Columnist
She was trapped on the court, signing autographs, posing for pictures, and you know what I remember thinking? She looks *miserable*.

Not at all like someone who's just played maybe the greatest basketball game of all time. It was weird.

Toby Sykes—Trudeaux's Best Friend
Nah, it wasn't weird. Not if you really know Lizzy. *I got it.*

Emily Murray—Philadelphia Sports Columnist
There was only one moment where I saw her smile. And even then it was subtle. This group of girls in the front row caught her attention. They were about her age, maybe a little younger. "Lizzy!" they said. "Lizzy, we *love* you!" They were holding up this big sheet of paper. Turned out they'd read the feature about Lizzy on ESPN.com and it'd inspired them to start a petition allowing them to play for *their* boys' basketball team.

Alou Achebe—Bells Center
The girls all had duct tape on their sneakers, like Lizzy.

43

have this dream sometimes. Okay, not just sometimes. I have it a lot. The setting's always the same—the playground basketball court—except it's different. It's surrounded on all sides by a cornfield like in *Field of Dreams*. The cornstalks are swaying in the wind, rustling. I'm alone for a minute. Then Mom walks out. She's glowing, sort of. She's wearing her frilly thrift-store wedding dress and white basketball sneakers, just like in the framed photo on the mantel.

Usually, we don't talk.

I just shoot.

She rebounds.

I shoot.

She rebounds.

It's perfect.

But tonight I decide to say something.

It catches her off guard.

"Hey," I say.

"Hey."

I shoot.

She rebounds.

I shoot.

She rebounds.

"So I have this big game coming up."

"Yeah. I know."

"You've been watching?"

She nods up at the sky. "*Terrible* seats. But yeah. Every minute."

We're not actually talking, I realize, but communicating telepathically.

I shoot.

She rebounds.

I shoot.

She rebounds.

"Something on your mind, Lizzy?"

"I set the record for points last game."

"I know. I saw. Remember?"

"Yeah."

I shoot.

She rebounds.

I shoot.

She rebounds.

"It just didn't feel right," I say.

"How do you mean?"

"I mean, it was *fun* . . ."

"But?"

"But it wasn't *me*, you know?"

"What do you mean? Sure it was."

"Not really, though."

"Ah. I get it. The . . ." She pretended to lift a phone to her ear.

"Yeah."

I shoot.

She rebounds.

I shoot.

She rebounds.

"So what do I do?" I ask.

"*Do?*"

"There's only one game left. Against Sidney."

"Like you always dreamed."

I shoot.

She rebounds.

I shoot.

She rebounds.

"So how you gonna play it?" she says.

"Play it? What choice do I have?"

She smiles. "You're forgetting something, Lizzy. But there's still time."

"What? Mom, what am I forgetting?"

I shoot.

But this time no one rebounds.

The ball rolls away.

She's gone.

I run blindly into the cornstalks—"Mom! Mom!"—but they're just a stage prop and behind them is a steep cliff and I fall and fall and fall and on the way down my phone starts ringing—"Hello? Hello?"—but even then it just keeps ringing and ringing and ringing and nothing I say or do matters.

44

t was my alarm clock. I was back in my bedroom, with the crappy wallpaper, the trophies on the dresser.

"What are *you* looking at?" I said to my poster.

"Nothin', rook. Just hangin'."

"Can you at least, like, look the other direction? It's kinda *creepy*."

"What is?"

"You watching me when I sleep."

"You *put* me here. Remember?"

I frowned.

"But hold on, let me try. Am I moving? Am I spinning?"

"Nah. Forget it."

"How about now?"

"Dude, you can't move. Just accept it."

I checked my phone and saw that I was up to 6.7 million Instagram followers. The #lizzylegend hashtag was still trending. I was still the lead story on ESPN.com.

Just a normal morning.

Before I rolled out of bed, I checked my texts for some reason. I scrolled back and found the one I'd gotten after the robocall. I'd forgotten all about it.

"What ya readin'?"

Dad.

With his freaking wizard powers.

Magically appearing.

"Nothing."

"You have a visitor."

"Dad, I told you I don't want to do any more interview—"

"He wouldn't take no for an answer."

And in marched Toby, fully decked out in new THE TOBY SYKES SHOW! swag, broadcasting again with his stupid phone. "Here we are, folks! The morning of the big game! Live inside the Trudeaux home, inside Lizzy Legend's *bedroom*!"

Dad covered his face and ducked out.

Toby spun slowly, holding out his phone. "Yep, there's her closet, her dresser, her trophies, her—whoops, don't mind those undies on the floor there—Lizzy! Lizzy Legend! How we feeling this morning?"

I glared.

"Obviously, she's a little tired after her record-breaking performance. That was a long flight home, wasn't it? Hey, let's take some questions from the comment section. @fame_game_99 asks: 'Hello, sir, I see you recently googled "how to get really really really famous and"'— Whoa boy! That's not a real question. That's some Insta*spam*. Ha-ha. Not sure how that got there. Nothing to do with my search history, I'm sure. Let's get to a *real* question, from @aussi_jenn: 'Lizzy, how do you feel being such an inspiration to so many girls out there?'"

"Um, it's nice, I guess. I don't know. I just play basketball."

When the "interview" finally ended, twenty minutes later, and it was just the two of us, I said: "What the heck, man?"

"*What?*"

"You can't just walk in and ambush me like that."

"What's the big deal?"

"I just woke up."

"Sleeping in now, are we?"

I hadn't even realized.

It was almost noon.

Normally, I would've been up for *hours*.

Practicing at the playground.

But what was the point?

"I have a big game tonight," I said. "I need to get ready."

I peeked down at my phone.

He caught me.

"What's up?"

"Nothing."

"You're being weird."

"No I'm not."

"Yes you *are*."

"I was just looking back at that old—"

Tink!

"What the—?"

A pebble hit the window.

Outside, a swarm of reporters were fighting for space in the street.

News vans, far as the eye could see.

The Press Monster had found our house.

The local guy, Chad Stephens, was clinging to a telephone pole.

He was the one who'd thrown the pebble.

"LIZZY!" he yelled, microphone extended. "LIZZY, CAN YOU TELL US—"

I backed away.

Closed the blinds.

Crossed my arms.

"Whose side are you on?" I said.

"What do you mean?"

"Are you with *them*?" I nodded toward the media. "Or with *me*?"

"With you. Of course."

"Good. Then I need you to do me a favor."

have a unique set of skills," Toby was saying, eyes narrowed, paraphrasing one of his favorite movies. "And for this task, I believe I am—"

"You sound like Batman holding in diarrhea," I said.

"Ha-*ha*."

"Well, whatever. Just make sure it works."

"Please. I've been training for this moment my entire life."

It was true. He *did* have a special skill that would finally be useful—drawing attention to himself. I needed two minutes to think without rocks hitting the freaking window or some reporter breaking down the front door. He opened the window and stuck his head out.

I mean, he *tried* to stick his head out.

But his flat-top wouldn't fit.

So he tilted his head and stuck it out sideways.

"Hear ye! Hear ye!" he said. "I have an important announcement, er, *proclamation* to make on behalf of . . ."

While he was reading from my social studies notebook in a Shakespearean accent, I closed the door behind me and sat on the steps, where it was quiet.

I took out my phone.

I reread the old text.

[RESTRICTED NUMBER]

Thank you.

Please keep this for your records.

Wish #39765488335251 has been granted.

Term Reply X – 01

The last line caught my attention.

Term Reply X – 01

Deep down I think I'd known it all along.

It could only mean one thing.

I had one credit left.

One wish.

Crazy as it sounds—

Part of me wanted to use it to unwish my wish.

To put myself back in control again.

To win or lose on my own merit.

But that was stupid.

Reckless.

No.

Instead, I would use it to *wish for more wishes.*

Like I should've done all along.

Like Toby had said.

That way, if I decided I wanted to selectively relieve myself of the power, I could. And if I decided I wanted it back, no problem.

Ultimate control, right?

My hands were shaking as I thumbed in my reply.

I wish for more wishes.

I closed my eyes.

Hit send.

I waited.

And waited.

And waited.

No response.

I typed it again.

Hit send.

I wish for more wishes.

Still no response.

Nothing.

Curious, I typed in just what the robo-text said after the word "Reply."

X – 01.

I deleted it.

Typed it again.

But this time just the *X.*

I hit send.

The phone rang immediately.

I jumped up.

It worked!

The mechanical voice.

"Hell-o."

"Hi it's me I don't have much time I need to—"

"Hell-o. How are you, to-day?"

"I'm fine, but I really don't have—"

"Your re-ver-sal has been re-ceived."

"Reversal? What re—"

"Thank you."

"I want more wishes!" I yelled. "I wish for more wishes! I wish for more wishes!"

"Thank you. Good-bye."

46

moped back into my bedroom.

Toby pulled his head back in and shut the blinds. "How'd it go?"

"Um, not so good."

"What do you mean?"

My hands were still shaking.

"You choked?" he said. "You choked under pressure?"

"I didn't *choke*," I said. "It just didn't let me make any more wishes."

"Why not?"

I shrugged. "It just said, *Your reversal has been received*."

"Reversal?" He paced around the room, shaking his head. "Whoa boy. Whoa boy. This is bad. This is *bad*."

"What?"

"It *did* occur to me."

"What?"

"But not until—"

"*What?*"

He tore a page from my social studies notebook.

"Hey!"

"Oh, now you're worried about your social studies quiz?"
I glared.

He crumpled the paper and offered it to me. "Shoot."

"Huh?"

He nodded to the trash can across the room. "Shoot."

"This is stupid."

"Just do it. Let's see."

I shot.

Perfect form.

Arm extended.

Wrist tipped down like the head of a swan.

Clank.

The paper ball hit the side of the can and fell on the carpet.

"Lemme try that again."

Clank.

Clank.

Clank.

Swish.

"There," I said. "See. It's fine. Right?"

But I knew it wasn't.

Toby held up his phone. "You know when you get those spam texts, and you can, like, reply *STOP* or whatever to unsubscribe?"

"Yeah?"

"I was thinking about that last line in the text. *Term.*"

"Term?"

"As in *terminate.*"

Oh, god.

I couldn't believe it. Just hours before the biggest game of my life, to be played on national television, and streamed live all over the planet—against Sidney freaking Rayne—I'd canceled the power. I'd voided the wish.

Dad poked his head in. "Hey, you guys ready to go?"

4th Quarter

CLEVELAND V. PHILADELPHIA

Lizzy Trudeaux

[Is handed the famous photo of her final shot.
Perfect form. Arm extended. Wrist tipped down
like the head of a swan. The ball is falling toward
the hoop.]

Toby Sykes—Trudeaux's Best Friend

[Is handed the famous photo of Lizzy's final shot.]

Lizzy Trudeaux

To be totally honest? I don't remember it very—

Toby Sykes—Trudeaux's Best Friend

Man, I'll *never* forget that day. Never ever *ever*.
Aliens could come down and zap me with a ray
gun and I'd still be like, *Uh, the day my best friend
went toe-to-toe with* Sidney Rayne? *And I watched
from the* front row? *Yeah, man. I remember that.*

Lizzy Trudeaux

[Sighs.] What I mean is, the memories are
there . . . but I'm not sure they're fully *mine*.
Does that make sense? It's like—you know how
when you read a book you have an image of
the characters in your head? One that's totally

yours? But then you see the movie and suddenly their faces are replaced by the actors'?

Toby Sykes—Trudeaux's Best Friend
I think what Lizzy means is it's like the *public* memory of the game—all the tweets, articles, interviews, and YouTube videos she's seen since—has overtaken, or at least blended with, her personal—

Rick "The Wizard" Trudeaux—Lizzy's Father
Something was a little off that day. I sensed it on the ride down. Lizzy had her big headphones on, like always, but she looked *worried*. I'd never seen that.

Toby Sykes—Trudeaux's Best Friend
So we get to the locker room, right, and there's this huge *mountain* of sneaker boxes waiting for her. I mean, there must've been like two hundred boxes. Nike. Adidas. Reebok. And1. Under Armour. Every brand you can think of. It was crazy.

Alou Achebe—Bells Center
Her friend was like—

Toby Sykes—Trudeaux's Best Friend
Dude, do you *see* this? It's Christmas! Ha-ha! And she was like—

Lizzy Trudeaux

[Genuinely confused. Lifts tattered sneakers.]
What's wrong with these?

Toby Sykes—Trudeaux's Best Friend

She was oblivious, man. [Laughs.]

Mike McCall—Bells Marketing Department

About an hour before tip-off, her friend—the
big black kid with the flat-top—corners me. He's
like—

Toby Sykes—Trudeaux's Best Friend

"Listen, dude, I need a half-dozen bottles of Wite-
Out, *stat.*"

Mike McCall—Bells Marketing Department

And I'm like, "Wite-Out?"

Alou Achebe—Bells Center

It gave her something to do before the game,
I guess, painting those sneakers, getting in the
zone. No one talked to her. It was like she was
meditating.

Harry Hawkins—Bells Guard

I'd never seen someone so focused, so calm.

Lizzy Trudeaux

I was freaking out. I was pretty sure everyone could tell, too.

Toby Sykes—Trudeaux's Best Friend

Lizzy got tickets for the whole middle school team. Everyone, even Coach Gulch and Tank. We were all in the front row, right behind the Bells' bench.

Jim Gulch—Ardwyn Middle School Boys' Basketball Coach

I leaned over to Sykes during warm-ups: "What's wrong with Lizzy? Why isn't she warming up?"

Toby Sykes—Trudeaux's Best Friend

[Raises eyebrows.] Uhhhhhhh.

Jim Gulch—Ardwyn Middle School Boys' Basketball Coach

"Why isn't she *shooting*?" She was just sitting there on the bench by herself.

Toby Sykes—Trudeaux's Best Friend

And I'm like, "Everything's fine, man! Don't worry about it!"

Alou Achebe—Bells Center
I can still see it. [Closes eyes.] The pregame
clock hits zero.

Harry Hawkins—Bells Guard
The horn sounds.

Toby Sykes—Trudeaux's Best Friend
The PA announcer leans into the
microphone.

Kevin Casey—Bells PA Announcer
"Ladies and gentlemen, please rise for the
national anthem."

Alou Achebe—Bells Center
The singer waddles onto the court in high
heels.

Tad Wexler—Bells TV Announcer
She brushes the hair from her eyes.

Mark McClaine—National TV Broadcaster
She lifts the microphone.

Jimmy Mack—Bells Head Coach
[Puts hand over heart. Lifts chin. Squints.]

Mike McCall—Bells Marketing Department

The players take the floor.

Toby Sykes—Trudeaux's Best Friend

Lizzy's finally got a uniform that fits. Her sneakers are bright white.

Lizzy Trudeaux

Sidney Rayne, the guy from in the poster on my wall, is immediately to my left. He leans in.

Sidney Rayne—Basketball Superstar

"Good luck, rook."

Mark McClaine—National TV Broadcaster

And out of nowhere, this fan runs onto the court.

Bill "Chalk" Rasner—Nationally Syndicated Sportswriter

He had on one of those full-body spandex suits. A green one.

Mark McClaine—National TV Broadcaster

The guy must've been three hundred fifty pounds.

Tad Wexler—Bells TV Announcer

The guy's prancing around, preening, pretending

to do his hair, obviously taunting Trudeaux, the only girl on the court.

Toby Sykes—Trudeaux's Best Friend
Everyone starts booing the guy.

Jim Gulch—Ardwyn Middle School Boys' Basketball Coach
Security's chasing him around the court. But he's quick for a big dude.

Bill "Chalk" Rasner—Nationally Syndicated Sportswriter
And then *bam*, he turns right into a left cross from Jimmy Mack.

Kevin Casey—Bells PA Announcer
Eighty-year-old Jimmy Mack.

Tad Wexler—Bells TV Announcer
The guy goes down.

Toby Sykes—Trudeaux's Best Friend
Hard.

Emily Murray—Philadelphia Sports Columnist
He's unconscious. He's like this big green

blob, a human loogie, on the court. Jimmy
knocked him out cold.

Alou Achebe—Bells Center
They drag him off the court by his legs.

Toby Sykes—Trudeaux's Best Friend
Within seconds, it's trending on Twitter.
#humanloogie

Lizzy Trudeaux
There was a fan on the court?

Toby Sykes—Trudeaux's Best Friend
See what I'm talking about, man? This girl? She's
in her own *world*.

Lizzy Trudeaux
I was talking to Sid. I'd had this conversation in my
head a million times. I was like—

Sidney Rayne—Basketball Superstar
She told me she had a poster of me on her wall.

Lizzy Trudeaux
I told him that I looked up at that poster every
night before bed and I thought, *Man, Rayne's a
punk. If I could just get one shot at him . . .*

Sidney Rayne—Basketball Superstar

[Laughs.] I said, "Well, here's your shot, rook. Don't blow it."

Jim Gulch—Ardwyn Middle School Boys' Basketball Coach

Sidney was laughing about something. I'm sure Lizzy was talking [trash].

Alou Achebe—Bells Center

They final get the big green dude off the court. The horn sounds again. The ref comes forward with the ball.

Harry Hawkins—Bells Guard

The centers bend their knees, lift their arms.

Toby Sykes—Trudeaux's Best Friend

Everyone lifts their cell phones.

Emily Murray—Philadelphia Sports Columnist

Philly won the tip. It was hard not to with Alou Achebe as your center. He could reach up and change the lights if he wanted to. We were all curious to see who would be guarding Trudeaux. We were all hoping it'd be Sidney—and it was.

Tad Wexler—Bells TV Announcer

Oh man, that first possession. She weaved through

a half-dozen screens, like always, but Sidney fought through every one of them. She couldn't shake him. He was the best pure athlete—by a long shot—that she'd ever faced.

Mark McClaine—National TV Broadcaster
Coach Mack called a time-out. He was all over the refs about Sidney's defense. He wanted them to call a foul. He was screaming like a baseball manager who's just charged out of the dugout. Spit was flying everywhere. The refs crossed their arms and ignored him.

Jim Gulch—Ardwyn Middle School Boys' Basketball Coach
I actually remember what Jimmy said. He limped back to the bench, stopped, and said over his shoulder, "Hey, Tommy"—Tommy Michaels was the head ref—"hey, Tommy, I can't get a T for what I'm *thinkin'*, can I?" Tommy rolled his eyes. "No, Jimmy, you can't get a T for what you're thinking." And Jimmy said, "Good. Because I think you *suck*." All the refs broke up laughing. That was Jimmy.

Alou Achebe—Bells Center
Lizzy was frustrated in the huddle. She looked like she was gonna punch someone. No one knew what to say, not even Coach Mack, and then out

of nowhere this *guy*—he looked like one of those
dudes you play pickup basketball against—this
goofy dude behind the bench tears this piece
of paper from a notebook and passes it into the
huddle.

**Jim Gulch—Ardwyn Middle School Boys' Basketball
Coach**
I had this idea—a play—I saw it in my mind, this
flash like an X-ray—so I drew it up real quick and
passed it to Lizzy.

Jimmy Mack—Bells Head Coach
Yeah . . . I remember that. I nearly blew my lid. But
then I seen what was *on* it. And I thought: *Hey, that
just might work!*

**Bill "Chalk" Rasner—Nationally Syndicated
Sportswriter**
Coming out of the first time-out, the Bells lined
up in this bizarre formation. Alou was at the top
of the key, just beyond the three-point line, and
all the other guys were lined up along the sideline,
like they were cheerleaders. Trudeaux started at
the *far* foul line, opposite Alou, about sixty feet
away. They inbounded to Alou, and Alou just stood
there with the ball high above his head. Trudeaux
got down like she was in the starting blocks and

203

sprinted forward. Everyone held their breath as she got closer and closer. Just before impact, Alou lowered the ball. She took it like a handoff and went straight through his legs. [Laughs.] Sidney was too big, of course. He had to slide around. Lizzy came out the other side and was wide open. She jumped to shoot—

Tad Wexler—Bells TV Announcer
But then she just landed with the ball.

Ovid Green—Bells Color Commentator
[Shakes head.]

Emily Murray—Philadelphia Sports Columnist
Traveling. Turnover.

@polli_wanna_cracka—Indianapolis, Indiana
what the heck was THAT????

> **@make_it_rayne_23—Cleveland, Ohio**
> sidney got the girl SHOOK!

> **@philly_yap—Philadelphia, Pennsylvania**
> she ain't scared man she's TROLLIN' these fools

Ovid Green—Bells Color Commentator
It was no secret that Lizzy wasn't, let's say, *pleased*

with how she'd been welcomed into the league. The network carrying the game had supposedly Photoshopped her chest to look bigger beneath her jersey in the pregame promos. A thirteen-year-old girl! It was sick. So a lot of people, myself included, thought that first possession was a protest to all that.

Emily Murray—Philadelphia Sports Columnist
It was brilliant. I loved it.

Lizzy Trudeaux
I got so into the game that I forgot. I forgot the power was gone. I remembered at the last instant and, I don't know. I froze. I messed up.

Deepak Lobsang—Cleveland Head Coach/ Spiritual Guru
That's why she's a legend, in my opinion. She does this stuff that transcends the game. Like that protest shot. She has this way of exposing the hypocrisy, the bias, that's been right beneath the surface in sports and society the whole time.

Lizzy Trudeaux
I was scared, man. That's what it comes down to. I was scared that I'd miss and everyone would laugh at me. That I, playing as myself, wasn't good enough.

Rick "The Wizard" Trudeaux—Lizzy's Father

We made eye contact as she ran back on defense. I pounded my heart like, *You got this. You've been working for this your whole life. Don't back down.*

Emily Murray—Philadelphia Sports Columnist

She didn't shoot again on the second possession, but she made one of the most beautiful passes I'd ever seen. It was like she knew she was this magnet drawing all the defense's attention toward herself, and she used that to create openings for her teammates. Brilliant.

Rick "The Wizard" Trudeaux—Lizzy's Father

I smiled. I knew right away. Okay, tonight she's playing *point guard.*

Harry Hawkins—Bells Guard

She wouldn't shoot. It was weird. But she was good enough playing point that we were right in the game. We were this crappy last-place team, but she made us all better.

Jimmy Mack—Bells Head Coach

That's what a great point guard *does.*

Bill "Chalk" Rasner—Nationally Syndicated Sportswriter
The assists started piling up. Sidney's competitive, so he started doing the same. He started throwing these crazy passes too.

Emily Murray—Philadelphia Sports Columnist
It was tied 56–56 at the half. A lower-scoring game than the one in LA, but the tempo was still breakneck. Lizzy was always looking to push the ball. Every single time. I said to my colleague, "Okay, she has to get tired *eventually*, right?"

Toby Sykes—Trudeaux's Best Friend
[Grins.] They obviously don't know Lizzy.

Jimmy Mack—Bells Head Coach
[Runs bubblegum cigar beneath nose.] I wasn't takin' her out no matter what.

Bill "Chalk" Rasner—Nationally Syndicated Sportswriter
The beginning of the third quarter was one of the craziest sequences I'd ever seen. It was like Trudeaux had given Alou a high five in the locker room and her magic had rubbed off. First time down, Alou took a dribble—always a scary sight—

and heaved up a three-pointer with, like, twenty seconds still left on the shot clock. It looked like a soccer throw-in. Everyone in the arena put their hands on their heads like *WHAT ARE YOU* . . . But then the ball swished through. He ran back down the court, firing his hands like pistols, smiling from ear to ear.

Deepak Lobsang—Cleveland Head Coach/ Spiritual Guru
Three in a row. Alou Achebe comes out to start the third quarter and drains three straight. What can you do? How do you even block his shot if you want to? A *ladder*?

Emily Murray—Philadelphia Sports Columnist
Lizzy was still piling up the assists.

Tad Wexler—Bells TV Announcer
Then Harry Hawkins caught fire. *He* hit three in a row. Philly went up double digits.

Sidney Rayne—Basketball Superstar
The game was turning into a blowout.

Deepak Lobsang—Cleveland Head Coach/ Spiritual Guru
I called a time-out. I knew just what we needed.

Sidney Rayne—Basketball Superstar
Sometimes, instead of drawing up a play in the huddle, Coach just reads us these weird riddles that he has scribbled on little scraps of paper in his pocket. He was like—

Deepak Lobsang—Cleveland Head Coach/ Spiritual Guru
[Draws two stick figures on coach's whiteboard.] Two monks are staring at a flag blowing in the wind.

Sidney Rayne—Basketball Superstar
[Shakes head.]

Deepak Lobsang—Cleveland Head Coach/ Spiritual Guru
The first monk says, "The flag is moving." The second monk says, "No, the wind is moving." Their teacher walks by, glances up, says, "No wind. No flag. *Mind* is moving."
I could tell they weren't really getting it. They're not quite on my level.

Leonard Galloway—Cleveland Guard
Coach had lost his mind. Sid took over. He was like, "Yo, listen, this is what's gonna happen."

Harry Hawkins—Bells Guard

They started fouling us.

Alou Achebe—Bells Center

And not just anyone.

Harry Hawkins—Bells Guard

They started fouling our worst shooters.

Emily Murray—Philadelphia Sports Columnist

It definitely went against the "spirit of the game," as they say. But it worked. Philly's big men kept bricking free throws. Cleveland rebounded, advanced the ball quickly, ran their offense, and chipped away at the lead.

Tad Wexler—Bells TV Announcer

The other thing the fouling did was give Cleveland a chance to catch their breath. The constant fouling neutralized Lizzy's superior endurance.

Bill "Chalk" Rasner—Nationally Syndicated Sportswriter

I've had clogged toilets that flowed better than that third quarter.

Mark McClaine—National TV Broadcaster

The Philly fans were out of their minds. They were like—

Toby Sykes—Trudeaux's Best Friend

Boooooooooooooooo!!!!!!

Tad Wexler—Bells TV Announcer

Every time you looked up, the Bells' lead shrank.
Fifteen points. Thirteen. Eight. Six. Two. Then it
was tied.

Emily Murray—Philadelphia Sports Columnist

It was a cheap strategy. But it worked.

Ovid Green—Bells Color Commentator

Finally, the game got moving again. The Philly fans
gave a big mock cheer.

Tad Wexler—Bells TV Announcer

The whole fourth quarter was back-and-forth.
We were "on the seesaw," as we say. Philly was up
one, then Cleveland was up one, then Philly was
up one. Then it was tied. We got to the final media
time-out—

Toby Sykes—Trudeaux's Best Friend

And that was when it started, I think. That was the
first time I heard it.

Alou Achebe—Bells Center

It was during a TV time-out. Coach Mack

was drawin' up a play on his hand, the way he always did. "Okay, you start here—"

Harry Hawkins—Bells Guard
It's weird—Coach Mack, most times, he's practically *deaf*. But it's like he can focus with his ears the way you focus with your eyes. Like he can squint his ears. Those big, droopy ears. He stopped drawin' the play, closed his eyes, and listened.

Jimmy Mack—Bells Head Coach
[Closes eyes. Listens.]

Bill "Chalk" Rasner—Nationally Syndicated Sportswriter
It started in the upper levels, the nosebleeds, where the working people sit.

Toby Sykes—Trudeaux's Best Friend
LIZ-ZY LEG-END (clap clap clap-clap-clap). LIZ-ZY LEG-END (clap clap clap-clap-clap).

Bill "Chalk" Rasner—Nationally Syndicated Sportswriter
When chants start like that—and I don't mean the LET'S GO BLAH-BLAH crap they pump through the speakers nowadays—when a spontaneous chant starts up like that, it's like a few people

rubbing some sticks together. It takes a minute to catch, but when it does, the flame spreads quickly. It gulps down all the oxygen in the place.

Sidney Rayne—Basketball Superstar

Yeah, we all heard it. How could you not? But if you're a competitor, then in that moment you want nothing more than to shut that crowd up. It fuels *both* teams, just in different ways.

Alou Achebe—Bells Center

It was a cool moment. It was like—you know thunder and lightning? How the lightning strikes and *then* you hear the thunder? It was like everything was reversed. First you heard this huge, booming chant, the thunder, and then the thought flashed inside your head. You thought: *This is it. This is her moment. I'm about to witness history. I'm a part of it.*

Lizzy Trudeaux

I knew this was my moment. It was time to step up. I couldn't be afraid anymore.

Toby Sykes—Trudeaux's Best Friend

Coming out of the time-out she looked over at me—well, I *thought* she was looking at me, but she was looking at her dad. They have this weird language where they can say entire sentences without actually talking out loud. Must be a father-daughter thing.

Rick "The Wizard" Trudeaux—Lizzy's Father
[Narrows eyes. Crosses arms.]

Lizzy Trudeaux
[Nods.]

Mark McClaine—National TV Broadcaster
That last minute will go down in history. Basketball history, at least.

Tad Wexler—Bells TV Announer
They ran this beautiful play coming out of the time-out. A double screen. Lizzy came off it tight, just like you're supposed to, shoulder to shoulder. She curled off it, caught the ball at the top of the key.

Ovid Green—Bells Color Commentator
She was wide open.

Tad Wexler—Bells TV Announcer
Wide open.

Ovid Green—Bells Color Commentator
Just like at the beginning of the game.

Tad Wexler—Bells TV Announcer
But this time she didn't hesitate.

Sidney Rayne—Basketball Superstar
She rose up.

Ovid Green—Bells Color Commentator
Perfect form. Absolutely flawless. Totally fluid.

Sidney Rayne—Basketball Superstar
The ball looked different coming out of her hand.

Mark McClaine—National TV Broadcaster
It wasn't a line drive like the last game, like we'd
seen before.

**Bill "Chalk" Rasner—Nationally Syndicated
Sportswriter**
It had this gorgeous arc to it. A moon shot.

Toby Sykes—Trudeaux's Best Friend
Clank.

Mark McClaine—National TV Broadcaster
It hit off the side of the rim and went out of bounds.

Tad Wexler—Bells TV Announcer
Everyone in the arena gasped at the same time.

@hate_the_playa_not_tha_game_99—Oakland, CA

ewwwwwwwwwww

@jedi_jump_shooter—New Orleans, LA

watches trudeaux catch ball

watches ball float toward rim

stares at tv in disbelief

@hate_the_playa_not_tha_game_99—Oakland, CA

ewwwwwwwwwww

Mark McClaine—National TV Broadcaster

She kept her cool. It didn't faze her.

Lizzy Trudeaux

I was mortified. I was reeling. I couldn't believe it.

Jim Gulch—Ardwyn Middle School Boys' Basketball Coach

So now it's Cleveland's ball. Tied game. Thirty-five seconds left. The crowd's on their feet. "DE-FENSE! DE-FENSE!" Sidney clears his teammates to the corners and dribbles until the shot clock's running down.

Bill "Chalk" Rasner—Nationally Syndicated Sportswriter

Trudeaux was on him, crouched in her stance, forcing him left.

Lizzy Trudeaux
He went right anyway. I couldn't stop him.

Bill "Chalk" Rasner—Nationally Syndicated Sportswriter
Sidney was too strong. He went right, pulled up at the elbow.

Jim Gulch—Ardwyn Middle School Boys' Basketball Coach
Lizzy recovered, but Sidney just soared straight up over her. She couldn't do anything about it. Sidney let it go—clean release, perfect backspin.

Mark McClaine—National TV Broadcaster
It swirled around.

Leonard Galloway—Cleveland Guard
Spun out.

Toby Sykes—Trudeaux's Best Friend
I'm jumping up and down. Yes! Yes! Yes!

Ovid Green—Bells Color Commentator
Alou snagged the rebound and handed it off to Lizzy. Ten seconds left. Me? I'd call time-out. But she didn't. She took off.

Mark McClaine—National TV Broadcaster

She went *flying* up the court. It was incredible.

Bill "Chalk" Rasner—Nationally Syndicated Sportswriter

Sidney was with her the whole way, hands high above his head so he didn't foul her.

Ovid Green—Bells Color Commentator

Five seconds left. I can still see it. She's in front of the Bells bench, dribbling with her right hand, almost shoulder-high.

Mark McClaine—National TV Broadcaster

Sidney's eyes go wide. He can't resist.

Jim Gulch—Ardwyn Middle School Boys' Basketball Coach

You can see the visions of glory dancing in his eyes.

Bill "Chalk" Rasner—Nationally Syndicated Sportswriter

He lunges for the ball.

Lizzy Trudeaux

[Smirks.] *Gotcha.*

218

Mark McClaine—National TV Broadcaster

She pulls the ball hard across her body—"draws the curtain," as they say.

Toby Sykes—Trudeaux's Best Friend

Her dad's famous move.

Jimmy Mack—Bells Head Coach

Get 'em leanin' one way . . .

Mark McClaine—National TV Broadcaster

Whoosh.

Toby Sykes—Trudeaux's Best Friend

She said it was like the whole arena vanished.

Lizzy Trudeaux

Suddenly, I was back at the playground.

Toby Sykes—Trudeaux's Best Friend

Three . . .

Lizzy Trudeaux

All alone.

Toby Sykes—Trudeaux's Best Friend

Two . . .

Lizzy Trudeaux

There was no sound at all. No wind. Nothing.

Toby Sykes—Trudeaux's Best Friend

One . . .

Lizzy Trudeaux

Just me and the basket.

Bill "Chalk" Rasner—Nationally Syndicated Sportswriter

She pulls up at the foul line.

Wilson James—Photographer

I'm beneath the basket. I lift my camera as she lifts the ball.

Bill "Chalk" Rasner—Nationally Syndicated Sportswriter

All her shots were beautiful. But that one especially.

Deepak Lobsang—Cleveland Head Coach/Spiritual Guru

I remember it happening in slow motion. Probably because I've seen the replay so many times. Trudeaux's leaning forward, ever so slightly. The ball's just above her eye level. Her

guide hand comes off. The ball's on her fingertips.
She pushes it forward. Her wrist tips down like
the head of a swan. Beautiful. She's watching
the ball, wide-eyed. I'm watching it. *Everyone's*
watching it. It's floating toward the rim, spokes
spinning.

Mark McClaine—National TV Broadcaster
The ball hits the front of the rim. It skips forward,
hits the backboard, hits the front of the rim again,
bounces straight up, swirls around twice, dips
halfway in, and then . . .

Toby Sykes—Trudeaux's Best Friend
It drops in.

Rick "The Wizard" Trudeaux—Lizzy's Father
It drops in.

Sidney Rayne—Basketball Superstar
It drops in.

Mark McClaine—National TV Broadcaster
The horn sounds.

Tad Wexler—Bells TV Announcer
Bells win! Bells win! Bells win! She did it! She did it!
Lizzy Trudeaux did it! Bells win!

Toby Sykes—Trudeaux's Best Friend
Yes!!!!!!!!!!!!!!!!!!!

Lizzy Trudeaux
I blinked, and I was back in the arena. For a second,
I didn't know where I was.

Ovid Green—Bells Color Commentator
There's nothing like a game-winning shot at the
buzzer. *Nothing.* There's this incredible energy,
this swell that starts in your toes and shoots up
through the top of your head. *Boom!* That happens
to all twenty thousand people at once, and it's like
the roof explodes off the building.

Mark McClaine—National TV Broadcaster
God, I love basketball.

Toby Sykes—Trudeaux's Best Friend
It was wild, man. All the Bells players were jumping
around on the court, celebrating. *I* was jumping
around on the court. We all were. Coach Gulch.
The whole middle school team. We were just
jumping. I was looking around for Lizzy.

Tad Wexler—Bells TV Announcer
Lizzy was at midcourt with Sidney.

Ovid Green—Bells Color Commentator

They hugged. He leaned down and said something to her.

Sidney Rayne—Basketball Superstar

[Smirks.] That'll stay between us.

Chad Stephens—Channel 7 News

Yeah, I was the sideline reporter. I knew I had to get to Lizzy, get her reaction. This was the biggest moment of my career!

Tad Wexler—Bells TV Announcer

It was hilarious. I watched the whole thing. This cheesy sideline reporter, this guy Stephens, from Channel 7, he comes sprinting out from beneath the basket, holding his microphone. "LIZZY! LIZZY! LIZZY!" He's almost to her and then—

Bill "Chalk" Rasner—Nationally Syndicated Sportswriter

Bam. This humungous black kid with a flat-top comes out of nowhere and body-checks the reporter.

Tad Wexler—Bells TV Announcer

Stephens goes flying.

Lizzy Trudeaux

The most athletic thing Toby's ever done. By far.
[Laughs.]

**Bill "Chalk" Rasner—Nationally Syndicated
Sportswriter**

So now it's just the two of them there at
midcourt—best friends—and the black kid pulls
out his phone and starts recording, broadcasting
the whole thing live, no stupid questions, they're
just dancing, just pure joy, they're dancing all
goofy, laughing—

Tad Wexler—Bells TV Announcer

And then all her other middle school teammates
join in, even the big goon-looking kid.

**Bill "Chalk" Rasner—Nationally Syndicated
Sportswriter**

This wild dance party breaks out on the court,
and all the kids are broadcasting it live as it's
happening, while all the adult broadcasters
look on in their fancy suits and cameras and
microphones, pointless, irrelevant.

Toby Sykes—Trudeaux's Best Friend

I didn't notice this in the moment. But you can see

it on YouTube. In the middle of all this craziness—
I'm doing the worm at midcourt—Lizzy sneaks
over and—

Lizzy Trudeaux
[Looks up at Dad.]

Rick "The Wizard" Trudeaux—Lizzy's Father
[Presses lips together.]

Lizzy Trudeaux
[Presses her face into his chest.] That smell just
washed over me, man. Old Spice and gasoline. I
peeked up at the rafters, and I knew Mom was
looking down too. It was the happiest moment of
my life.

47

So yeah.

As you might imagine, it's been pretty crazy since that final game. I've decided to stay offline for a while—it's just too much—but Toby's been updating me on the latest developments. He says the original video of me shooting at the tryout is now at over six hundred million views. The one of the no-look shot in New York has five hundred seventy million.

And the crossover? The game-winning shot against Cleveland? 1.2 *billion*.

i let u have that one, Sidney said to me last night.

I laughed. *oh yea?*

didn't wanna ruin ur special moment . . .

Except now I'm not talking to the poster on my wall anymore. Now I'm talking to the *real* Sidney. He's busy 'cuz his team's still in the playoffs, but we text sometimes and talk trash.

So yeah.

Things have changed.

48

ut in other ways things are kinda the same. I still hate math class, for instance. I asked Dad if I could drop out of school because, you know, I'm a professional basketball player and all now—a free-agent point guard, to be specific—but he said [Dad voice]: "If you're gonna live under this roof, you're gonna make up every last—"

So yeah.

That's another thing that's the same.

And always will be.

Dad's still stubborn.

He didn't tell me, but I know from snooping through our mail that he's started to apply for loans so he can open his own auto shop, so he can make his own hours. It'll be hard because of all his debt, but, um . . . have I mentioned that he's stubborn?

49

Toby's still my best friend. And he's still a jackass. The last episode of *The Toby Sykes Show!* had forty-seven thousand viewers, a personal record, and as you can imagine, he won't shut up about it. We took the train down to Philly the other day, to the Mack Center, just like we did on that— jeez, I was gonna say all those *years* ago.

It *feels* like years ago.

But really it was just weeks.

Crazy.

So we took the train down and found Coach Mack boxing up all his stuff in the locker room.

"They finally fired you?" I joked.

"Only took five thousand years," Toby added.

"Got me a better job," Coach Mack said.

"Golden State?" I guessed.

He frowned. "What the heck am I gonna do in *California*?"

"Good point."

"New York?" Toby said.

"St. Ann's," he said, closing up the final box.

I laughed.

He crossed his arms. "I ain't jokin', kid."

"What age?"

"Seventh and eighth grade."

"*Head* coach?" Toby asked.

Coach Mack glared. "First assistant." He clamped a bubble-gum cigar between his teeth. "You done all right, kid. But you got a lotta work ahead of ya. Don't get lazy on me now."

"I won't, Coach."

I was over by my locker. My Bells jersey was still hanging there. And right beside the jersey, where I'd pinned it, was the tryout list from when I'd been cut from the middle school team. The paper was all wrinkled and faded. I folded it up and put it in my pocket. Call it a souvenir.

The three of us all walked up the tunnel to the empty arena—just like that first day—and stood at the edge of the gleaming hardwood. "You seen that Lizzy Trudeaux play?" Toby asked Coach Mack like I wasn't there.

"Yeah, I seen her."

"Not bad, right?"

"Eh, she's all right." He nudged me, smirking. "For a girl."

50

Somewhere, right now, at this very moment, some little boy is standing in front of a mirror, singing into a hairbrush. Out back, his little sister's on a stump, delivering her inauguration speech to an audience of squirrels. Up the street, the police chief's kid is backed against a fence, hands in the shape of a gun, saying to his partner, "Are you hit? Are you hit?" The Girl Who Watched Too Many Disney Movies is twirling down the sidewalk in a homemade ball gown, bluebirds fluttering all around her.

And over at the playground, on the ghost-lined basketball court, a girl with duct-taped sneakers is smearing dirt under her eyes like war paint, preparing for the biggest, most important, most pressure-packed shot of her life.

That last one, of course, is *me*.

I'm back here, where it all started.

It's a little rainy this morning, but hey—

There are no rainouts in basketball.

51

got up early, like always, so I've already swept the court from end to end. I weeded the cracks in the lane. I zigzagged between little orange cones. I dragged the twenty-pound tire. And now I'm counting down to the final shot.

Three . . .

Two . . .

One . . .

The ball swishes through.

I jump up on a rain-warped bench, pump my fist.

She did it!

She did it!

Lizzy Trudeaux's done it again!

I'm just uncorking an imaginary bottle of champagne when, out of the corner of my eye, I spot a mythical figure. He hasn't been seen around these parts in a long time. I'm so stunned, I dribble the ball off my foot.

The Wizard—disguised in a cheap baseball cap and a gas station shirt—picks up the rolling ball and spins it on his finger. He's coming straight from a twelve-hour shift, so he must be exhausted, but he doesn't complain. He sits on the ghost-lined court with his elbows hooked outside his knees.

I sit beside him.

"Missed one," he says, nodding at a stray weed that's shot up through the cement.

I reach over.

Pluck it at the root.

"If you're gonna do something," he says.

"*Yeah, yeah.* I got it."

I reach into my pocket—my personal savings bank since the age of five—and I take out a folded-up envelope. Inside is an eight-thousand-dollar check, my first and only pro paycheck, signed by Mr. Hal Kurtz, owner of the Philadelphia Bells.

I give it to him like I've always dreamed.

Well, I *try*.

But he won't take it. The stubborn old goat.

I lean over and force it into the front pocket of his gas station shirt.

"I'll just deposit it for ya," he says, frowning, and looks away.

52

The rain has stopped. It's still cloudy, but a few rays are breaking through, shining on the abandoned factory with all the windows knocked out. Wet plastic bags hang limply from the barbed-wire fence.

"I can't sleep sometimes," Dad says, still looking away, his knobby elbows still hooked outside his knees.

I think he's talking about *regret*.

About all that he had in front of him once, and lost.

And I want him to finally open up, to pour out his guts once and for all.

But I'm wrong.

He's not talking about regret.

He says: "I just lay there thinkin' about all the things you're gonna do. My heart starts racin'. I think of all the things you're gonna see, the people you'll . . ."

He stops.

This is the most consecutive words I think he's ever said in his *life*.

He narrows his eyes.

Presses his lips.

And I understand completely.

53

Dad picks himself up off the court, dusts his hands.

"Look at you," he says, glaring down at me.

"*What?*"

He pats the check in his shirt pocket. "You've been a trust-fund baby for, what, *thirty seconds*? And you're already lounging around like a bum?"

"Oh, *please*," I say, laughing.

He offers me his hand.

But I knock it away.

And I pick myself up.

ACKNOWLEDGMENTS

I probably wrote a million words and threw them all away before I got to Lizzy. It's been a long road here to the beginning. I'd like to thank the following for their help along the way:

My early readers—Mark Smith, Liam Moriarty, Jim O'Brien, G. W. Hawkes, Phillip Le, Jason Finau, Meaghann Schulte, Becca Venuto, and Kevin Casey—for your wisdom and encouragement.

My all-world agent, Melissa Edwards, for listening to my ridiculous pitch about a girl with duct-taped sneakers and magical powers and thinking *yeah, this could work.*

My wonderful editor, Fiona Simpson, and the team at Aladdin Books—Mara Anastas, Elizabeth Mims, Steve Scott, Samantha Benson, Caitlin Sweeney, Sara Berko, and illustrator Oriol Vidal—for taking the girl with the duct-taped sneakers and getting her ready for prime time.

My students over the years (too many to name) who have challenged and inspired me.

My family, who put up with me locking myself away on vacations . . .

Quentin, you're not old enough to read this yet, but soon you will be—and that's the cool thing about books, my words are right here where I left them for you.

Zelda, you'll never be able to read because you're a dog, but you're sleeping beside me as I write this, and I feel bad.

And, finally, most of all—Georgia—I'm thankful not just because you helped me figure out this story (although you did), but because you've transformed the whole way I see the world. I love ya.

A PERFECT FRIEND

REYNOLDS PRICE

A PERFECT FRIEND

ATHENEUM BOOKS *for* YOUNG READERS
NEW YORK LONDON TORONTO SYDNEY SINGAPORE

Atheneum Books for Young Readers
An imprint of Simon & Schuster Children's Publishing Division
1230 Avenue of the Americas
New York, New York 10020

Book design by Michael Nelson
The text of this book is set in Goudy.

Printed in the United States of America
2 4 6 8 10 9 7 5 3 1

Library of Congress Cataloging-in-Publication Data
Price, Reynolds, 1933-
A perfect friend / Reynolds Price.
p. cm.
Summary: Still grieving over the death of his mother,
eleven-year-old Ben finds solace in the special relationship
he forms with an elephant in a visiting circus.
ISBN 0-689-83029-7
[1. Elephants—Fiction. 2. Circus—Fiction.
3. Human-animal communication—Fiction.
4. Grief—Fiction. 5. Death—Fiction.] I. Title.
PZ7. P93163 Pe 2000
[Fic]—dc21
99-55397

FIRST
F
EDITION

FOR

MARCIA DRAKE BENNETT

and

PATRICIA DRAKE MASIUS

FIRST FRIENDS

BOOKS BY REYNOLDS PRICE

A PERFECT FRIEND 2000

FEASTING THE HEART 2000

LETTER TO A MAN IN THE FIRE 1999

LEARNING A TRADE 1998

ROXANNA SLADE 1998

THE COLLECTED POEMS 1997

THREE GOSPELS 1996

THE PROMISE OF REST 1995

A WHOLE NEW LIFE 1994

THE COLLECTED STORIES 1993

FULL MOON 1993

BLUE CALHOUN 1992

THE FORESEEABLE FUTURE 1991

NEW MUSIC 1990

THE USE OF FIRE 1990

THE TONGUES OF ANGELS 1990

CLEAR PICTURES 1989

GOOD HEARTS 1988

A COMMON ROOM 1987

THE LAWS OF ICE 1986

KATE VAIDEN 1986

PRIVATE CONTENTMENT 1984

VITAL PROVISIONS 1982

THE SOURCE OF LIGHT 1981

A PALPABLE GOD 1978

EARLY DARK 1977

THE SURFACE OF EARTH 1975

THINGS THEMSELVES 1972

PERMANENT ERRORS 1970

LOVE AND WORK 1968

A GENEROUS MAN 1966

THE NAMES AND FACES OF HEROES 1963

A LONG AND HAPPY LIFE 1962

A PERFECT FRIEND

BENJAMIN LAUGHINGHOUSE BARKS WAS CALLED BEN.
By the time he was nine, he asked his friends to
call him "Laugh." Laughinghouse had been his
mother's last name before she married his father.
But nobody wanted to call Ben "Laugh," nobody
but a red-haired boy named Duncan Owens, who
became his second-best friend. Ben was generally
friendly to young and old people, but even that
early "Laugh" didn't seem right for a serious person. His cousin Robin Drake was one year
younger, and she knew Ben as well as anybody.
She tried to call him "Laugher" for a while; but
when Ben's mother died the year he was ten, he
finally asked Robin to call him anything except
"Laugher."

He was the only boy in school who had a girl for his best friend, and he could usually smile at Robin's joking. After his mother died, though, Ben's outlook changed; and he went on feeling sad for a long time. Even a whole year later, he still missed his mother at night; and the sadness would keep him awake sometimes. Then he would lie very flat in the dark, with both his arms stretched down by his sides, and think about elephants to help him sleep. Sooner or later they always helped him. Just the thought of their power and the awesome gentleness with which they treated each other most times could ease his mind and send him on into sleep like a boat on a calm dark lake.

Some people love horses or tropical fish. Some are devoted to cranky parrots that can bite off a finger. Ben knew one boy who kept a mighty boa constrictor right by his bed—a snake that could choke him to death as easily as strangling a kitten. Ben Barks loved elephants long before he'd seen one. He sometimes wondered how that love started. Since he lived in a small quiet town and had never even been to a zoo, Ben guessed his mother had been the cause.

By the time he was three years old, his mother would sit with Ben at a kitchen table and draw good pictures of elephants with a pencil. When she was a

child, she'd seen an elephant in a traveling circus, and she and Ben's father had a few books and magazines with photographs of actual elephants who lived far off in Africa and Asia. But Ben's mother never copied those pictures. For some mysterious reason of her own, since childhood, the idea of elephants was planted in her head; and when she drew her idea on paper, the elephant always looked realer than any photograph—to her and her only child Ben at least.

Good as she was, she always asked Ben to draw along with her. At first Ben's drawings were funny, but they managed to look more or less like elephants. When Ben and his mother each finished a drawing, she would help him color his picture with crayons. Ben colored them red or blue or yellow— impossible colors.

His mother let him do that for a while. But when he was five and the idea of elephants was safe in his own head, his mother said "Ben, in Africa and Asia, all elephants are gray or brownish gray. Let's respect the way they really look." From then on Ben made his drawings true to life or as true as he could since he still hadn't seen a live elephant.

Soon after that Ben's mother mostly let him draw alone. He was his parents' only child; and

since they lived on the edge of town with few close neighbors, he had no playmates except his cousin Robin and occasionally Duncan Owens, when Duncan's mean father would let him play. Robin lived a mile away. On weekends she and Ben would ride their bicycles to visit each other, and then they'd act out the stories they'd read or seen in movies. Ben went to every movie that starred real elephants, and most times Robin went along with him. In a lot of their games, Ben would ride an imaginary elephant and sometimes let Robin ride behind him through the nearby woods. It could make them happy for a whole afternoon; and once Ben started school and could read, he spent many evenings reading about real elephants in his father's books.

That way he learned a lot about them. Elephants lived in good-sized families and guarded their babies carefully. They were stronger than anything else alive on land; and they had huge brains that made them at least as smart as the smartest other creatures—whales, dolphins, pigs, gorillas, and chimpanzees. The only thing elephants did that seemed wrong to Ben was butting down whole trees just to eat the top leaves. Now and then they also tramped down the gardens of helpless people who were trying to grow their food and live in elephant

country. Even one elephant could ruin a whole cornfield by just walking through it. And when they got angry occasionally, some elephant might badly hurt or kill someone. That would only happen, most times anyhow, when they felt their young were in real danger.

When Ben was seven the year after he began first grade, his parents surprised him by taking him and Robin to an actual circus that was visiting the nearest big town for two days. It was Ringling Brothers, the Greatest Show on Earth—or so it said on its red-and-blue posters. Ben knew the whole thing was his mother's idea, and he secretly wished that he could have gone with nobody but her. He liked his father and Robin; but he and his mother had spent almost their best times together, drawing elephants and trying to imagine their lives. His mother got tickets for the whole family, though. So Ben concealed his disappointment, and off they all went. The whole way there Ben had told himself silently to concentrate on the great sights to come and not to let Robin or his joking father keep him from seeing and memorizing every good thing and of course every detail of the elephant troop.

But before the show started in the huge main tent, Ben and the others walked through a long but smaller tent where all the circus animals waited. There were lions and tigers and leopards pacing back and forth in cages, looking fierce and lonely at the same time. There was one lone gorilla crouched down in the corner of a cage with the thickest bars of all. His face was as sad as anything Ben had ever seen—and sadder still because there was nothing anybody could do to cheer him up, short of sending him back to the African mountains.

Then the last thing before Ben and his family entered the main tent was two lines of elephants. One was on Ben's left, one on his right. By the shape of their heads, Ben knew at once they were Indian elephants, who were easier to tame than the ones from Africa, though even the smallest one was twice as tall as Ben's father. When they came into sight, Ben stopped in his tracks. However many elephants he'd read about or seen in movies, he had never guessed at the high excitement he would feel when he first saw one, alive and nearby.

He felt as if he were flying through space with just the power of his own two arms, and the speed had emptied the air from his lungs. But that didn't scare him. Ben had always liked a great many things

in the world around him. A well-played game or an arrowhead he might find in the woods could make him happy for hours. But the sight of these elephants made him happier than he'd ever been before. Joyful as he was, soon he got his breath back and counted the elephants carefully.

There were fifteen on one side, fourteen on the other—twenty-nine live elephants in all. They looked enough alike to be a single family; but each one of them was moving a little, side to side as if dancing alone with nobody near. None of them were looking at each other but were facing straight forward, chewing mouthfuls of hay. Each one had a small chain around an ankle, and each chain was hooked to an iron post in the ground behind. Of course they all could have pulled those up with no trouble whatever and gone anywhere they wanted to go unless men with powerful elephant guns shot and killed them.

Ben even realized that, with their famous strength, any one of them could take a single step, break free completely, and kill every person in the whole crowded tent. Their family together could tear up every building in town, including the water tank, and crush all the people. But they just continued their gentle dance and seemed not to make any

harmful plans. Ben could hardly believe he was in the same space with such peaceful and noble creatures. A few yards ahead of him, a human family with several children were feeding peanuts to one old-looking elephant. With excellent manners she was taking the nuts from the children's hands with the tip of her trunk and then transferring them straight to her mouth.

Ben's parents had moved on a few steps ahead, but now his father looked back and grinned. "Son, you want to buy a bag of peanuts?"

It turned out Robin was standing just behind him. She said "Oh yes!"

Ben mostly trusted Robin but hearing her say "Yes" made him want to say "No." Robin was wrong. To stand here and feed little dried-up peanuts to these enormous creatures seemed like a bad joke. Ben shook his head *No* and walked on forward, ahead of the others, toward the main tent. He knew his feelings were stingy-hearted, but all he wanted to do right now was be alone in a private place with all these elephants—or even just one. Nobody else but his mother would be near, and no other noise but the sound of her voice could be heard around them. He told himself that was crazy to hope for. And when he stopped at the main tent door and

turned to smile at his family, it was one of the hard-est things he'd done.

Under the main tent there were three wide rings on the ground. Ben's father had already told him how everything that would happen in the show would happen inside those rings at the same time. It would be up to Ben to figure out which ring to watch at any moment. If he wasn't careful he'd miss the best part. So all through the long and busy performance, Ben smiled at the clowns, felt scared for the man who went into one wide cage with lions and tigers roaring together; and he crossed his fingers for the men and women on the trapeze swings and high wires. Mainly he watched the elephants do every one of their acts.

For the first time Ben saw in person how patient they were and how respectful to the people who gave them orders with sticks and whistles. That much made him glad. He was sorry, though, that all their stunts were silly child's play thought up by the humans that owned them. He was sorry too that he still hadn't touched one or stood where one could see him clearly; but he wasn't sorry about the peanuts. Handing a peanut to an elephant would be like handing a penny to a king or giving a single scrap of bread to a starving orphan, bareheaded in the snow.

✣   ✣   ✣

It was soon after that when Ben realized he truly loved elephants in a stronger way than anything else alive but his mother. The simplest picture of any elephant would still catch his eye. He would sit down right then, study it closely; and soon he would feel the best kind of peace inside his head. He wouldn't have to wait till night came and then just ask them to help him sleep. So he went on drawing them better and better, and then he made models of them with clay. It gave him more pleasure than any other animal or friend, and no other kind of game could help him that much.

Ben often prayed that his father would buy him a baby elephant to raise. They had a broad field of grass and weeds behind the house. On the edge of the field was a small clear pond, and then the woods started. In the woods there were more trees than any one elephant could ever push down, or so Ben believed. He could easily imagine the pleasure of coming home from school each afternoon to find an elephant waiting and pleased to see him after such a long day. He had heard that elephants could speak with each other, over miles of distance, in sounds so low no human could hear them. Ben's ears were keen and he told himself he would learn to hear their secrets and to share his secrets with them.

He'd already had some secret talks with his family's dog. Surely an elephant would speak with him too. Couldn't his father place a want ad in some city paper and find a young elephant that might have outgrown its narrow home and needed more space?

But his father told him an elephant cost more money than they would ever own. It would also need more space and food than their field could provide.

Ben understood that but was badly disappointed, and he went on asking for an elephant in his prayers at night. What he mostly said in silence was "Please make me strong and gentle enough to be a good keeper for a real live elephant. Then let somebody give us one, and let it be happy in our back field." Ben had also prayed when his mother was sick. But she died anyhow in terrible pain with Ben at her bedside, holding her hand and begging to help her. So Ben knew his prayers were probably useless. They gave him hope, though—the kind of hope that lucky people have and everybody strongly needs. It helped Ben believe he would grow up someday and find the necessary time and money to bring the things he loved closer to him where he could guard them, day and night, from enemies, sickness, and unfair punishment.

✧   ✧   ✧

After Ben's mother died, leaving him and his father alone in a sad house, Ben's cousin Robin spent even more time than usual with Ben. She also missed his mother, who had been her favorite aunt. So she and Ben began to make up serious games about death. At first they looked for dead birds or insects to bury in shallow graves with flowers on top and rocks to show where the small bodies lay. Then Ben told Robin the legend that says that elephants who live in the jungle or on the plains will go to the same secret place to die. Just the ivory tusks of all the dead elephants would be of great value to find and sell; and since the elephants' graveyard gets bigger by the year, greedy people are always hunting for it.

Ben also told Robin that the legend was probably wrong, but that didn't stop them from spending long days pretending to hunt for the elephants' graveyard in the thick woods back of Ben's home. Every now and then either Robin or Ben would find a smooth white rock that they'd pretend was a genuine piece of a tusk or a tooth. Once they even found the long white rib of a big buck deer that had died long ago. They told themselves it was ivory for sure and that they must be very near their goal—the elephants' graveyard with all its treasure—but of

course they weren't. Deep down they knew there was no such place.

Robin was ready to go on hunting, but Ben just said "You can but I won't."

She understood why. Ben had given up hope of finding anything grand or rewarding. He also knew that in the real world of Africa and Asia, elephants would stop by the bones of their dead family members and turn them over very slowly with their trunks. Sometimes they'd stand and do this for hours as if they knew the bones were all that was left of some live creature that once took close care of them when they were young and could never be repaid.

After Ben gave up hope from such games, he and Robin gave up playing so seriously. She did once suggest that they ride through the human cemetery on their bikes. It was a small green place on a hillside, and at the bottom was a narrow river with a long sandbar that Ben liked to wade out to. Ben didn't suspect that Robin had a private plan, so he readily agreed to the trip. It was too cold to wade; but once they'd stood by the river and skipped flat rocks on the surface, Robin picked some cattails— tall brown and green plants—and started back

uphill alone, where they'd left their bikes. Ben eventually followed her until he saw she was squatting down by his mother's white gravestone. He hadn't been there since the day of her funeral, and he wasn't going now. Deep as his mother was buried in the ground, Ben was afraid he might hear her moan. He picked up his bike and called back to Robin "You coming with me or not?"

"Did you forget what today is?"

Ben said "It's a Wednesday sometime in January."

Robin had finished arranging the cattails in the jar for flowers that stayed by the grave. So she stood and smiled. "It's your mother's birthday."

Ben thought for a moment, then pedaled away slowly.

Robin thought he said "Don't you think I know that?" but she couldn't be sure. Till now she'd thought she understood Ben's sadness, but he'd just shown her that he hurt a lot worse than she'd realized, and she never again tried to change his feelings.

From then on what kept Ben hoping to grow out of his sorrow and run his own life was not games or dreams but more and more books about elephants with more accurate pictures. He also had his father, who was kind and tired but who seemed to need

Ben's company and help—even when they seldom spoke to each other. Even after Ben and Robin had given up wandering through the woods, he enjoyed her company at the movies or playing occasional indoor games. He never had to ask her again to let him keep his sadness private.

Ben also had a few good teachers who tried to help him onward, and most of the other children in school seemed to show they liked him. So he had other reasons to live on through his days and nights, neither too sad nor happy but without much hope that he'd have a life which felt rewarding. Sometimes he felt like a single young hawk, abandoned by its parents but learning to fly and hunt on its own. Most days, though, he felt like a boy who would never be stronger or have his own safe family and a job that he liked better than school.

It was two months after his eleventh birthday that the next wide door in Ben's life began to swing open, slowly at first. It started in school one day when Duncan Owens said to Ben "Remember that my dad knows the man that brings traveling shows to town—mostly bands and dances? Sometime this spring he's bringing a family circus with one ring. Let's us two go." Everybody, including

Ben, called Duncan "Dunk." It was maybe because his red hair always looked as if he'd been dunked by his heels in water and stood up to dry with his hair in peaks.

Ben had gone to movies with Dunk a few times but had to quit. Dunk talked too much all through the story. Up on the screen a good cowboy would aim his pistol at a furious rattlesnake, and Dunk would say "Why is he doing that?"

Ben would say "Because the snake might kill him. Use your brain, Dunk."

Dunk would give a bow in Ben's direction and say "Oh thanks, Great Wazuma." Both Dunk and Robin called Ben silly stuck-up names when he acted smarter than he was.

But in two more minutes, when the movie cowboy stopped to let his horse drink from a beautiful river, Dunk might say "Ben, you think that horse is really thirsty?"

Ben liked Dunk because he was funny and loyal a lot of the time. When Ben had gone every afternoon to see his mother the whole last month she was in the hospital, Dunk would wait in the hall to ride home with him. And the night she died, Dunk biked out to Ben's and stayed all night on the extra bed across from Ben's in case Ben needed to wake

up and talk or go outdoors in the January frost and sit in one of their usual places to stare at the moon and tell long stories about brave boys.

So Ben was glad he knew Dunk Owens, but he mostly went to the movies alone or with Robin Drake. They would ride their bikes straight to the theater from school, then ride on home in the early evening. Ben didn't mention the possible news of a circus to Robin or even to his father. But after a week of keeping the secret, he managed to leave school alone one afternoon. He biked to the office of the local newspaper, asked to speak to the advertising manager, and then asked the man if the circus news was true.

The man said "Son, I can't tell you that. If it's really just a one-ring circus like you say, I doubt it could even afford to buy ads. If they don't buy ads, then we won't know if they're living or dead."

Ben thanked him and turned to get back on his bike; but then he said to the man "You think they'll have any elephants with them—actual elephants, really alive?"

The man shook his head and gave a dry laugh. "If these circus people are half as poor as you say they are, they'll be lucky to have one moldy bear. Of course, way back when I was a boy, a man came to

town with a trained black bear. You could pay him a nickle, and the bear would dance with you and hug you when he finished—or anytime he wanted to! I didn't believe it but I paid my nickle, and—bless my soul—the old bear stood up and hugged me tight and then danced me around in circles till I was dizzy as any old drunk."

Dunk had said that the circus would come in the spring. Spring was still a slow three weeks away. So Ben decided just to wait through the final days of cold rain and see what late March or April might bring. For Ben, ever since his mother died, it was natural to keep his thoughts and dreams a secret from everyone but himself. That way he never had to look disappointed if his hopes failed to happen. But he had a calendar in his room at home; and before he lay down to sleep each night, he would cross off one more day of time. He could almost feel the warm breeze of spring moving toward him through the gray end of winter.

Toward the middle of March on a bright warm day, Ben and Dunk rode their bikes back from school. Ben stopped with Dunk at the long drive-way downhill to Dunk's house. Dunk wanted to keep riding around together, just laughing and talk-

ing and throwing rocks maybe. But Ben's father had told him to come home as soon as he could to mow the yard—or so Ben claimed.

Dunk said "Mow the *yard?* Our grass hasn't grown an inch all winter."

Ben said "Ours has. See you soon." Of course the grass didn't need to be mowed. Ben planned to be alone for a while and check on something he still didn't want to share with Dunk or anybody else.

One good thing about having Dunk as a friend was that you couldn't hurt Dunk's feelings easily. Not that you wanted to harm him on purpose; but in case you were careless or too sarcastic, Dunk mostly let it pass. Eventually you could rile him, but you had to scratch deeply. Dunk had a hard time at home with his father; so when he got out in public, he took most things that happened very calmly and waited for better luck the next time he saw his few friends at school. It was one of the main things Ben liked about him. This time Dunk just waved goodbye to Ben and sped down his driveway.

Then instead of heading home, Ben rode on to the far side of town, to the empty field where they had the county fair in the fall. If a circus was com-ing, it would have to come here. There was no other

piece of vacant land that was wide enough to hold even something as small as a circus with only one ring and a moldy old bear.

When Ben got to the field, the sun was setting; and fog was creeping out from the line of distant trees. The only man-made things he could see were a few light poles and some rusty garbage cans left over from the end of the fair. That was last October. Ben always liked to look around garbage cans. Sometimes he found scraps of old letters or postcards. Finding somebody else's words would often make Ben feel less lonely. He had a small collection of postcards he'd found, thrown away. They were mostly from other people's vacations, and they had bright pictures of strange wild animals and said dumb things like "How do you like my alligator suit?" when the picture showed a wild alligator with its mouth open wide and about two thousand teeth on display.

So even though it was close to dark, Ben biked over toward the beat-up cans. They were empty of all but bubble gum wrappers and some burst balloons. Still, he noticed some kind of small sign on the nearest light post. He rode straight to it and was truly thrilled to read what it said—

THE DREAM OF A LIFETIME!

ONE AND ALL!
FAMILY CIRCUS TO CHILL AND THRILL YOU!

*COMING FOR FIVE NIGHTS ON ITS WAY BACK NORTH
FROM WINTER IN FLORIDA!*

CARNIVOROUS CATS AND PONDEROUS PACHYDERMS!
CHUCKLESOME CLOWNS AND HIGH-WIRE HEROINES!

*FAMILY PRICES—COME MORE THAN ONCE!
MARCH 21-24TH*

Until that moment as the sun set deeper and the dark of the woods moved closer toward him, Benjamin Barks had been a fearless boy in most parts of his life. But now he felt as if long fingers in an iron glove were raking a deep cut up his spine. His whole body shook hard once and then again. In another few seconds he was almost scared, and he turned his bike to escape. But then he calmed a little and stayed in place beside the light pole and asked himself what was frightening here? Soon he understood there was nothing wrong with the place. There were no seen or unseen enemies lurking—just the same old empty field that, once every fall, gave room to a Ferris wheel and rides and the noise of a rinky-dink fair.

What Ben had thought was almost scary was the news that Dunk was right when he'd said a circus was coming. Dunk seldom lied but sometimes he got his news reports twisted. And for Ben, so soon after his mother's death, circus news might be too good to handle. But what this sign announced was no county fair with prize pigs, cows, and giant apple pies. It was promising a circus, in this small town, and very soon. The most exciting thing of all, of course, was the place on the sign where it bragged about pachyderms.

While there was still enough light to see it, Ben reached out and touched the actual word in bright red ink. He knew that a *pachyderm* was normally an *elephant*, and the sign promised more than one—big weighty creatures. The thought of those wondrous animals coming to this tame field was still too good to risk talking about with anybody, however kind or friendly. Just thinking about it too much in his own mind could make it go away. So Ben decided, more than before, to keep on waiting and watching in silence.

That much happened on a Friday afternoon—no school the next day. When Ben got home safe from the fairgrounds, it was already dark. But his

father was still not back from work, and the only light in the house was the one Ben always left on for times like this. Coming into the empty house alone was hard enough, but coming in the dark was almost too hard. As he unlocked the kitchen door, the telephone rang. He sprinted to answer it.

It was Robin. "You OK?"

"Sure" Ben said, though he breathed too fast.

"You sound like you're scared. Where have you *been*, Mr. Laughinghouse Barks?"

Ben didn't like telling anybody his plans, but somehow he'd never stopped Robin from asking for detailed reports on what he did or was planning to do. Now he laughed and told her "Maybe you'll *know* in a hundred years or *so*." When he realized that his answer rhymed, he sang it to Robin a second time like a teasing song.

Robin loved country music so she sang right back. "Then I'll keep *livin'*, long as you keep *givin'*."

Ben said "What have I given you, since Christmas anyhow?" Last Christmas he'd given her a good harmonica, and she'd learned to play it—any song you could mention and some she'd made up.

She kept on singing in her fake country voice. "You ain't give me not a penny—"

Ben finally had to laugh. He knew that Robin was a genuine friend, and her voice could cheer him when most others couldn't, but now he had to start cooking supper, so he kept quiet.

Robin waited as long as she could. Then she said "All right, Chef Barks, go do your magic with steak and potatoes."

That was what Ben's father ate three nights a week. Ben said "For your information, General Drake, we're having macaroni and cheese."

"And something green please—a salad or spinach. You've got to eat *green* stuff more than you do, or you'll never get grown."

Ben said "Then I'll run out and mow the yard right now with just my teeth." Ben had almost hung up before he remembered to ask Robin if she was doing OK—he hadn't seen her at school that day.

Robin moaned and groaned. "I've got a strep throat, but I'm so tired of *bed*."

"Want me to drop by tomorrow and see you?"

"Yes" she said. But then "No, I'm dangerous— you know, *contagious*. I've still got a fever."

Ben said "Call me when you know you're safe, and I'll bring some ice cream." Robin would have walked on her hands through flames to get her

favorite ice cream, which was peppermint, though she liked all flavors.

She groaned again but ended with a smiling sound. "Good. I'll hurry." As usual she hung up with no word of goodbye.

After Ben had put his jacket in his room and checked upstairs for any burglars that might be hiding, he came back down and set the kitchen table for supper. He turned on the oven to thaw the frozen macaroni and cheese, and then he went to the dining room to do his homework while he waited for his father.

An hour later Ben's father still hadn't come home. That wasn't strange; he was often as late as nine o'clock. So Ben turned the oven off, went back to his homework, but then leaned down on the table and fell entirely asleep. Soon he was dreaming that he sat in a chair in a field very much like the field out back. His head was turning in all directions like radar scanning for planes or storms till an elephant came to the edge of the woods and stood there, shy, looking out toward him and curling her trunk to show she might be friendly if he was gentle enough. She was a middle-sized Indian elephant with a deep notch in her

broad right ear and a bracelet of small bells around one foot.

The sight of her there was so good and strong that—still asleep and lost in his dream—Ben stood up from the table and started walking toward the kitchen door to go out and meet her and tell her his name at least and ask for hers. But before he put his hand on the knob, a sudden owl's cry ended the dream. Ben was standing in the kitchen with nothing but the smell of macaroni and cheese to keep him company.

So now while the memory was fresh in his mind, he took a clean sheet of paper and drew—for the first time in all his tries—the picture of an elephant so much like real life that he almost thought she would speak his name and tell him secrets the two of them could share in the long time they might spend together. Ben knew it was the truest picture of an elephant anyone had ever made, and it pleased him more than anything he'd done with his hands in all his life.

He held the drawing out in front of him and spoke to it as he might have spoken to a friend if he'd had any friends but Robin and Dunk. "You know what it feels like inside my head, and you're the only living thing that does." He didn't know

exactly what he meant by that, but the words themselves made his pleasure turn into actual happiness
that lasted through his father's return and a dried-
out supper past bedtime.

Those last days of winter crept by, dim and
rainy. On school days when the sky was still dark,
Ben would wake before his alarm clock rang. His
father liked to sleep as long as possible, so Ben
would dress and go down quietly to start the coffee
in a chilly kitchen. Then he'd trot outside, as the
sun made its first streaks on the sky, to feed old
Hilda. She was Ben's mother's dog and was fifteen
years old, deaf, and mostly blind.

Ben and his father were always trying to persuade
Hilda to sleep in the main house but she always
refused. She'd sit by the kitchen door and wait there,
upright all night long, until they let her go back to
her cot in the shed by the garage. There she slept on
a pile of worn blankets in the one low room. Old as
the shed was, it was warmed at nights by its own oil
stove and covered with a bright tin roof. Hilda's corner was also lit by a dim bulb, night and day, to let
her know—in case her blind eyes could see the
faintest shine—that members of her family still lived
in the main house and remembered her needs.

So as always the first thing Ben saw when he entered was his own reflection on the opposite wall from where Hilda lay. Years ago his mother had fixed this space for Hilda, and then she'd propped an old cracked mirror low down on the wall and kept it polished. When Ben got old enough to notice, he asked his mother what the mirror was for in a place where so few people ever came.

"It's company for Hilda, son. It lets her feel she's not so alone."

Ben had said "We could get another dog. Then she'd have real company."

But his mother had just said "No, son, this is what Hilda wants."

It hadn't occurred to Ben, so long ago, that Hilda might have also spoken to his mother.

But now he stood in the freezing morning air and took a slow look at his own face and body. That was something he very seldom did, and at first the sight of himself was shocking. He was thin and a whole inch taller than he remembered. His hair was longer than his mother would have liked, and his wrists were showing at the ends of his sleeves—all his clothes were too small now. There was one change that Ben liked, however. His face was plainly more nearly grown, more like a boy maybe

fourteen years old and not just eleven. Ben put out a hand and covered the mirror's image of his eyes. They looked as though they were seeing too much. Then he turned back to Hilda.

Old and deaf as Hilda was, she'd generally still be asleep when Ben walked in. But once she heard him, her tail would start a quick thumping on the floor. Then very slowly she'd manage to stand and turn her head up to trace Ben's moves as he opened the can and made her breakfast by stirring in the water he'd brought from the house. When Ben's mother had found Hilda so long ago—a lost puppy by the road—Ben wasn't even born. So she was the only dog he'd ever had; and because of that maybe, they had a deep calm friendship.

In their early days together, Hilda was still young and strong. She loved to hunt frogs and little fish in a stream near the house. But long before dark every afternoon, she'd come to where Ben was— building houses with his blocks on the floor or drawing pictures at the kitchen table. Then she'd lie beside him as close as she could get. It was back in those early days that Ben sometimes thought the dog was speaking to him. She didn't speak the way dogs speak in movies by moving her lips and using plain words. She'd turn her wide eyes to meet Ben's

directly. And then when they'd each looked deep into one another, Hilda might put words into Ben's head in a voice that was strange but clear. They'd be silent words but he'd hear them all the same.

He knew he wasn't imagining her voice. As time passed they talked more often, yet there were times when Ben tried to ask for help and Hilda couldn't reply. Still, when she did her help was trustworthy; and her voice was always soothing to hear. It was as real as his own voice in school, solving problems at the blackboard. So he had no trouble in believing that the bond between Hilda and him was real. He'd had something like it before with a deer he saw more than once in the woods. So he went on listening whenever Hilda spoke, though he told nobody else, not even his mother.

At first Hilda would say things like *Can we go outside and lie where the sun's warm?* Later she would ask Ben to tell his mother to feed her more than she normally got. Later still as Ben started school, Hilda began to tell him true things about his life—how he'd like other children but somehow feel more lonely around them than when he was alone. But those words slowly stopped with the years; and by the time Ben visited Hilda the morning after his dream and the realistic elephant drawing, it had

been maybe four years since Hilda spoke a word to Ben. All through his mother's sickness and her funeral, Hilda never said a thing, though Ben could tell she understood everything in the house or the hospital. And she'd been as sad as Ben was. In fact the old dog had seemed so forlorn that Ben couldn't even ask her to help him with her silent messages or her warm companionship, stretched on the floor.

This morning, though—as winter was starting to fade—Hilda waited till Ben had mixed her food. He knelt beside her to set her bowl down. Then her eyes met his.

In the next five seconds, Ben heard her say *I'll be leaving soon but you'll be fine. Don't worry; you'll be happy.*

Ben whispered back to her. "You don't have to go. This is your free home as long as you want it."

Her voice had sounded thin and stranger than ever, and she paused to let Ben calm back down.

Then he said "And don't you worry about me, Hilda. I'm a lot smarter than I was last year." He hadn't really understood Hilda's words.

So she managed silently to say another sentence that Ben could hear clearly far down in his mind. She said *This thing that's coming will help your whole life.*

Keeping his voice silent too, Ben asked her exactly what thing she meant.

But Hilda was finished for that day at least. She wouldn't meet his eyes again. She just ate her breakfast and crouched back down to sleep through another day of her tired old age.

Ben knelt once more, though, and stroked Hilda's broad head. Just the feel of her warmth and the strength of her skull told him what she'd meant. He said it to himself. "She means the circus will somehow save me." It felt like good news, like something he'd waited a long time to hear. So he stood up smiling. But all the way back toward the house, he asked himself "Save me from *what*? Dad and I both are a whole lot stronger than we were right after Mother died. Why do I need a dumb little one-ring circus?" He could think of no answer, and he wondered again why any sane person should believe a talking dog, but the thrill he'd felt at the sight of that one word *pachyderms* on a sign at the fairground rose in him again.

By the time Ben was back in the house, his father was seated at the kitchen table with a cup of coffee, a plate of toast, and the day's newspaper. He mumbled a few words of greeting while Ben washed

his hands and got his own cereal. As Ben took his place across from his father, he still felt as good as he had with Hilda. He was almost afraid to speak to his father now and run the danger of harming that feeling.

The silence was easy enough to hold on to for the first few minutes. Mr. Barks kept on reading the paper; but then as Ben stood to wash his bowl, his father said "Son, there's a one-ring circus coming to town. Will you pay for my ticket? It'll sure be expensive. But remember I took you when you were a child—and to Ringling Brothers, the biggest of all." Mr. Barks was teasing about the free ticket. Almost as much as Ben, though, he wanted to go. He'd had a hard time too through all these months, and he'd kept as quiet with his sadness as Ben.

Ben said "Sure, I'll take you every night—it's four nights, right? Are tickets on sale yet?"

Mr. Barks checked the paper. "At the music store, it says right here in the ad. You know where the music store is?"

Somehow Ben didn't care about music. He thought he would learn to want music in high school, but he knew where the record store was on Hickory Street.

✢   ✢   ✢

That afternoon Ben biked into town. School hadn't been out for more than twenty minutes, yet the music store was already full of teenagers ganged up in the little listening booths. In each one anywhere from two to six boys and girls were smoking and playing new songs and halfway dancing or hugging each other and pretending true love. Ben didn't know them, so he told himself he wouldn't have to worry about the stuff they were doing.

Maybe he and his few friends would act the same way eventually. For a whole year now, Ben had understood that no human being can foretell the future. And the smartest child can't predict his luck for the next two minutes. In gym class you might sink a stunning shot, then do it again five minutes later. But then you might get home late from school and find that your house had just burned to the ground.

At the back of the music store, there was one old lady at the ticket window; but she was reading a magazine so ancient it was falling apart. She had a narrow face and a long pointed nose that made her look more like an anteater than a normal woman, but Ben didn't mind that at all. When the lady looked up from the magazine and saw Ben standing there, she cried out *"Whoa!"* His silence and nearness had scared her.

He said "I'm sorry. I do that a lot—scare people, I mean. I guess I'm too quiet."

The lady said "Son, don't apologize. I wish every child alive in the world was as quiet as you." She pointed toward the front of the store and the music that was blaring even louder from the teenagers' booths. Once she'd stuffed a finger in each of her ears and shaken her head, she smiled and quickly came back to normal. "Can I sell you some fun?" There were posters behind her for wrestling matches and a show that promised to feature live fleas in a chariot race and authentic mountain dancing.

What she'd said about fun confused Ben for a moment. Then he also smiled. "Is a circus really coming to town?"

"Best circus in the world. Or so they claim. Don't they all claim that?"

Ben said "You guarantee they've got live elephants?"

"What makes you think they do?" She looked genuinely serious.

Ben said "I saw their poster at the fairgrounds a few days ago."

"And it claimed they had elephants?"

Ben said "Oh yes."

The lady said "Then it's bound to be true. People go to prison all the time for lying to the public. I feel fairly certain that circus folks wouldn't lie about their show." But then she faced Ben and winked an eye to admit she was fooling. "Son, if you buy a ticket and they don't have elephants—one elephant at least, in good working order—then you come back here, and I'll refund your money. I'm Firefly McCoy; just ask for me." When she saw Ben's smile, she said "Are you laughing at *Firefly?* Go right ahead. My name was Mother's first idea when she was still all drugged from having me. So I've had to live with people's dumb reactions all my life."

Ben said "Nothing sad about your name to me— at least she didn't name you *Lightning Bug.*"

The old lady laughed. "You've got a point there; but if you come back for that refund, just don't tell my boss. He'll gouge my gizzard out and fry it for supper."

By then Ben had what was left of his Christmas money in his hand. And he knew he should be smiling, but his face clouded over. He didn't want to risk being badly disappointed in this mysterious show, so he put the money in his pocket again.

The lady said "Look, are you an elephant boy?"

Ben recalled, right away, that *Elephant Boy* was

the name of an excellent movie he'd seen a few years ago. It was set in India where elephants are plentiful, and the boy in the story could talk to elephants as truly as Ben could talk to his dog. Still he told the lady "Yes, elephants are my favorite thing—in the whole world, I mean."

The lady was clearly more than surprised. "You love elephants more than human beings?"

Ben thought about that. He knew it sounded strange, but it probably was true. So he said "See, there's really no question at all that elephants are better than people. They always take good care of their young, they never kill anything unless they really have to, and they talk to each other over miles of distance in voices so deep we can't even hear them."

The look of surprise that had been on the lady's narrow face made it get even longer, and her eyes squinted shut. Then she shook all over like a cold wet dog. When she looked up again, she said "Aren't you the Barks child?"

Ben's father was the last grown member of the Barks family still left in town; so Ben said "I must be, yes."

"Aren't you sure?" the lady said.

"My dad is Billy Barks. Is that who you mean?"

The lady paused to turn that slowly over in her mind. Finally she said "I'm talking about the man whose wife just died—him and his young son."

Ben said "My mother died a whole year ago—even longer now. It only feels like yesterday."

"Then that makes you the boy I thought you were." The lady smiled but not in the pitiful way Ben dreaded from most of the people who'd known how much his mother suffered in her last days.

Ben said "All right. Now you know" and tried to smile again, but his own face clouded over too. He felt as if he'd admitted to a crime—something that awful for which he'd have to be punished every day through the rest of his life. He couldn't think of anything else to tell the lady, so he said "Is there something you want me to do?"

She said "Oh no, I've never met your family. I just read about your mother's death in the local paper and meant to send you a sympathy card that very same day, but then I forgot it. See, both my parents died when I was your age; and I wanted to tell you that I know it's a shock but you'll survive. You'll grow up stronger than any child in *town*."

Ben thanked her and felt a little dazed for a moment, the way he'd felt when Hilda suddenly spoke that morning. Then he burst out laughing

and said "The trouble is I live in the country, not the *town*."

The lady laughed too but said "Personally, I think you'll be the strongest child *anywhere*."

Any serious praise always embarrassed Ben, and this time he started to turn and leave.

But the lady said "Wasn't I selling you tickets— two circus tickets?"

Ben said "*Three* tickets, please—me and my dad and my cousin Robin Drake." Until that minute Ben hadn't planned to take Robin. He thought she might say something crazy that would ruin his concentration on the elephants. He'd already thought the same thing about Dunk; Dunk would act like more of a clown than anything the circus could offer. But at the last minute, Ben couldn't neglect Robin. She'd been good to him when his life was a lot harder than it was now; she deserved all the fun he could give her.

The lady said "Which night? They're here for four nights, though I can't imagine where they'll get that many willing spectators."

Ben asked if she had any tickets left for Thursday night. He'd thought he should wait till Thursday and give the circus a night to practice. So he fought his eagerness down and asked the lady if she

had any tickets left for Thursday, the second night.

"Thursday?"—she looked at her drawer. When she faced Ben she said "Gosh, it looks like I only have a few hundred left! How many dozen will you be needing?" Again she seemed serious.

Ben said "Just three, please—one, two, three." He showed three fingers so she understood he didn't mean dozens.

When she held the tickets out to Ben, she finally grinned.

So he took them from her bird-sized hand and paid her with the last of his Christmas money—six whole dollars.

As the lady folded the money and Ben turned to leave, she suddenly called him back. "Hey, listen."

When Ben looked back she whispered again. "You remember now—if the whole thing's awful, bring your ticket stubs back; and I'll give you your money."

Ben said "Are you saying it's not worth seeing?"

Her whisper went even deeper and softer. "Not exactly, no. But it does sound *tiny*—compared to Ringling Brothers, you know. And I don't want to cheat you, scarce as money is."

Ben thanked her one last time and left, expecting to feel depressed by her words; but the sun was

bright, and that clear fact plus the thought of the old lady's name—Firefly McCoy—kept his spirits up. His hope survived for the whole trip home and on into the night.

That night, though the circus had still not arrived, Ben went to sleep with no anxious feelings. That was because he'd learned not to lean on thoughts of the future, even when the future seemed sure to be good. In the dark of his room, he slept on deeply till three in the morning. Then something woke him—a sound in the room or just outside. It didn't scare him but he sat upright in his sheets and looked at once toward the window. At first he saw nothing but a very dim glow from the thin young moon. Still, he kept on waiting there till something began to fly past slowly, time and again, and brush the open window. What large bird would be flying at night? It might be a barn owl, hunting mice, or a confused hawk or eagle that had been waked up as quickly as he by some strange noise. But that didn't seem likely.

Then very gradually in the midst of the window, the faint outline of a human head began to be visible, stroke by stroke as if Ben were painting it himself with a brush and dark brown ink. The head had

short hair and was faced away, looking past Ben's room and into the night. Ben could somehow tell that, in spite of the short hair, this might be his mother—his mother the way she'd looked as a girl, long before he was born or before she'd known his father.

The air was chilly but Ben knelt on in the midst of his bed and stayed as still as he could, hardly breathing. He was almost sure he didn't believe in ghosts and demons. Yet eventually he thought that this person, high up and just outside, might be the spirit of his mother. Like most people he dreaded the thought of dead things returning—if there were such things. But ever since his mother died, Ben had missed her enough to welcome her back in any way she might choose to come. So he whispered three words toward the window. "Please. Yes, please."

Then whatever it was, and however it might have looked in the daylight, the head at the window started making a peculiar music. And Ben started hearing a high kind of singing. At first the song was like the feelings of a lost sad child; and Ben even put out a hand toward the window to let the spirit know he was friendly, though he didn't stand up or walk any closer.

Right then Ben heard his father's footsteps

move past the open door. The boy held his breath. As much as he liked his father, Ben wanted this minute alone for himself.

But his father didn't pause or speak, just went slowly into the bathroom and shut the door.

Maybe because Ben had reached out toward the face at the window and the curious song it sang, the music quieted down from then on and gradually faded away in the dark. When the air outside and the air in Ben's room—and Ben himself—were calm again, the head at the window turned very slowly and faced straight inward.

It was his mother, yes—his mother returned for just these moments. And yes, she looked like pictures Ben had seen from long ago when she was near his present age. Her eyes met Ben's and they felt so kind that he was reminded of what he'd nearly forgot since she left—how she'd almost never said a mean word to him in his whole life with her. And now he realized how she'd been the finest human being he'd known or might ever know in the long years to come (Ben had always thought he'd live a hundred years).

He was so happy in the sight of her face that he felt no need to speak or move. He did wish she'd sing again, one of the songs he'd loved as a young

boy, late on the nights when he'd have trouble sleeping. But no song came and no real words. In the next long minute, though, he felt an understanding spread deep down inside him, an understanding that he'd only felt with animals before—with poor old Hilda and the hawks he'd seen in tall bare trees and that buck deer, long ago in the woods, that spoke Ben's name and told him the world was a fine place to live, hard but fine.

Still kneeling in his bed now, Ben's mind shared his mother's mind completely; and while she still didn't say real words, he understood she was watching him gladly. He also knew she was doing all she could to help him grow and be happy as often as possible, the way he used to be before she left. By the time he understood that much, her face had gradually begun to disappear. Over the next five minutes maybe, she faded till there were no signs at all of her visit or her gladness. And once she was gone, Ben felt a little of his sadness return. But he was still tired, so he lay back flat on his bed and slept before he could lose this fresh good memory. He didn't even hear his father walk past, back toward his own room, and pause to check that Ben was safe.

In his way Mr. Barks missed his wife at least as

much as Ben did. But once she'd died she never came to his window looking like a girl again and sang or spoke to him in silent words. So he thought the smile on Ben's sleeping face must come from some enjoyable dream. He bent to smooth the boy's tangled hair and found it was hot. Then he touched Ben's forehead to check for fever. Finally he decided that Ben wasn't sick, but it didn't occur to Mr. Barks to think that the boy was already warm with hopes for something as small as a one-ring circus and a few old clowns and worn-out acrobats, and maybe some elephants.

Alone again, deep in sleep, Ben was resting every part of his body and aiming his hopes toward the first full day of spring, which was close.

When that day came it was warm and dry, and the sun was as clear as a washed new window. School had been hard and slow for Ben since he knew that tonight was Wednesday, the first circus night—or was meant to be, if the circus had turned up and got itself ready. In such a small town, it would have been normal for half of Ben's school friends to talk all day about the excitement of going tonight or later in the week.

Ben even waited for some boy to say he'd waked

up early and gone to the railroad stop near the fair-grounds to watch the elephants unload the tents and the lion and tiger cages. But nobody said the word *circus* one time, and Ben began to wonder if he'd just imagined the whole thing. He didn't ask any questions, though. He didn't want to hear even one boy or girl laugh and say he was dreaming again. Even worse, somebody might say he'd already seen the tents and the cages and that the whole thing was a pitiful mess—just a small-town show.

When the school day ended at three-thirty and Ben went out to find his bike, Dunk and Robin were already waiting for him. There was no way for Ben to ignore them politely; so he just thought silently *Don't say "circus"—either one of you, please. And don't make fun of anything about it.* Then he rode off a few yards ahead of them.

Dunk and Robin came on a little way behind. They both knew Ben too well to crowd him when he took the lead. But Ben could hear their conversation, and again they never mentioned the circus. So once he got to Dunk's driveway, Ben stopped and waited. When Dunk and Robin reached him, they also stopped and waited for Ben to say what happened next. He took a few breaths and said

"I better get home—got to feed old Hilda."

Robin said "You feed Hilda every morning, I thought."

Dunk said "You're not forgetting poor Hilda? I could come on and help you—she likes me, remember?" Dunk knew that Ben claimed to hear the dog speak every now and then. He didn't know whether to believe it or not, but he knew not to mention it in Robin's presence. Still, when Ben didn't answer, Dunk said again "I'm at least Hilda's second-best friend."

It was true. For reasons of her own, when she wouldn't go to anyone else, Hilda would stand up and let Dunk scratch behind her ears and call her crazy names.

But Ben said "Thank you, Sam. I've got a busy evening." Sometimes when he was trying to leave Dunk behind, Ben would call him "Sam," which was Dunk's first name—Samuel Duncan Owens.

For a moment Dunk looked disappointed.

So Robin said "Dunk, you can come home with me. Looks like a good day for pitching horseshoes." Her father had a horseshoe pit in the backyard, and Robin was as good at the game as almost any boy, but all winter long the pit had been too muddy.

Dunk gave it a moment's serious thought. He

had a lot of sisters who gave him a hard time, and girls hadn't started to interest him yet, so he didn't want to spend his free time pitching horseshoes with one more girl. He silently decided he'd ride toward the fairgrounds and see what he saw out there. He thanked Robin for the invitation, though, and just told Ben he'd see him whenever. He knew not to mention his fairgrounds plan to Ben. Lately for some reason Ben had gone silent to Dunk about the circus. He hadn't even mentioned buying tickets. Dunk would wait a day or two before asking why. And with that he waved Ben and Robin good-bye and went on his way, standing up on his pedals and pumping fiercely.

When he rounded the corner and went out of sight, Robin said to Ben "You mad with Dunk?"

"Not that I know of—why?"

Robin shrugged to show her usual sense of mystery with Ben's weird doings. They were half the reason she liked him so much. The other half was the fact that they were cousins.

Ben never tried to be weird to anybody, but he knew he struck some people as unusual. So he balled up both fists, screwed his mouth up into a frown, and said "I'm just mad with the whole world today." He meant it as a joke; he didn't want to

have to explain why he'd left Dunk behind.

But Robin nodded. "I know *why* you're mad. Every time you're mad I know the reason." She looked right at him and waited for an answer.

Ben faced the ground and didn't speak.

So Robin said "You *know* I understand your moods. I'm the key to your secrets, O Mysterious One!"

Ben finally laughed. "Not now, you aren't—I'll bet you a quarter."

Robin held out her palm to claim her reward. "You're worried about this circus in town."

With a gap between the words, Ben said "What–circus?"

Robin made a long face to mock his solemn look, and she imitated his voice exactly. "*What– circus?*" Then she laughed too. "The circus you've been waiting for all winter, with the live pachyderms." When Ben's faced stayed long and baffled-looking, Robin said "*Pachyderms?* You've heard of them?" When Ben still didn't smile, Robin said "Live elephants—your favorite thing on Earth after Robin, your wonderful cousin that you love so much."

Ben laughed even harder. Robin had always been better than anybody else at helping him know

how strange he could be. When he calmed back down, though, he looked straight into her pale gray eyes and asked her "Why would I be nervous if I truly love elephants and they're nearby?"

Robin said "Because they're the only thing you ever really loved—them and your mother."

Ben knew that Robin was nearly right. Nobody had said it out loud before, and it shamed him badly. What about his father and his cousin and his life, not to mention the human race and all mammals? So he said "I'm working on doing better, Robin."

She took a very long look at Ben's face as if he were sick with an awful plague and she was deciding whether to nurse him or run. Then she finally said "You could fool me, boy. You still look like a hungry lost puppy by the side of the road."

Ben let his eyes droop. Then he moaned three times, puppy style. When Robin raised her face to the sky and gave a long wolf howl, Ben said "What are you doing tonight?"

She looked at him hard, as if he'd lost all his marbles at once. Then she said "First, I'm getting my hair dyed purple with green polka dots. Then I'm going to the finest nightclub in town with a handsome hotshot you haven't met." There were no

nightclubs anywhere nearby, and Robin was still just ten years old.

Ben said "No you're not."

"I beg your pardon. I make my own plans."

Ben reached for his wallet and pulled out all three circus tickets. He brushed the top ticket with his lips—a mock kiss. Then he passed it to Robin.

She studied it like a hand grenade that might blow her sky high. After a long ten seconds, she said *"Tonight?"*

"Yes, madam." Still straddling his bike, Ben gave a low bow.

Robin said "Me and who else?"

Ben did his best to imitate the voice of George Washington or somebody else from days of old. "Your noble cousin Benjamin Barks and Benjamin's father."

Robin was on the verge of feeling happy that Ben might like her this much, but she had to check one other thing first. She waggled her ticket in front of Ben's face and said "Did you buy these or was it your dad?"

Ben used his George Washington voice again. "I—Benjamin Laughinghouse Barks—purchased these with my own hard-earned precious cash money." And again he gave his formal bow.

Then Robin felt safe to say just the right amount of thanks that wouldn't embarrass Ben. "I'm a happy soul, brother—all thanks to you." She'd never called him *brother* before (she didn't have a brother); but she'd use the word with Ben the rest of their lives at important times.

By seven o'clock the evening was clear and a good deal warmer than the day had been; but when they reached the fairgrounds, there were few cars in sight.

Mr. Barks said "I hope everybody but us doesn't know something bad about this event."

It was the kind of easy remark that Ben had tried not to hear all day. Instead of shutting his father up, though, Ben tried to calm him. He said "You're always telling me not to judge too fast or *I'll* be judged. *I* think this show is going to be fine."

Robin said "Me too."

But Mr. Barks said "Well, you've got to grant that it does look *little*."

And that was true, Ben had to admit. There was one tent as big as a good-sized house and another tent, close by, that was half the size. In the early twilight Ben could see four cages with bright steel bars. They had red wheels with golden spokes but were

very still now, and the animals in them were crouched out of sight or weren't there at all. No sign of an elephant anywhere.

Though she knew not to do it, Robin couldn't help whispering "Pachyderms, pachyderms, oh where *are* you?" When she looked toward Ben, he was facing the floor of the car and frowning. Robin understood he was burning now in fear and shame. So she said "Let's get out anyhow and find the cotton candy. I'm buying our treats." Robin always tried to carry her share of any load, financial or otherwise.

Ben was hoping the smaller tent would be where the elephants were waiting; but after everybody was holding the cotton candy, they entered the tent and Ben's hopes fell. The whole space was nothing but a dressing room for clowns and acrobats. They seemed like creatures from a pitiful planet, and they paid no attention to the few ticket-holders who walked right past them as they changed their clothes. None of them were completely naked for more than a few seconds, but most of the men had their shirts off, and a lot of the women were crouched beside mirrors, slathering crimson paint on their lips and chalk-white powder all over their

faces. Not a single clown or acrobat seemed to care who saw them half dressed like this.

Ben thought they seemed like people whose bodies were nothing but toys that they were mistreating intentionally. Maybe they were people who hated each other. Or maybe they were actual brothers and sisters who just spent too much time together. Whatever, Ben rushed his father and Robin through the awful mess and into the main tent. All Ben could hope was that somehow the elephants were hidden away and would turn up soon.

But they didn't. The clowns did silly stunts that were loud and easy to laugh at. They'd tie firecrackers to each other's shirttails and howl when they popped. They had a little dog that was funnier than they were. It could do back flips, six or eight in a row, and come up grinning. The acrobats bowed to the bleachers as if they were servants and the crowd was rich. Then they climbed tiny ladders far upward. There they swung and hurled each other through space in dangerous circles and swoops far up toward the top of the tent with no safety net.

A chubby man with a curly mustache walked into a flimsy iron cage with a lion, a coal-black pan-

ther, and a tiger. With a long leather whip, he made the three cats restless enough to snarl and reach their sharp claws toward him. But Ben suspected the man had given them some kind of drug since they never stood straight up on their hind legs or charged the man, who was smiling of course and soaked with sweat.

There were trained seals playing simple music, more dogs romping like actual children with children's clothes on. There were four trained horses playing circular games and a man who said he was the tallest thing living, which might have been impressive until you thought of a grown giraffe or a redwood tree. Still, he was close to eight feet high, though all he did was to walk around grinning and collecting applause.

After an hour or so of such ordinary foolishness, neither Ben's father nor Robin had said anything about the absence of pachyderms. Ben himself had halfway given up hope and was starting to laugh with the people around him, most of whom he knew by sight if not by name. He knew he'd feel disappointed when he got home, and he wondered if he'd have to tell Hilda she was wrong in her good prediction. But for now he was here with his favorite kin—that would have to be enough. Then

an unexpected thing broke on him like the best surprise of an ideal Christmas.

A boy and a girl, little older than Ben, ran forward from the far dark door of the tent to the brilliant spotlights and bowed to all directions. They were dressed from neck to toe in white costumes that clung to their excellent bodies like skin. When they'd finished bowing they faced each other as the small crowd clapped. They took a long moment, checking each other's eyes—for safety maybe—and then the boy leaned forward a little. The girl leaned to meet him, and they touched their lips together very lightly before they turned and ran to a pair of ropes that hung from the absolute top of the tent.

Until that instant Ben had felt that kisses, with anyone but your family, were either embarrassing or comically sickening. But here and now he felt otherwise—strongly and with a secret new thrill. The boy and girl didn't pause long enough for Ben to think about what they'd done.

Almost before his eyes could follow, they'd seized the two ropes and pulled themselves, as easy as walking, to a little platform almost out of sight. It was that far above. There they stood in the dark till a spotlight discovered them. Then they smiled again broadly and bowed to all sides.

Ben was impatient with so much bowing. He wanted to yell out "Do your dumb *act!*" Nonetheless his eyes were fixed on them.

Robin was also fascinated. She leaned to Ben and said "Do you think they're brother and sister or cousins?" Robin cared a lot about who was who in families.

Ben said "They're acting like husband and wife but I don't know."

Robin laughed. "They're not much older than you!"

Ben kept his eyes on the couple but said to Robin "All over the world there are millions of people younger than me who are already married and have their own children."

Robin generally laughed when Ben turned solemn, but she often believed Ben's strange ideas. This time, though, she guessed he was wrong. As she faced him to say so, the voice of the circus ringmaster blared out. "Ladies and gents and kids of all ages, prepare yourselves for the pride of our show. All the way from the snows of farthest Michigan, we bring you that dashing team, the astonishing Ringoes—Phyllis and Mark, loving twins. Young as they are they'll attempt for you now a feat of strength and skill unparalleled on the planet Earth

until this very moment. If you're caring people we hope you'll pray—and pray very *hard*—for, as good as they are, the astonishing Ringoes need your hopes in this new dare!"

Ben's father could tell that Ben was anxious—his face was pale and his fingers were clenched. He leaned to Ben's ear and said "Son, they wouldn't try this if they couldn't do it."

Ben nodded but wanted to shut his eyes.

Robin by now was watching just Ben. She also leaned toward him but said something far more typical of her own dark outlook. "I think they'll both be squashed jelly beans in another two minutes, don't you?"

At first Ben half believed her and almost nodded his head yes, but then he realized that he somehow trusted the ringmaster—a man who looked worn-out but also trustworthy. So he just told Robin "I'm betting they're safe." And from then on he kept looking up as the spotlights waved around like torches, and the drummer in the four-man band began a nervous roll that raked everybody's nerves and scared many adults, not to mention children.

The astonishing Ringoes clasped each other closely and hugged each other once but didn't kiss again. Then they reached above them and took two

separate trapeze bars hardly wider than their hands. With huge smiles still on their pink and white faces, their eyes turned serious as they planned their feat. Phyllis took the leap first; then Mark right behind her, not two yards apart. Quickly it turned out that both bars were connected to a single wire, amazingly thin. And once they'd jumped, one after the other, at first they slid fairly slowly down a sloping wire toward the ground by the dark tent door.

Still, Ben shut his eyes for a moment and thought *If they really had elephants, they wouldn't have this act—that wire could snap; it's way too risky.*

Then the whole band joined the snare drum at once. To the loud blasting of horns and snares, the Ringoes were only twenty feet from the ground. They were picking up speed; but with no sign of any net or cushion to ease them, they were bound to slam hard into the ground any instant.

Ben felt a high wave of sadness come on him, so he spoke out loud to Robin and his father—*"Excuse me please!"* He meant he was sorry for buying the tickets and forcing his family to watch this disaster.

Then in the band the cymbals crashed. And next, to the crowd's outright amazement, the Ringoes landed one-by-one on another platform ten feet off the ground. It was dimly lit and shaky, and it

had a black drapery all around and beneath it, but it had thin railings on the back and sides. So Phyllis and Mark only wobbled a little as they landed and stopped. They managed to keep upright and graceful, and they bowed as the spotlight found them again and blazed them in what seemed like all the light from an actual star—that strong and white. The audience rushed to its feet, yelling hard. Ben and his father and Robin stood too and joined the wild cheering.

Before it died down the Ringoes turned their backs to the crowd and faced the dark night just beyond the tent door.

Then their shaky platform began to revolve slowly to the right till it faced the people. Just as applause was beginning to die, two men on the ground reached up toward the Ringoes and pulled down the long drapery beneath them. That revealed the grand surprise. The platform, with Phyllis and Mark still on it, was delicately balanced on the back of an elephant—a genuine pachyderm—alive with its trunk curled up to its forehead, waving a brand-new American flag.

Ben's father grinned broadly and cheered even louder. Robin, who seldom touched other people, put her right arm around Ben's waist and hugged

him toward her. They were still standing up, but Mr. Barks and Robin might well have thought that Ben had turned to a statue there between them. He was that quiet and motionless, just watching the elephant steadily as it slowly moved on into the ring.

Once it got there it turned around in all directions, still saluting with its trunk and the flag, while the Ringoes kept on waving happily. When the elephant was facing the bleachers to the left of Ben and his family, it lowered the flag right to the ground and left it there. Then it started another whole turn around the ring.

A few people standing near Ben gave a gasp— the flag is never supposed to touch ground except when a soldier that's holding it dies.

But before Ben or anyone else could think it had picked out a single person to salute, the elephant stopped in place again. And again it was facing the bleachers to Ben's left.

When the ringmaster trotted near and stopped eye-to-eye with the elephant, he put his arms out level beside him. Then he lowered both arms; and the elephant lowered itself down slowly, hardly tipping the Ringoes on their platform. Then it lay down fully, so Phyllis and Mark could leap to the ground. As the cheering rose again, the twins from

Michigan came to the elephant's solemn head and kissed it gently above the left eye. The elephant took no notice of them but stayed on its belly in the sawdust ring. Through the whole act it had stayed as dignified as if this were Asia and it was at home in a warm green thicket surrounded by free food, family members, and no real enemies that mattered enough to trouble its sleep.

The ringmaster beckoned for the elephant to rise. It stood up slowly. At another signal it began to turn like a great clock-hand, almost that slowly. The ringmaster told the crowd that "Sal, as we call her, is our grandest possession. She's the single remainder of our elephant family, and as you've seen we save her for the crowning moment of our show. She comes to us here from the far land of India. She's twenty-four years old and lives up to her name every day. We call her Sal but her full name is Sala, which means *sacred tree*. She's sure been a sacred blessing to us ever since she came to these happy shores. Make her feel welcome in your town, please."

From her size and gentleness, Ben had already guessed that Sal was female. And as she stayed on, turning in the ring, he was already wondering what other elephants she might have lost. Had they died

or what? Ben tried to catch her eyes through the slight distance that lay between them. If Ben could be sure Sal truly saw him now, he might be able to hear thoughts from her, the way he'd got real help from Hilda.

But Sal kept turning as the audience clapped a modest welcome. If she saw any single person in the bleachers, she gave no sign of recognition. Then at a final word from the ringmaster, she left the ring at a funny running pace and was out of the tent into darkness too soon.

A little applause still spattered as she vanished, but Ben was sitting quietly. He was fixing the sight of her body in his mind in case he never saw her again. His heart was still a little fast, and blood was still pumping hot through his head, but really he'd never felt calmer in his life. With all the disappointment he'd had, this latest minute had been almost enough reward to cancel the sadness and fill him with a full set of hopes for life. Again and again he could hear the words of Hilda's prediction—*I'll be leaving soon but you'll be fine. Don't worry; you'll be happy.* He almost believed she'd told him the truth and that he could trust her from here on out.

After that there was still another half hour of acts, ending with the famous stunt where a tiny

automobile drives in and then eighteen normal-sized clowns unpack themselves from inside the car to the wonder of all. Ben watched them patiently, hoping that Sal would come back again and close the show but somehow she didn't. Even in the final parade, when every other member of the circus trooped by (including the cats in separate cages pulled by horses), there was no sign of Sala; and the ringmaster never mentioned her as he told the crowd "Good night. Come again!"

Neither did Robin nor even Ben's father say the word *Sala* or mention an elephant when they stood to leave. As they all stepped out of the tent into nighttime, Ben took a quick look around. There seemed to be nothing but the same few animal cages on wheels, some clowns undressing, and the scattering crowd. Ben heard several of them mention acts they'd truly enjoyed, but again nobody mentioned Sal and her small part.

So Ben began to wonder if he'd made it all up, out of pure hot hope. He couldn't recall doing anything quite that elaborate in his life till now. He still believed that what he'd seen at his bedroom window a few nights ago was really his mother, returned somehow. He understood that he was the kind of per-

son who saw and felt things that he couldn't mention or people would laugh and think he was crazy. But had this whole circus—or Sal's part anyhow—been another good dream that wouldn't last long?

As they got to the car and the three of them sat close together on the wide seat, Ben decided he'd wait till his father or Robin spoke of the elephant. If they didn't in the next five minutes, then Ben would know he was in some kind of serious trouble with his mind. His mother had always told him he leaned on hope too hard. He dreamed too much. She'd say "Ben, don't make so many *plans*. Life will mostly let you down."

Then at the first red light, Mr. Barks said "Why do you two think that poor old elephant did so little work tonight?"

Somehow it almost made Ben angry. He quickly said "She's not an old elephant. You heard the man say she's well under thirty. She might live a century if people treat her right."

Robin said "I think she's bound to be lonesome. She's got nobody to be with but clowns and a few mangy cats that are halfway asleep. I'd be lonesome too."

Ben couldn't disagree so he sat on quietly as his father drove ahead. To calm himself, he tried to see

nothing but the car's headlights as they lit their fast way through the thick trees.

At last Mr. Barks said "Benjamin, we thank you for the tickets and the fun."

Robin said "Amen."

Mr. Barks said "But tell us about that elephant—was Sala her name?"

Ben knew he'd have to speak now. He couldn't just sit in silence all the way home and turn the memory over and over for his pleasure. So he said "Sala, yes sir. It means *sacred tree*. They call her Sal."

Mr. Barks said "What's sacred about an elephant?"

Ben said "Maybe this one behaves really well. But elephants mostly behave very gently. Still, if you treat an elephant bad—if you beat it or keep it from getting its water and food—then one day it may turn on you like a *snake*. They'll throw you to the ground with that mighty trunk; then they'll kneel down and crush you to pulp with their foreheads. It's happened in a lot more zoos and circuses than people admit—they keep the news quiet so as not to scare people."

Robin said "They crush you to *pulp?* Boy, I wish you hadn't told me. I'll never feel safe around one again."

Ben said "That's half the pleasure of knowing them. Big as they are, they mostly won't crush you. But you've still got to face that risk when you see one. Even tonight, as kind as the Ringoes were, Sal might have got mad for some private reason and squashed them and that dumb ringmaster. Then she might have charged the bleachers and stomped us to jelly."

Robin shut her eyes and shuddered hard.

Mr. Barks said "Don't exaggerate, son. And don't blame the ringmaster. He had too much to do, but I thought he handled his job fairly well."

"You're right," Ben said. "He treated Sal fairly well, considering where they were. I guess I was sorry he told us her story in public like that—her birthplace and losing her family and all. I'll apologize to him when I get a chance."

Robin said "Do you *know* him?"

Ben didn't answer her.

In a couple of minutes, though, Mr. Barks said "No, Robin, Ben doesn't know the ringmaster yet. Let's leave it at that." He didn't glance at Ben or say another word, but he'd shown Ben two important things. This father understood a lot about his son, especially why he kept so many secrets; and he wasn't trying to scare Ben off. If the boy had some

plan to visit the circus another time to meet the ringmaster and get to know Sala, it was fine by his father. He trusted him that much.

And here tonight Ben felt at least some thanks to his father. Robin sat on the seat between them, so Ben leaned forward to his father and gave him a semi-comic salute with his right hand. "Aye aye, sir," he said. "I'm outward bound." That was an expression Ben had heard in war movies. He thought it meant that ships had been launched toward enemy bases or submarines were firing torpedoes.

Ben somehow felt he was truly airborne, on his own wings, and was maybe headed toward his grown life, however far off it might prove to be. And finding a way to know Sala in the coming few days would be the next step. Somehow he would have to manage to know her and to let her know about his love for her— and for her kin all over the world— tonight and forever.

That same night after they'd stopped for ice cream, dropped Robin off at her house, and then gone home to sleep, Ben had an unusual dream. It wasn't sad or scary. It was just a plain story, a story that seemed natural and very much like his daily life. He was walking through some woods that at

first he didn't recognize. Then he came to a wide creek with deep fast water, and he knew that these were the woods he and Robin sometimes explored when they acted out movies they'd recently seen. He looked around to see if Robin was lagging behind him, which she mostly was; but there was no sign or sound of her. He even called her name and she didn't answer. So he was alone.

In the dream Ben sat on the bank of the creek and looked up toward the tops of the trees. After a long quiet wait, with bright sun pouring down on his body, he gradually thought that maybe the world had disappeared. Maybe every other place and person had vanished, leaving him and this creek and these few trees entirely alone, with no friends or family—no wild animals or tame ones either. He thought about that; and it didn't seem bad, not if the world had disappeared painlessly. For a few quiet minutes, it seemed an excellent way to live. But just as Ben got to the edge of feeling afraid of loneliness, he heard a rustling in the woods beyond the creek.

In another minute, as the dream rustling changed into thundering footsteps and Ben stood to run if necessary, a creature broke into sight and stopped. It was still more than half concealed in dead leaves and sticks. And it faced him directly—he was

clearly its target, whatever it was. For a moment somehow he thought it was Hilda. But if it was Hilda, then she'd grown terribly tall and heavy. At last the creature stepped forward slowly; and though Ben knew this was really a dream, he also knew that this was Sal, the elephant from that night's show.

She came on right to the edge of the creek and took long drinks of the clear cold water. To do that she had to suck water up into her trunk, then bring it to her mouth. When she'd finished that Ben spoke to her in a normal voice. "Sal, come on and get me. It's just us two left alive in the world."

She seemed to understand that. She didn't disagree. Her eyes stayed calm and fixed on Ben. After a moment of silent waiting, she gave him a greeting very different from what she'd offered in the circus. She had no American flag to hold, no humans on her back, no platform for the Ringo twins. What she did was to pull one leg far back and bend that knee. She also lowered her head and looked down. It lasted ten seconds. Then she stood back upright.

That amounted to what Ben thought was a bow. People in his world had long ago quit bowing seriously to others. In news from Japan, though, Ben had noticed how the Japanese people bowed low to each other and especially to strangers. Right or

wrong, he gave Sal a solemn bow in return for hers. Then again he held out a beckoning hand and urged her to cross the deep water toward him. He knew that elephants, and most other mammals, can swim like fish from the moment they're born.

But Sal wouldn't come toward his hand. She plainly meant that Ben should come across to her, wading or swimming. He could swim well enough, and he thought of Hilda's promise that his meeting with Sal would change his life in excellent ways. But he waited in place, alone on his side.

At last after what seemed a very long time, Sal lowered herself into the water. Her eyes never moved from Ben's face, where he stood still waiting.

Ben suddenly thought he might have made her angry. He knew she could break every bone in his body with two light slaps from her trunk, but Hilda's promise stayed clear in his mind. Hadn't she more or less said *This thing that's coming will save your life?* He knew the chances were surely even that he'd be dead in another few seconds. But he felt no fear. In fact Ben was smiling when the dream broke off, and he was awake in the dark in his bed again. At first he was sorry the story had ended. But then as he lay looking up to the ceiling, he decided the dream was the final proof of what he'd more than half decided

to do tomorrow. He'd go to the fairgrounds and try to find Sal.

When he'd made that plan, Ben fell back asleep with no more dreams or waking till daybreak.

Next morning the sky was completely blue. By the time Ben finished his breakfast and walked to Hilda's shed, the air was warming. He recalled how seldom Hilda had spoken in recent years; but today he thought that Hilda might have some extra thing to tell him, some more advice. While he mixed her food, she kept her thoughts very much to herself; and even while Ben watched himself in her mirror, she stayed silent. So before Ben left he told Hilda what he'd noticed about his face this morning—he looked even older than he had the day before.

It felt as though he were growing the way plants grow in nature movies, almost too fast. But that didn't worry him or change his plan. It seemed so important that Ben had to remind himself to pet old Hilda before she took a few brief minutes to roam the yard and smell every tree. He didn't mention last night, though. He'd wait to see how today turned out. Then he could either tell her good news or just not bother her with any disappointment.

✤   ✤   ✤

During lunchtime at school, Dunk brought his two mashed-potato sandwiches and sat by Ben in a shady corner of the loud cafeteria. Ben knew the first question Dunk would ask, but he didn't try to stop him.

With his mouth full Dunk said "I hear your whole family went out last night."

Ben said "You heard right."

Dunk said "I was hoping you felt like I was kin to you."

Ben said "You're my good friend but no, Dunk, we're not kin."

Dunk said "So why didn't your *friend* Dunk get invited to the circus with your tiny family?"

In hopes of sparing his friend's feelings, Ben told Dunk a lie. "See, Dunk, Dad bought the tickets; and he's been hard up for money lately."

"Ben, I could have paid my own way." Dunk turned his pants pockets inside out, but they both were empty.

Ben said "You know we couldn't ask you to come with us and then make you pay your way. You can go on your own any night it's still here."

Dunk said "Yeah, 'on my own.' *That's* a whole lot of fun."

Ben said "Ask Robin; she'll gladly go again."

Dunk's sisters were chatterboxes and had left him, for now at least, with very little interest in girls. So he made his comical sour face. "*Robin?* I'd rather take Phil Campbell, sick as he is." Phil Campbell was Dunk's dog, older than Hilda and crazy enough to lunge at almost any moving thing.

Ben went back to eating his green beans and pork chop. For a while he tried to feel guilty for leaving Dunk out last night, and he was almost on the verge of feeling selfish when Dunk broke in.

Dunk had tried staying quiet to show he was hurt, but finally he had to ask his main question. "So how *was* that little bitty run-down flea-bag circus?"

Ben couldn't help laughing. Finally he said "You got it! It was very little bitty and mighty run-down."

Dunk said "And that one pitiful pachyderm should have been in the elephant's graveyard—right?"

Ben wondered if Dunk hadn't somehow also been at the circus the previous night. "By any chance were you hiding in the bleachers?"

It was Dunk's turn to laugh; he doubled over and chuckled longer than was necessary. When he'd got himself calm, he shut his eyes dramatically and said "Ah, you know me—the invisible phantom. I go where I want, and none can stop me!"

Ben said "Where were you sitting? Could you see us?"

Dunk laughed some more and then was halfway serious. "Relax, Mr. Stuck-Up. I wasn't at the circus, no. But see, I can get inside your mind any night I want to. All you have to do is fall asleep, and I can send my mind right into your bedroom and crawl through your eardrum and *listen*."

Thickheaded as Dunk could be sometimes, that almost sounded possible to Ben. But he ignored it and took up for Sal. "Dunk, the elephant was kind of sad but she's not old."

Dunk shrugged his shoulders. "Have it your way. Did she tell you any secrets?"

When his mother was dying and Dunk was so kind, Ben had told him a little about how Hilda had talked to him long ago but wouldn't speak now. And ever since, if Ben and Dunk disagreed in private, Dunk might bring up that one thing and almost threaten to make fun of it. So now Ben told him "No, Dunk, she didn't speak. Don't you think it's about time we gave up acting like three-year-olds?"

Dunk thought about that while he finished the last half of his sandwich. Then he took a long gulp of milk, belched loudly, and said "Oh pal, I've been

a grown man for months now. I'm glad you've decided to catch up with me."

Ben laughed almost as much as Dunk had before; but when he stood up to head back to class, he didn't say a word about his afternoon plan.

By lagging behind at the end of class to talk to Miss Elmers, his art teacher, Ben managed to leave school alone at four o'clock. There would be at least two hours of light before sunset, but he still rode as fast as he could to the fairgrounds. He hid his bike in a clump of low pine trees and walked toward the tent and the few wagons nearby. He was almost there before he saw the first sign of life. He heard it actually—a very deep roar from the only lion. He recalled from last night that it was in the biggest cage, and he walked right toward it.

Ben was not more than five steps away when he thought the cage might somehow be open. The lion might rush down on him in an instant. But the thought didn't scare him. Any day before this Ben would have stopped and gone back a safe distance to check. Today for some reason he felt ready to face whatever happened. As he reached the side of the red cage, the lion was right up against the bars, looking out as if he'd expected Ben every minute

since last night here at the show. Ben also moved up to the bars and met the lion's eyes directly. Mostly it's a bad idea to meet the eyes of any strong creature, wild ones especially. But this was the lion who'd seemed so tame in the show, and the look on his face now seemed to Ben even more peaceful.

The lion kept his face close, touching the bars; but he lay down flat on his belly and plainly invited Ben to rub his nose and muzzle.

Tall as he was for his age, Ben's arm could barely reach high enough to touch the lion. He tried, though, and after he'd lost his balance and fallen against the bars, the lion lowered his enormous head with its golden mane. Ben took a good look and saw how kingly even this cooped-up cat still was. He thought "Please don't let anything happen now that either one of us regrets." Then Ben tried again and finally reached the lion. With only a little burst of nerves, Ben patted the lion's damp nose and the broad dry muzzle that hid the crushing jaws and teeth. He even reached far enough in to scratch the short hair on the back of the lion's right front paw. It was the size of a normal dinner plate and strong enough to claw down an antelope or zebra on the plains or a human being taller than Benjamin Barks or anyone he knew. Yet here it was letting

him actually touch that paw at the end of a strong leg—a grand wild thing.

From close behind Ben a man's loud voice said "If you want to give him your whole arm, just keep on doing what you're doing now."

Ben hadn't heard anyone's footsteps, and the nearness and loudness scared him more than what the man said. He jerked his arm back out of the cage.

The lion rose up as quickly as a bad storm and gave a deep roar so powerful it seemed to shake the world around them.

Ben had never stepped back from the cage, and he saw that the lion's eyes were locked on the man who'd come up near them from behind. So several times Ben said "Calm down, *calm*" to the lion and soon it did.

It lay back down and looked to Ben; but before it could try to know him and maybe exchange some thoughts, the man put a heavy hand on Ben's shoulder. "I didn't mean to scare you there, son; but you were in *danger*. That cat's named Trouble and you could have been in deadly trouble if I hadn't caught you." When Ben had turned and faced the man, the man put his hand out. "I'm Duffy Brown. Weren't you here last night?" Duffy was not much taller than Ben, but he weighed a lot more, and his voice was

nearly as deep as the lion's. He was trying to make his dark eyes flash to show he was strong, but they looked a lot gentler than he intended.

Still, it took Ben a moment to see that this crumpled little man was the circus ringmaster. The man still held out his hand; so Ben shook it, told the man his own name, and said "Yes I was here, with my dad and my cousin."

Duffy said "See, I knew you'd be right back today."

"How did you know that?"

Duffy said "I saw you when the show was over. You were walking away but you were still lit up like a *lamp*—you were that excited."

The story didn't seem likely to Ben, but he didn't try to correct the man. He just said politely "If you know my thoughts, you'll know I'm hoping to see your elephant."

For some reason Duffy laughed and shook his head no. Then he said "I'm afraid that can't be arranged."

Once again Ben wondered if he'd somehow imagined the whole appearance of Sal last night. But hadn't Ben's dad and Robin confirmed that the show was real? Had he dreamed that too? He said to Duffy "I hope she's not sick."

Duffy's voice went down to a whisper, and he moved a little closer to Ben. "She's not really sick but, see, she's the boss's personal pet. He doesn't want anybody to scare her—she's been through so much stuff here lately."

Ben nodded. "Last night it seemed like you mentioned her losing some kin. Is that true, sir?"

Duffy went on whispering. "Just call me Duffy—everybody else does. You probably read about us in the paper. Small as we are, we had four elephants up till last summer. Then over the fall and winter, three died. Just stopped eating, got weak, and died pretty quick."

Ben asked "What caused it?"

"The vet in Florida—where we spend the winters—he couldn't explain it. I told the boss just what I thought but he wouldn't listen. He wouldn't believe anybody could be so mean as to poison creatures like Emma, Agnes, and Ravi—smart as they were. See, we'd had a young guy named Bert Beazley working with the animals for nearly a year. Bert was a peculiarly *quiet* fellow, barely spoke to anybody, even me, though he talked a lot to the cats at night. Then the boss caught him striking old Emma one day. Emma was the head girl of all our elephants, gentle as a puppy; but she never seemed to like Bert one bit.

"After a while Bert decided she was snooty; and he'd hit her with his prod, up near her forehead and around her eyes. I saw him and told him he'd better watch his step. If an elephant really turns against you, you can wind up worse than a grape on the floor. Like I said, the boss wouldn't believe me; but then he caught Bert in the act one day. Boss nearly tore him apart with words—told Bert he'd fire him the instant he heard of any more cruelty to *anything*. After that Bert worked for another three weeks. Then one night he just disappeared, and a few days later all four elephants started acting peculiar." Duffy stopped there as if the story were told. He stepped up, put his face to the lion's bars, and told the creature how much he loved it.

The lion suddenly growled in what Ben thought was an affectionate way. But it silenced Duffy and when he gave no sign of saying more, Ben had to ask "Are you telling me Bert somehow poisoned the elephants?"

Duffy said "I guess I am. The day after he left, I found some green powder strewn in their hay—just a small handful. At first it looked suspicious to me, like arsenic poison; but I didn't think much more about it. With all kinds of animals living around you, you see a lot of peculiar chemicals—things to

kill rats and fleas, you know. Anyhow, by the time the elephants started getting sick, it was too late to do anything about it."

"So all the others but Sal got sick?"

Duffy said "Oh no, Sal got sick too and lost a lot of weight; but she came through when the three others failed. It broke nearly all our hearts, I'll tell you. And it nearly bankrupted the boss and the show. We're staggering still and we may not make it."

Ben said "What kin were the others to Sal?"

Duffy said "To tell you the truth, we never were sure. A ringmaster had to say that to his public—that they were a family—but none of us was working for this show back when the elephants were young. Even the boss bought the show when the elephants had been here for years, so we always just called them sisters. They lived in peace together anyhow." Duffy paused a moment, then laughed and said "Which most sisters don't!"

Somehow that made Ben want to see Sal more than ever. He said "If Sal is here right now, I'd sure like to see her."

Duffy waited. "You're not a big criminal, are you?"

The question seemed serious but Ben had to laugh. "Sir, I sometimes think I'm stark *crazy* on the

subject of elephants; but I'm no real crook." Then like Dunk, Ben turned his pockets inside out and held his hands up to show they were empty. "The worst thing I've ever done was to shoot a bird with a B.B. rifle the day I got it. I've never used it since."

Duffy went silent and turned around slowly in every direction. Then he said "Look, the boss is in town right now. I don't want to make him mad. He loves this creature—"

Ben said "I love every elephant alive, all the ones I've heard about anyhow. Since I was a child, I've wanted to have an elephant to care for."

Duffy shook his head, frowning. "Whoa, boy! An elephant takes steady care round the clock. They may look strong but, if you take them out of the jungle, they're fragile as light bulbs." He looked around again and then whispered "Come on now with me. If anybody stops us I'll say you're my nephew—I'm your Uncle Duffy."

Ben whispered too. "Where *is* everybody?" He meant all the clowns and other performers.

"They're off in town somewhere like the boss. They take every chance they get to run wild. Still, somebody might come back and find us; so say you're my son—"

Ben said "No, your nephew. Your nephew,

remember?" He remembered to look back and give a short bow and a wave to the lion, who still watched him closely, though Ben had all but forgot it was there, hearing everything they said.

By then the lion looked like something that deserved the name Trouble as Duffy had said. He could no doubt swallow a boy, age eleven, in record time. Ben waved again, then followed Duffy onward in silence.

To Ben it felt like a five-mile walk—he was that excited and his mind was that hot. Would Sal be hid underground somehow or in one of the trailers with the blinds shut tight? Maybe she was there in the dark pine woods, somewhere near his bike. But where Duffy led him was straight to the far back side of the main tent. Last night Ben and his family hadn't noticed the single small tent with all flaps shut.

At the main flap Duffy looked around again. Then he quickly undid a knot in the rope and lifted the flap just enough to let Ben through. Then he followed the boy in.

The sky outside had been so bright that Ben's eyes took awhile to adjust to the dim place he stood in. The first thing he could see clearly was a deep bed of hay under his feet. Then he caught the mix-

ture of smells that he recalled from his other circus visits—a mix of dry hay and the strong but clean-smelling dung that comes from creatures who eat only grass and straw. Then Ben could see that Duffy had stepped ahead of him and was whispering again.

Ben could make out words like *My girl* and *Honey* and *Safety*. By that time he could see Sal standing in place with her trunk laid lightly across Duffy's shoulder. *Sweet Sal* were the words that first came to mind when Ben saw the whole enormous shape of an elephant not more than four steps beyond him. But he waited for Duffy to notice him and tell him what to do.

Finally Duffy looked back and asked Ben his name. When Ben had given his three full names, Duffy said "Sal, this boy Benjamin here is a great admirer of you and your family. You ready to meet him?"

Sal reared her trunk up into the air above Duffy's head and smelled Ben through the space between them. Then she reached the trunk out toward him.

Ben could see the moist pink skin inside her nostrils, and he remembered how the first circus elephants he'd seen years ago had begged peanuts from the crowd. Now here was Sal maybe asking for food

and Ben had nothing. Again he did what he'd done for Duffy. He turned out his pockets and showed his empty hands.

Duffy said "Don't worry. Sal doesn't care what you've got to give her. Just tell her you like her, in your own voice."

That was the first time Ben realized that he'd never in his whole life said a word to a live elephant. He stepped forward now and took the end of the great trunk in both his hands. Then he said as clearly as he could manage "Sweet lady, hello. I'm just a local boy; but I'm happier to be here with you today than anywhere else I've ever been."

Duffy snorted, laughed, and said to Sal "You don't believe a word of that, do you, darling?"

Whatever she thought, Sal left her trunk in Ben's hands all the same; and Ben tried to say what he meant in better words. "I don't know why, lady; but I'm feeling *better*." And so he was. Just holding the serious weight of the trunk seemed to Ben like a privilege—the thick dry skin and the hundreds of delicate muscles that made a trunk even more useful than any human hand.

Ben was so involved in those feelings that soon Duffy had to say "Keep talking to her, son. She needs a lot of talk."

Ben asked him "Why?"

Duffy said "She's alone as a child at the North Pole. Can't you see that?"

Ben stared into Sal's eyes and thought he could see the kind of look he'd seen on children at the orphan's home on the south side of town. It was thoroughly lonesome and nearly hopeless but was also ready to laugh if anything or anybody would give it a chance. Of course Ben knew that, strictly speaking, elephants don't laugh; but in movies he'd seen them play with one another, and he strongly suspected that almost every living thing could understand happiness and feel it at times. So he wanted to talk to Sal in whatever way she might like or need. Duffy was standing too near him, though. And Ben needed privacy before he could fully open his heart. He stepped a little closer to Sal and then said "Mr. Duffy, could I just be in here with her alone for a while?"

At once Duffy shook his head. "No *way*. Boss would kill me *dead*." But he thought about it and finally said "I'm going to pat you down like they do with real crooks in jail. Is that OK?"

Ben said that it was.

So like a policeman Duffy patted his way down Ben's shirt and pants. He even looked again at both

of Ben's hands. Then he said "I'll be waiting right outside here. You talk to her kindly, and I'll give you warning if anybody's coming."

Ben said "Thank you, sir." And as Duffy reached the flap, Ben said "Please don't listen to us. It'll just ruin the visit."

Duffy smiled. "Son, Sal can do a lot of smart things; but Sal can't talk, not that I ever heard."

Ben nodded to show he agreed, which he didn't—not yet anyhow.

And then Duffy was gone.

Sal lifted her trunk again and smelled the air beyond Ben's head to prove to herself that she and this boy were alone together. When she knew that was true, she stood in place, rocking from side to side. She accepted Ben's presence as a natural fact, and that made a change in her loneliness.

Ben leaned down and swept up an armload of hay. He held it close to his body but near enough to tempt Sal to eat.

Her trunk pulled a few strands loose and carried them to her mouth, then more and more.

When she'd eaten it all, Ben still kept his arms hugged tight to himself; and Sal probed inside Ben's grasp to find any last hay, as if the ground weren't covered around them.

As Ben accepted Sal's tickling gladly, he said aloud "This is one place I've always dreamed of being." Then he wondered how weird or dumb that would seem to other people his age or to his father. What he didn't wonder, not then, was whether Sal could hear what he said; and did she know his meaning?

But as Ben's hands came up again and took her tickling trunk and he laughed, he slowly began to feel a kind of rumbling, very low and deep in his bones. It was like the first faint signs of an earthquake or the bass line of music too far off to hear. At the start it came in short bursts. Then Sal laid her trunk on the top of his head. The weight was so heavy Ben thought he would soon be forced to duck out or at least to kneel at her feet in the hay.

Just as the weight turned painful, Sal suddenly lifted her trunk; and deep inside his chest, Ben heard a few sounds that seemed like words. They were so soft he couldn't really hear them well. But he stayed where he was, standing near Sal; and slowly he began to understand her. The first message was so dim that it seemed to be more like a far-off moving picture than words. Ben shut his eyes to focus on the message, and slowly all around his mind a new world opened as his thoughts moved forward.

A whole new place took shape in his mind. It was so clear that Ben didn't pause to wonder whether it was real or a dream. There were trees much bigger than any he'd known, and the path he was walking now in his mind was a narrow path through thick dark grass that came almost to his ears. After his mind had walked a long way, Ben finally stopped to take a deep breath; and then he heard the first clear words from this new world. They came from a little way behind him, and they came in a tone that sounded like the voice he had hoped Sal would have. To Ben's mind alone she finally said *Behind you is safe. All around you is safe. Be fearless now.*

Ben didn't think he'd been afraid. There was nothing about sweet Sal that scared him. Even if Duffy's boss should burst through the tent flap at that moment, the worst he'd find would be a young boy who plainly wouldn't harm a living thing. Still, Ben appreciated the message and he whispered back. "I'm thankful, lady. But don't stop guarding me. I'm still in trouble a lot of the time." He wasn't exactly sure what he meant, but he knew it had been true this whole past year.

Sal was swaying side to side by then, the way trapped creatures often do. But she said nothing else.

"I could try to stay here with you—"

Sal gave him no answer.

"Does that mean I should leave you now?"

Again no answer.

Ben wondered if anything he'd said or thought had been wrong or mean. He asked Sal please to excuse him for any mistake. He said "See, I've only talked with a dog up till now. I'm not much good at conversation." The whole idea of conversation with this strange creature was so amazing that Ben had to laugh. Sure, he'd known Hilda all his life; but walking into a small private tent and having an elephant answer your voice seemed to Ben as wild as speaking to the ocean and having it speak back in words you could hear.

What Ben had just said seemed to free Sal. She sent him some words about *learning to cross the lines in nature. It's much too hard for most of your people to talk to me or anything like me.*

Ben said "My people? I'd give up everything to be one of you." As long as he'd loved elephants, he'd never wanted to be one before. Was what he'd just told Sal a lie? Was it some kind of insult? Ben waited to see what she'd do with the strange idea.

Her body swayed on in place as before, her trunk rummaged in the hay but she didn't eat, her eyes

seemed fixed on nothing nearby. Was she hearing some sound Ben couldn't detect? Was the boss back from lunch and walking this way? Was Duffy worried and ready to come back in and stop this?

None of those questions got answered at once; but in a few seconds Ben heard clear words like *Help* and *Promise* and *Don't fail me, please; I've been failed before.*

Ben suddenly knew what he had to say, and he told Sal clearly what he meant to do next. He said "Don't worry. I'll get you out of here. See, I live in the country with my father. The only friend that hangs around much is my cousin Robin, a girl who's a whole year younger than me. We've got a big field and woods and a creek; and except for an old dog that once was my mother's, we've got nobody else at all to care for. Dad thinks the place will be too small for you, but I think you'll love it and will want to stay. Anyhow we'd be together at last, and nobody else could come between us unless we changed our minds and asked them to be with us always."

Years from now when Ben got close to falling in love with the girl he'd marry, he would say words at least this serious and certain. For now they were brand-new and pouring from him like water that has just broken through a high dam. For now he

paused while Sal rocked gently and listened maybe, though she didn't say Yes, No, or Maybe.

In the silence Ben heard a new man's voice. "Who's in there with her?"

Duffy's voice said "A boy. A harmless boy that just loves elephants and wanted to meet her. He bought three tickets and came last night with his dad and his cousin—"

The tent flap was all but torn off in haste; and there—with the daylight flowing in around him—stood the boss of the circus, Bo Grimlet. He was short and no taller than Ben, but his face had the fury of a hot blast furnace. He looked like an actual human being but one that could melt other humans with his anger just by meeting their eyes and staring hard. Once Mr. Grimlet had checked out the sight of Sal and seen she was safe, he was staring at Ben.

But Ben spoke first. "Sir, I'm Benjamin Laughinghouse Barks, a local boy. I live here in town—or just outside. My father's an insurance agent and rides around town and the county all week, selling policies to people. I'm in the fifth grade in the only school in town; and elephants, without any doubt on Earth, are the thing I love after my parents and the home we have."

Oddly, Mr. Grimlet said "Who's your pitiful mother then?"

Ben said "Sir, there was nothing pitiful about her. She died last year."

As he said that, Sal said the one word *No* so plainly that Ben looked back to see if Mr. Grimlet heard her.

Mr. Grimlet's anger hadn't cooled yet, and he walked right toward Ben with both fists clenched.

Ben tasted a mouthful of fear like cold pennies laid on his tongue.

By the time he got close enough to see Ben's size and his actual age, Mr. Grimlet had calmed down enough to stand next to Ben and not strike him down and then lug him from the tent. He looked at Ben from head to toe slowly. "You're halfway reliable-looking anyhow."

Ben said "Yes sir."

Mr. Grimlet reached down and took both of Ben's wrists. "Let me see the palms of your hands."

Ben knew the boss was looking for poison—maybe arsenic or cyanide—so he spread both hands. They were clean of all but the honest dirt of a day at school.

Mr. Grimlet turned both Ben's hands carefully, side to side. He looked at the hay on the ground

beneath them and kicked it aside, still looking for any poisonous powders or hypodermic needles that Ben might have used to kill this final elephant, the show's last hope.

Ben's voice broke in. "Sir, I'm as harmless as any boy you know. Like I said, I worship elephants; and Sal is the only one I've seen close up. I came out here after school today, and Mr. Duffy kindly let me in when he'd checked me out to be sure I was safe."

Mr. Grimlet was slowly warming up. He had his hand on Sal's trunk now—she had stopped her swaying and was standing like a statue—and he said to Ben "You know she's bad off?"

Ben said "Are you talking about Sal?"

"You bet I am. I'm the man that owns her. She's lost her family and, for all I know, she may be poisoned too. The stuff that vicious rascal used on her sisters was mean and slow acting. So only time will tell about Sal." At that, Mr. Grimlet put both his hands on Sal's forehead and leaned against her. Actual tears ran down his cheeks, and he didn't try to hide them.

Ben could see that Sal's eyes were still on him, so he came close enough to touch her also. He said to Mr. Grimlet "I'm planning to be a veterinarian someday."

Somehow it struck Mr. Grimlet as funny; he gave a short laugh. But then he said "That'll be too late for Sal and me, won't it? It's a fine choice, though. You'll do a lot of good." He stepped aside and waved Ben closer to where Sal waited.

Ben moved close enough to lay his head against the broad trunk; and as soon as he touched her, he heard the word *Stay*. Ben looked to Mr. Grimlet—surely he'd heard her too?

But apparently Mr. Grimlet hadn't. He'd pulled a small folding knife from his pocket and was cleaning his fingernails.

So Ben said it aloud to Sal. "I wish I could sleep right here with you till the circus leaves."

Sal didn't answer him.

But Mr. Grimlet smiled and looked up. "That would be against all my rules and regulations. I have to give these creatures their rest. All this traveling is hard on their nerves. If you slept in here, you'd keep Sal awake all night and you know it."

Ben said "I could put my sleeping bag there in the corner and not say a word. She could sleep like a baby and so would I."

Mr. Grimlet faced Sal. Was he speaking to her in his own kind of silence and was she replying? Whichever, he looked back to Ben and said "Son,

I'll give you free passes to the rest of the shows. But no, you go along to your home now and let Sal rest. She's working tonight." He reached into his deep vest pocket, pulled out several free passes to the show, and gave them to Ben. "You can come tonight and come back tomorrow night—Saturday night will be the last show. Those are passes for two; bring any friend you've got."

Ben was still leaning against Sal's trunk, but he took the passes reluctantly. "Thank you, sir. I can't come back tonight, though. My dad'll be home alone, and I'll need to stay with him." Ben knew his father wouldn't need him tonight; but now that he'd had this time alone with Sal, he didn't want to see her in a crowd right away.

Mr. Grimlet said "All right, but that leaves you Saturday—cheer up, boy! Come out here and talk to her Saturday afternoon, and then you'll see her in the last show that night." Mr. Grimlet let his words settle for a moment. Then he pointed toward the open tent flap, meaning Ben should leave.

So Ben told Sal he'd see her tomorrow, and he turned to walk out. At the flap he looked back and asked Mr. Grimlet if he could maybe travel with the circus this summer and take care of Sal. As wild as

that sounded, Ben knew how much it might matter in his future.

Mr. Grimlet said "No, son. You're just too young and it's too hard a life. You come back tomorrow morning or afternoon like I told you, and she'll be glad to see you. Be sure you let Duffy know you're with her, though. Don't come in here by yourself alone. You might get hurt or you might cause damage."

As much as Ben hated to be thought of as a threat to Sal, he said "Yes sir."

Mr. Grimlet said "I want you to promise me now—look me in the eye and swear you won't hurt her."

Ben raised his right hand. "Yes, I swear." Then he lifted the tent flap. As he stepped outside he thought he heard another word from Sal. It sounded like *No* again but Ben left anyhow—what choice did he have?

Most of the way home in a chilly evening, he felt like a traitor to the best thing he knew. Yet the memory of Sal's beautiful head and body was still in the midst of Ben's mind as he biked on faster in the gathering dark. When he had just half a mile to go, he was feeling those different things at once. He was partly a shameful traitor, partly the most loyal lover

on Earth, and partly a cold boy alone in the night, a little afraid and racing for safety.

At home the kitchen light was on, and there was Ben's father looking out the window and waving when he saw his son. Ben propped his bike by the back-porch steps and walked to the door. The first quick sight of his father helped him. This man had never done an unkind thing, not to Ben at least.

But now his voice was almost harsh. "Where on Earth have you been, boy? I've been worried sick."

Ben remembered what he'd forgot in his happiness—he was now his father's only family, and he'd scared him by not coming home in time. It was past six o'clock. He was two hours late, and he hadn't started his share of the supper. If he told his father the honest truth, it would maybe show that he thought more of Sal than anybody else. He could just say he'd been with Dunk or Robin.

But Mr. Barks said "I called Dunk and Robin. I even called your teacher, Miss Elmers. Nobody knew where you might be. I was just about to call the police when I saw you rolling in."

So Ben knew he had to tell it straight; no white lies would do. "Sir, this afternoon after school, I

stopped by the fairgrounds for just a minute to look at things in daylight. And then to my complete surprise, I met the elephant's owner and keeper; and I got to see her—up close in her private tent. She's the finest thing I've ever—"

Mr. Barks stood silently; his face was still frowning. At last he turned to the stove and stirred a big pot of black beans. Finally he said "I ought to have known you'd try that trick. I wish you'd phoned me, I'm not feeling all that well here lately. I thought you knew that much anyhow."

Ben said "Yes I did. And I'll make it up to you. I'll clean out the whole garage next week." That was a long-delayed promise he'd made more than once before.

Mr. Barks was taking corn bread from the oven, and he didn't face Ben. "Wash your hands please and help me serve this. If you don't want it, we can take it to the homeless." The thought of hauling a whole pot of beans to the three old men who slept by the bridge made Mr. Barks laugh unexpectedly.

Ben joined in and soon they were in their usual places, eating beans and rice. Almost nothing was said for the first five minutes. Ben knew it was best for him to stay quiet till his father decided what to talk about, if anything.

In a while Mr. Barks looked up and said "Did you ask how much they'd charge to sell her—your elephant friend?"

That nearly bowled Ben over in his chair. "Are you saying we might try to buy her?"

His father searched Ben's eyes as if he thought the boy had gone crazy. He even laughed a little; but then he said "No, son, I'm sorry. I didn't mean to tease you. We couldn't buy her, even if we had the room and the money. I was just wondering if they meant to sell her now her family is gone."

"I think she matters to them more now than she ever did before."

Mr. Barks thought about that and nodded. "She must eat ten bales of hay every day."

"Even more—plus a lot of raw cabbage and old produce they get from the stores wherever they are." He was making that up, but he estimated it had to be true.

Mr. Barks said "Was she glad to see you?"

Ben wondered if he should mention now that Sal had found her own private way to speak to him and hear what he said. If he told anybody it would be this sad but patient man. And Ben was almost ready to say his most secret words—"She speaks to me, Dad." But they stopped in his throat.

He coughed once and then said "I wouldn't claim she seemed *glad* to see me, but she acted very politely and she touched me."

"Son, you understand elephants can kill anything they want to in an instant? Even lions run from them."

Ben felt like saying "I know a lot more about this than you." But he finally nodded. "Lions won't come near them. But see, Sal was mostly raised in America; so she's a lot tamer than anything wild."

Mr. Barks said "I've seen tame dogs rip a black bear to shreds. Anytime you get near an elephant again, don't forget who they are."

Ben said "That may be tomorrow morning."

"What happens tomorrow?"

Ben pulled out the passes for Saturday night. "The circus boss gave me these, completely free, when he saw I loved Sal."

Mr. Barks reached out, took the passes from Ben, and studied them carefully. "They look real, don't they?"

"Oh they are—from the boss. You want to go with me?"

Mr. Barks thought it over. "Thanks but no, I've had my share—and I enjoyed it. You know Dunk would give his right arm to go."

Ben shook his head. "Dunk would get in the way."

"The way of what?"

Ben said "Me and Sal. He'd be telling jokes, doing hand tricks to show everybody he's nut number one. Dunk's fine when all you want to do is laugh."

Mr. Barks seldom looked at Ben with the hard cold eyes he turned on him now. "What do you tell your friends about me when I'm not around?"

Ben was baffled. "Tell me what that means."

Mr. Barks waited to calm his voice. "It means that if you can talk that way about Dunk Owens, you'll talk that way about anybody else."

"Dad, Dunk is not kin to us. He's a boy I know at school."

Mr. Barks said "He's stuck by you through some mighty hard times. You don't have another friend as good to you as Dunk, and I don't see any substitutes lined up to take his place. I mean, Robin loves you but she's close kin. Dunk's the friend to cherish. Notice I don't have one. When I was your age, I was cruel as you are; and look at me now. I'm a lonesome man whose wife has died, and all the company I've got in my life is a coldhearted son who'll leave my house in another few years, and here I'll sit till I drop dead."

Ben was stunned by his father's words. He'd known how sad his father was this whole past year, but he'd never heard words like this before. First, Ben was sure they were partly unfair. Yet he could see that the man was sober. Then Ben realized that his father must have thought such things many times in the past but kept them private. Suddenly without waiting to think back through the months and years, Ben understood that what his father said might be true and fair. He'd need to think it over later.

By then Mr. Barks was eating again and not facing Ben.

So Ben said "Sir, I'll try to do better." And for a long moment, he thought of asking Dunk to go with him.

Mr. Barks said "Try." Then he looked up finally and gave a big smile as faked as a clown's.

So Ben said "Try—absolutely. I will. I'll start Monday morning." He ate the last of his beans and bread; and finally he said "I'm weird, I know, but I don't want to share Sal with anybody else. I've just got tomorrow morning and evening to see her once more. Then she's *gone* for good. This'll likely be my last chance, forever, to be with an elephant right up near me."

Mr. Barks said "What's this about tomorrow *morning?*"

"The boss told me I could visit Sal one more time in her private tent. Then she'll be needing to rest before the show. And then they leave."

"Late Saturday?"

Ben said "I guess so."

His father said "You could go back tonight. These passes aren't dated."

"I know. But I want to stay here tonight."

Mr. Barks had finished eating by then. He stood and took his plate to the sink. When he looked back to Ben, he seemed much younger than he had for a while. He even looked like the man he'd been when Ben was a great deal younger than now. Before Ben could think of anything to say to thank his father for so much care, Mr. Barks looked down at his watch. "I'll drive you to the fairgrounds. You can call me when it's over. I'll come back and get you." Mr. Barks had done very few things to Ben that called for an apology. He wasn't apologizing now, just making a genuine offer.

But before his father could speak again, Ben said "I don't like to be gone so much."

Mr. Barks said "I hope you're not worried about me."

"Not worried, no sir, but—like you said—I'm getting older by the week; and in a few years I'll be leaving home. So I'm staying here now as much as I can." Ben smiled as though he were partly joking, but he wasn't and he knew it.

Mr. Barks laughed again briefly. Then his face turned serious. "Son, you've got to start having your own separate life. You've already grown four inches this year. I understand that and I surely don't want to keep you locked up where you don't want to be."

Ben nodded again but looked at his hands and thought in silence "Where I want to be is alone with Sal, but that won't happen at the circus tonight. Tomorrow morning is my best chance."

Once Ben had gone upstairs to do his Monday homework, he kept hearing his father's hard words—hard but maybe at least half fair. Had he ever spent two minutes thinking of ways to cheer his father or ease his loneliness? Honestly no. Ben had lived his own life, doing just what he wanted when he had any choice. By the time he was ready to undress for bed, he knew his father's words were fair and—more than that—true. Ben suspected they'd never quite leave him, the rest of his life, and he was right.

✛   ✛   ✛

But of course all night it was Sal who came and went in Ben's quick dreams. Still they didn't wake him. So far as he knew, there were no strange creatures or spirits outside to brush his windows. The dreams that passed through his mind were as real as his visit this afternoon to Sal's own tent. Oddly, though, again and again she sniffed his body from top to toe; but she never spoke to him. Ben tried to send silent words to her—about how glad he was to know her and how these days with her had changed his outlook on all his future.

From here on, he really would start to study hard to be a veterinarian maybe fifteen years from now. He'd be the kind of vet who works for a zoo and heals big animals of all the harm that comes their way because they're captured and can't find the natural herbs and medicines that grow in their native parts of the world. In his dreams Ben told Sal that more than once and in great detail, but she still never spoke. She didn't seem sad or the least bit sick, but she kept her silence.

In the dreams Ben of course was badly disappointed, but somehow he knew this was make-believe. He even told Sal in his normal voice "Girl, this is not real. This is nice but wrong. Tomorrow

morning we'll both be rested and can share each other's thoughts again."

In the dream Sal nodded as if to say *Yes*, and that freed Ben to roll to his side and sleep like a worn-out boy till morning.

The morning itself was bright and warm. Ben woke up early before his father, so he hurried to dress and feed Hilda. Again Hilda looked no worse than ever, a tired old dog who seemed mildly glad to see him and watch him fix her food. But again she seemed to have nothing to tell him. In fact she seemed to avoid his eyes, so he set her bowl down and gave the top of her head a few rubs. Something told Ben not to try to persuade her to say more than she'd already said. Her news might turn out to be hard or sad; and if that was so, he'd rather learn it as it happened in his life, not from this poor creature that his mother had raised from an orphan pup.

Instead Ben hurried back inside to fix his own breakfast of cereal and toast. He worked as quietly as he could manage so as not to wake his father. Then he sat to eat it in the silent kitchen. Several times he had to slow himself down. He had no idea of when Mr. Grimlet and Duffy would give Sal her

morning bales of hay, but he didn't want to get to the fairgrounds too early and risk running into a tough clown or acrobat who might think he was some kind of poisoner and run him off or call the police. He was thinking through that when he heard his father's footsteps coming down. That reminded Ben how he had promised to clean out the garage, and he dreaded that his father might want him to do it this morning.

But no, Mr. Barks just said hello; then got his own food out and sat down to eat behind the newspaper. He'd hardly looked at the first page, though, before he said "Bad news."

Ben waited but his father just kept on reading in silence. So finally Ben said "Please tell me what's *bad*."

Mr. Barks looked up. "Oh I thought you'd already read the story." He turned the front page toward Ben, and there was a picture of Sal almost surely. It looked enough like her anyhow.

Ben felt a little frozen in place. He didn't move closer to the paper to read whatever news it told.

His father took the paper back. "It says the show has lost three elephants lately. Mysterious causes. And the owner is scared this last one's in trouble."

Ben said "And that's all? Sal's still all right?"

His father looked closely at the paper and nodded.

"It seems they think she's in good health but they're worried anyhow. She's under close guard."

Ben felt relieved. "I knew that much. Her keeper told me yesterday."

"And he still let you go in and see her?"

Ben said "Yes, he trusted me. And so did Mr. Grimlet, the boss. I told you, Dad."

"You didn't tell me they left you alone with an elephant in danger."

Ben said "I wasn't alone with her more than three minutes unfortunately."

"Maybe that was lucky."

Ben said "How?"

"No one could think you were poisoning the old girl."

"She's not so old, sir. And how many poisoners have you ever heard of as young as me?"

Mr. Barks said "You've got a point. But if you're heading back out there this morning, you want to be extra careful with yourself. Don't be alone with her, and don't try to interfere if you see anybody trying to harm her. Just call the boss."

Ben was relieved that his father had no objections to his morning plans, so he didn't try to say that he'd defend Sal with all the strength in his body if necessary. He only said "Sir, she's surrounded with

people who care the world about her. And she's three states away from where her sisters got sick."

Mr. Barks was listening but he gave no answer.

So Ben got up, washed his plates, put them away, and then said "Dad, I'm off to the fairgrounds—OK?"

"You want me to drive you?"

"Oh no, sir. I need the workout."

His father looked toward him for maybe ten seconds; and then, for the only time Ben could remember, he said "Will I ever see you again?"

That was so strange it upset Ben, but he didn't want to show it. He laughed out loud and said "*Again?* You'll be sick of the sight of me long before I leave."

Mr. Barks said "Maybe. Somehow I doubt it." But then he laughed too and waved Ben away.

By the time Ben got to the fairgrounds and hid his bike in the woods, it was ten o'clock; and a few men were standing around in their underwear talking to women in bathrobes and slippers. Ben thought he recognized the Ringoes from the high-wire stunt with Sal two nights ago; but he dodged his way behind wagons and cages, pausing just once to speak to the lion that had liked him yesterday.

That way he managed to get almost to Sal's tent without being stopped, but then he ran headlong into a man who had to be the giant—the world's tallest man.

He was three times as tall as Ben anyhow; and though he didn't grab him, he said "Stop *there!* Who in the devil are you, little buster?"

Ben made a mistake. He said "Sir, I'm Mr. Duffy's and Sal's good friend—see, I'm just a young boy." He could hear how silly that sounded, so he held both hands out to show the giant he wasn't armed and to prove he was a boy after all, not a small but desperate crook. When the giant kept standing there, watching in silence, Ben tried again. "Who are you, please?"

At last the man said "I'm the ogre they keep here to ward off trouble. My real name is Pat, but my circus name is Otho."

At that he made a move toward Ben to seize him by the neck. His arms were longer than most men's legs.

But Ben jumped back and said "Tell Duffy I'm here. Duffy knows me *well.*" When Otho kept coming, Ben jumped again. "Tell Mr. Grimlet. *He* definitely knows."

That stopped Otho. He looked a little stunned

to hear the Boss's name, but he went on looking at Ben's face in earnest. Then at last he said "Oh then *you're* the one."

Ben said "The one *what?*"

"They told me Sal had a good friend coming sometime this morning. But the way they talked, I thought he was big—a hotshot anyhow."

Ben laughed a little and said "Oh no, *you're* the hotshot, Patrick."

The giant looked more stunned than before. He knew he'd told Ben that his real name was *Pat*, but no one had said his whole name *Patrick* since his own mother died in Ireland long ago. Pat's awful temper could change in an instant; and hearing his full name from Ben won his heart. He paused to give his head a great shake and clear his mind. Then he pointed beyond them toward Sal's tent. Just his pointing hand was the size of a huge ham hanging in the store. It could have torn down old city walls in King Arthur's time.

Or so Ben thought. Yet even though Otho had turned into Pat and seemed kind enough, Ben knew he had to be more careful than he'd been last night. He couldn't risk taking the blame for anything bad that happened to Sal today or later. So he said "We need to tell Duffy or Mr. Grimlet I'm here."

Pat said "They're busy right now, counting last night's money. I can let you in the tent, though; and then I'll tell them you're safely here." When Ben still looked reluctant, Pat waved him on again toward Sal. "They trust you, boy—they *told* me so."

So Ben turned and went directly to the laced-up flap of Sal's tent.

Just as he untied the first knot of the rope, one of the men in underwear yelled "You leave Sal alone!"

Pat yelled back "Shut your mouth, clown. I'm running this show."

Everybody in sight, including a pair of tall pink poodles, nearly fell down laughing.

And Ben went on inside the small tent. The instant he shut the flap behind him, he heard a word—*Welcome*. When he looked Sal was already reaching toward him with her trunk. It was as fine as any welcome he'd ever received, except for the night his mother came to him and promised him a life. So Ben went toward Sal, and she wrapped him in—very strongly but gently—till he stood right up against the base of her head. At first Ben worried that, if she tightened her grip at all, his bones would crack. But her grip stayed steady. And as he stood there, Ben silently wondered if Sal knew exactly how tightly to

hold him. He wasn't afraid but it did occur to him that, if he'd been a young elephant, she could surely have held him much tighter than this.

Sal's voice said a new thing—*Safe. Now never leave here.*

That eased Ben completely and he stood on calmly, glad to accept how much she liked him—if that's what it was.

Very gradually over maybe two minutes, Sal relaxed her grip and went back to her habit of swaying from side to side. But her eyes were on Ben.

By then Ben was sorry he hadn't brought big pocketfuls of the nuts he and Robin gathered months ago—pecans from the edge of the woods. Ben had thought of bringing some to Sal before he left home, but then he'd thought that bulging pockets might look suspicious, so he'd left the nuts. Now as Sal rummaged through the hay at her feet and occasionally reached down to search Ben's pockets, he thought he'd step outside and find the peanut man and hope he'd sell some nuts this early in the day. Dumb as it seemed, feeding peanuts to the biggest land creature on Earth, this creature was hungry.

But before Ben had even turned toward the tent flap, Sal understood his plan and said *Stay.*

So he stayed. At one side of the tent, he saw a green barrel. Ben brought that forward and sat in front of Sal, touching her trunk when she reached out toward him but mostly just feeling peaceful in her presence.

Sal seemed to feel the same.

In another few minutes Ben realized that they hadn't spoken for a good while now. He didn't want to ruin their contentment with too many silent words or ideas; but he knew they only had this much time to be together. After this they must separate, likely forever. Out loud he asked Sal to tell him about her life, from the start till today.

Through another long space of time, she sent him nothing that was like clear words or an actual story. It felt like nothing but more and more of the peace they were sharing.

So Ben went on and tried to tell her his story, in silence and in the fewest possible words. It amounted to this—*I was born in this town a long time ago. Or so it feels to me. I had parents that were kind and fair up till last year when my mother got sick and died too soon. My father and I still live in the same house. It's out on the edge of town with some deep cool woods and a creek and a field, and I've got no real complaints about the place. I have my own room; and my* best friend—my cousin Robin, who's a girl—lives close by. I do all right at school; and like you heard me say last night, I hope to be an animal doctor when I'm grown. The main reason why I'm trying to know you in these few days is, I'm in love with you and have been ever since I was a little boy. I love you and, after you, I love most all the elephants alive. I'm the only boy or girl I know who feels this way; it may have a lot to do with my mother. Long ago she started me to drawing you, and she started reading to me about you when I was almost a baby. All through the years she'd encourage me to keep on learning more about you. Then she got sick and died when I was ten; and ever since, I've wanted more and more to know you and love you, close up like this, and understand everything I can about you. See, I've talked to one other animal creature—our old dog Hilda—so I've wanted to talk to you also. And now we have.

Sal had stopped her rocking by then and was completely still except for quietly turning the hay at her feet with the tip of her trunk. But she didn't seem to speak.

If so, Ben couldn't hear it. He waited as long as he could bear to wait. Then he stood up and shut his eyes and thought as strongly as he'd ever thought anything—You told me it was safe here and that I should never leave. You couldn't believe how much I'd like to be with you, the rest of your time, and then come with you wherever you go next. But I've got reasons to stay at home. I've got my duty to finish school and to stay awhile longer with my lonesome dad. Still I'll try to find you when I'm a little older. Till then please don't get too sad yourself and please try to keep Benjamin Laughinghouse Barks in your memory. He wants you to have a full good life, not alone like now; and he'll be your loyal friend forever. Think about him.

Sal took maybe two or three minutes to hear that and think it through. Again her trunk came up in the air and felt very slowly through the top of Ben's head; then down to his hands, which were open and lying palm-up on his knees. Then she sent this silent message toward him. At least you can guess how my life feels. I don't know where I'll go from here, but I'll try to keep you somewhere in my mind.

Ben was glad to hear Sal say that much, but he was also worried. With her present loneliness and her life on the road among nightly crowds of strangers, Sal was in more trouble than Ben could handle. He didn't try to conceal his worries. He said to Sal You're strong and well—I'm pretty sure of that. You'll get some more company as soon as Mr. Grimlet gets his insurance money. More than anything, I'd love to buy you from him and rescue you now. But

see, I couldn't help my mother much either when she needed help so badly. And I'm still trying to get over that. Ben paused there to see if anything else might need to be said.

Sal was as still as anything stuffed in an animal museum. She was like something Ben might have made in his wildest dreams when he was six or seven years old. It seemed as if he could get another few boys, and somebody's pickup truck, and take her home to stay forever. But then Ben thought he heard two more words—*You will.* He was so shocked that he spoke out loud. He said "I will *what?*"

Sal's answer rumbled like a far-off train in the midst of a storm. *You'll get over that. Your mother is safe. I need you now.*

Ben was as happy as he'd ever been. He was also bitterly sad. A beautiful creature, that he'd prayed to know, was asking for him; and he was so tied down in his own life that he couldn't follow her. He whispered it out loud. "Oh Sala, I can't. Please understand why and forgive me please."

Her eyes were still fixed on Ben, but for the first time they looked blind or unreal like the white-rimmed black glass eyes of a doll. And then very slowly Sal pulled against the chain that tied her back left leg to an iron stake. The chain held tight. Sal

made no second try to free herself; but in the next minute, she started her swaying again, side to side. She didn't seem angry but she took up a big mouthful of hay, half shut her eyes, and began to chew.

Ben understood that she wouldn't speak again, not to him this morning. He sat back down on the stool to make up his mind what to do. He'd never been in a situation as hard as this. If he'd thought, for instance, that Sal would get sick soon and die of the same mysterious thing that killed her family, it might have hurt him less than this feeling that he'd deserted her when she asked for help. Today Ben had to face the fact that the gift he'd hoped for through most of his life was maybe possible—a live elephant actually wanting to live beside him—but he couldn't take it.

Ben hadn't cried since the long night after his mother's funeral. He wondered whether tears wouldn't start any minute if he sat on here, and what would the clowns and acrobats think if they saw him leave with red eyes and cheeks? He stood up and told himself to say a simple goodbye to Sal and then head home. He had chores there; he could even take Hilda for a walk to the creek if she'd go that far. And thinking of Hilda he thought how wrong she seemed to be when she told him this

meeting would help his life. Her old age must be clouding her mind. This elephant wanted nothing that Ben could possibly give.

He tried again. *Sal, you know I've got a pass for tonight's show. Should I come or not?* When Sal didn't answer, Ben said *Do you want me to come? Please say.* When no words came he said *It might just hurt both of us too much.*

Sal said *Not me.*

Or had Ben imagined that? He asked her to repeat her meaning.

But before she could say it again or refuse, two hands spread the flap of the tent wide open; and at once Sal's trunk went up in the air to scent the new body.

Ben thought it had to be Duffy or maybe Mr. Grimlet, but it was Dunk Owens. Of all the people it might have been, Dunk was almost the last one Ben would have guessed. How in the world had he known to look here?

Dunk had stopped just inside the flap and was staring at Sal, plainly amazed. Ben sometimes teased Dunk by calling him the Great Mouth-Breather— his nose was often stopped up from allergies. And now Dunk's mouth was open wide enough to catch a softball.

Sal reached past Ben as if she knew Dunk as a separate friend.

Ben was so worried at being unable to stay with Sal that the sight of Dunk was actually welcome. Maybe Dunk could think of some good way to solve the problem. But as Dunk stepped toward him, Ben had to say "You can't come in here. It's strictly off limits."

Dunk said *"You're* here."

"I've got the boss's permission, see? Please leave right now or we'll both be in trouble."

Dunk pointed behind him to the world outside. "Your dad told me you'd be somewhere around here. Then some men out there—they told me where you were."

"What men?"

Dunk said "Two fellows out there walking on stilts—they're ten feet tall."

Ben said "They're clowns and they had no right to tell you anything."

Dunk spoke more quietly than usual, but he dared for the first time since Ben's mother died to challenge his friend. "Ben, speaking of *rights,* who gave you the right to treat old Dunk like mud on your shoe? Ever since I told you this show was coming, you've dodged me and left me out of everything."

Ben knew that was true; but since Sal also seemed sad about him and was standing here, he couldn't find the words to tell poor Dunk how sorry he was. Dunk would be around always. Someday soon Ben could ask for forgiveness. So he turned back from Dunk to Sal and told her silently *I'm leaving now. If you say so, I'll come to the show tonight and tell you goodbye.*

If Sal understood him, she gave nothing back. She was rocking again and chewing hay as if that mattered more than anything near her.

Outside the tent Ben and Dunk were walking quietly toward the woods when someone shouted Ben's name out behind him. He looked and it was Duffy. Duffy was waving Ben toward him. For a moment Ben thought of pretending not to hear.

But by then Dunk was yelling to Duffy. "He's here. Here's your man!"

So Ben led the way, and Dunk came with him. The new spring sun beat hard on their backs.

When they got there Duffy shook both their hands. It was so unusual for Dunk to shake hands with an adult that he laughed and wiggled his hand in the air as if Duffy's strength had broken his fingers.

Ben was sadly disappointed that Sal hadn't

urged him to come back again, so he had no strength to get mad with Dunk. He just asked Duffy "Is anything wrong?"

Duffy wasn't smiling. "When I was a boy I heard it was rude not to speak to grown-ups who'd been kind to me."

Ben said "I'm sorry, sir. My friend here turned up unexpectedly, so I got flustered and left in a hurry."

Duffy said "But you shut up Sal's tent good. That was one thing you did right."

Ben said "There was no way I'd risk harming Sal."

Duffy said "Did she show you she knew you? Sometimes she pretends not to know people. It's either to tease them or to show she doesn't like them."

Ben said "At first she seemed glad to see me. Then she got fairly sad and stopped noticing me."

Duffy said "She does that to everybody lately. I told you the boss thinks maybe she's sick like the others before they croaked. I'm sure, though, that after this long a time it's nothing but grief. Nobody's poisoned her. She'll slowly get well."

That was good news to hear. If Ben had been alone, he might have loosened up and told Duffy the whole story—how he and Sal had talked and

how she'd turned against him now. But Dunk was too close. Dunk would tell the whole world that Ben had gone loony and was talking to beasts. Ben just said to Duffy "I wish I could help her, but there's not enough time."

Duffy said "You've got your passes for tonight. She'll see you in the crowd—she notices everybody she's ever known. And maybe you'll get to speak to her later when she's finished her act."

Ben said "I thought you were headed straight out."

Duffy said "No, the boss is a religious man. He won't make the animals, or any of us, work on Sunday. We'll head out just after dawn Monday morning." He waited as if to let that sink in. Then he said "Go on now. I've got to get Sal fed and rested for the evening show. Look for me tonight and at least say goodbye. If you're half as polite as you need to be, maybe I'll loop back by here someday and give you a job as my elephant boy. I'll have a better job by then—more *pachyderms* to tend to."

It was the first time Ben had heard him say that word. Privately he figured Duffy had little chance of working elsewhere. Duffy was too old, too fat, too slow-moving. Ben gave a short wave of his hand and looked behind him.

As Duffy turned to go, Dunk said "Mr. Duffy, you got any more of those passes left?"

Duffy said "Sorry, boy. Those come from the boss, and he's gone right now."

Dunk's face fell. He had no money of his own for a ticket, and his father would never give him any. But he knew Ben well enough not to ask who was going with him tonight.

Before Duffy had turned again to leave, Ben had already headed toward the woods and his bike. From behind, to Dunk's eyes, Ben looked small somehow and hunched on himself almost as if his back were broken and he was in pain. So Dunk half trotted till he got within four steps of his friend. When Ben didn't pause and didn't look backward, Dunk kept his distance. And they didn't speak, though they rode off together, aimed the same way.

Dunk lived considerably nearer to town, but he showed no sign of turning off at his own drive-way. He rode with Ben the whole way out to the Barks's house. When they got to the drive, they paused on their bikes; and Ben was on the verge of telling Dunk goodbye when he suddenly felt a wave of loneliness pouring over him. At such times Ben mostly went off alone and walked in

the woods or rode to Robin's and joined with her in acting out the plot of some movie they'd recently seen or a story they'd read. That would usually raise his spirits.

Today, though, before Ben could say a word, Dunk did a strange thing. He said "Look, I know you're smarter than me. You and your folks live nicer than we do, and none of your family beats you the way my dad beats me. But I don't really feel jealous of you. To tell the truth, in my mind you're still my favorite person. So I wish you'd have more patience with me and teach me some things that would make me less of a loud jackass."

As Dunk said that, Ben's loneliness deepened. For the first time he saw how his own weird pride, and his wanting to be alone for all that really mattered to him, had forced Dunk to run down his own good nature—nobody Ben knew was any more honest or loyal than Dunk, not even Robin; and she was his cousin. He kicked in the gravel, trying to think of a way to say that. But when he looked up, Dunk's face was so unusually solemn that Ben nearly laughed. Then he managed not to.

Dunk was plainly saying what he meant. For instance, till now he had only once let Ben know how his father beat him. Maybe Dunk, after all,

knew things Ben didn't know—serious things about pain and shame and how to last through them and come out laughing. Maybe Ben should learn those things at least and whatever other secrets Dunk might know. Ben looked past Dunk to the edge of the woods—he was giving himself a moment to think. On a high bare limb of the tallest tree sat a red-tailed hawk, an enormous bird, nearly the size of a full-grown eagle. It seemed to be watching both boys very closely. So Ben said "Dunk, there's a hungry-looking hawk. He thinks you look tasty."

Dunk flung his arms out toward the bird. "You can *have* me right now. I'm not much good for anything else but truly I'm *tasty!*"

Ben silently thought "That may be the truth." But what he told Dunk was "Whoa, not so fast. You've got to go with me to the circus tonight."

Normally Dunk would have thrown down his bike and hopped around happily, yelling "Wahoo!" But now he kept on staring at the hawk till it spread its wide wings, flew on upward, and was soon out of sight. Dunk still didn't look back to Ben, but he told him "You want me to stay here with you all day? I haven't got anywhere else I want to be. I could help you clean out the garage like you've been promising your dad you would.

And then we could head for the circus early."

Ben glanced at his wristwatch. It was a Lone Ranger watch he'd bought from a boy in school. The boy had claimed the watch was broken and only charged Ben half a dollar. But in the three years Ben had worn it, it told perfect time. Since the long nights he'd spent last year, hearing his mother suffer, he seldom looked to his watch—time was too slow. But as he looked now, it said twelve noon. His father's car was gone from the yard, and he had to eat lunch, so he said to Dunk "Let's make some fresh banana sandwiches and see what happens."

Dunk had never eaten a whole banana—his mother said they cost too much. He didn't drop his bike, but he finally did throw his arms up again. He said "Wa-hoo, Benjy Boy, banana *time!*" When Dunk really wanted to tease Ben, he called him *Benjy*; and Ben would howl, which he did right now as they biked down the drive.

By midafternoon the sun had shone so brightly for hours that the March air was almost hot. Ben and Dunk had wandered in wide circles, imagining that a comet made of solid gold had landed last night and must be found soon; or it would fall into

evil hands. When the game wore out, they worked their way back toward the creek and built an elaborate dam that soon backed up a deep pool behind it. At first Ben tried to stay clean, but he finally gave up and waded into the pool with Dunk. They'd rolled their jeans above their knees, but in no time they were soaked to the waist. So Ben led the way to a clearing farther up the creek, and they lay down there to dry off and rest.

With dark red mud Dunk had painted Indian markings on their faces. Then after they'd lain awhile in silence, they propped up on their elbows to talk. But the sight of their markings made them seem really strange to each other. They felt as if they were talking to somebody they'd never met. Still it helped them somehow to be more honest than they usually were.

Dunk started by saying "That elephant didn't live up to your hopes."

It was such an odd idea that Ben took a good while to try to understand it. He finally said "You asking a question or telling me news?"

Dunk said "I'm saying that, since I told you the circus was coming, you've been living for this week; and it hadn't turned out like you expected."

Ben had known for a long time that Dunk, with

all his craziness, was keen-eyed as any Indian brave in the movies or in real life on the prairies. But Dunk didn't often try to say what he knew. Whatever he thought, he'd mostly just grin and make fun of himself. Ben knew, for instance, that when Dunk's dog Phil Campbell vanished for six weeks last Thanksgiving, Dunk tried to act as if it didn't matter. Ben had noticed, for years, that Dunk trusted Phil more than any of his family; so Ben had tried to be extra friendly to Dunk in the days after Phil disappeared. Now he waited awhile and then asked Dunk "Can you talk to Phil Campbell?"

Dunk said "Talk to *who?*"

"Your bulldog."

Dunk crossed his eyes and stuck out his tongue. But then he got calmer and said "Dogs are dogs, Ben. I mainly talk to *people.*"

Ben nodded. "You know I talk to Hilda; she talks back to me. Not often, not every day but some mornings when I least expect it."

Dunk crossed his eyes again and kept them crossed. "Does she speak in Spanish or Dog or what?"

Ben said "Your eyes are going to stick that way." He put out a hand and covered Dunk's eyes to make him look normal. Then he said "Get serious. We

can speak without words. Hilda started it when I was maybe six. I'd be sitting by her and then very slowly I'd feel her voice seeping into my mind."

Dunk said "Have you had your brain tested lately? Boy, you may be in *trouble*."

"Don't lie to me—I know you talk to Phil sometimes."

Dunk waited a long time before he looked at Ben with a serious face and said "When did you hear Phil and me say a word?"

"Just once—that night you biked out here when your dad had beat you bloody and my mother made you spend the night. Remember? Phil had followed you and stayed on the floor by the side of that extra bed in my room. It was late and dark, but I could tell you two were talking."

"Then what did we say?"

Ben said "I couldn't hear that. See, I think that people who can talk to animals speak private words that nobody else knows."

Dunk was still facing Ben. "Phil saved my life and I let him wander off Thanksgiving Day and stay gone so long—" Dunk's eyes almost filled with water. He was never ashamed of anything his body did.

Ben said "Dunk, don't you think Phil is old

enough to die? You know dogs sometimes wander off and die alone, so they don't scare us and make us try to stop them."

Dunk nodded but said "Phil may be old enough, but don't you try to help him wander off again." He looked straight ahead past the creek to a tall beech tree. This one had an owl asleep on the shortest limb. At last Dunk said "You tried to talk to that elephant, didn't you?"

"The elephant's name is Sala, Dunk. You can call her Sal."

"Did Sal tell you anything?"

Ben said "Not enough."

"But you understood each other?"

Ben said "I thought we did for a while. Then she turned quiet and wouldn't look at me or say another word."

Dunk sat up and took a long look at Ben. "You seem to have all your arms and legs still."

Ben said "What does that mean?"

"It means that pachyderms can get really *mad* if you break their rules."

Ben said "Listen, I told you everything you ever heard about elephants. Don't try to teach me, O Wise One."

Dunk said "All right. What did you tell Sal?"

Ben said "Cross your heart you won't tell a word of this to anybody else."

Dunk crossed his heart and raised his right hand as an extra promise. Then he lay back on his elbows again.

Ben sat up so he wouldn't have to meet Dunk's eyes. He saw that same sleepy owl in the beech tree and said these words in that direction. "I talked to Sal twice. The first time was yesterday afternoon and that went fine. It was all about safety—how we'd keep each other safe. Then this morning I'd been with her for maybe twenty minutes when you came in. See, you have to know this first—the other three elephants in the circus died a few months ago. They were maybe Sal's sisters, and so she's been gloomy.

"Today I tried to tell her I knew how she felt. Yesterday, like I told you, she said I was safe in her tent forever. Today I was trying to give her the same kind of feeling by telling her how I loved her and all her kin and how I'd love to stay right with her for the rest of our lives but that I had duties to help my father and would have to stay here till I grew up. I told her I knew she'd be safe on her own—"

Dunk was impatient to know one thing so he broke in. "Did you tell Sal that your own mother died?" Dunk had gone in to speak to Ben's mother

several times after she was bedridden; but knowing how it all hurt Ben, he'd never mentioned that fact again.

Now the actual words of Dunk's question made Ben shiver, even in the hot sunlight pouring down. Finally he said "I mentioned it, sure."

"And after that Sal wouldn't speak anymore?"

Ben said "More or less. She might have been starting to speak when you got there, but the sight of you stopped her."

"Whoa, pal. That's one piece of blame you can't lay on me. Before Sal even saw I was there, she was sad as could be. I saw that the minute I walked in her tent. If I was you I'd run off with her and live in the circus the rest of my life."

Ben said "Yeah, but you don't love your dad the way I do."

"You got *that* right. I may have to kill mine if he doesn't kill me first."

Till now Ben had always thought that Dunk was exaggerating when he talked of harming his father, but now he sounded serious. Ben said "Better not. See, I won't be able to drive a car for five more years; so I couldn't pay you visits in prison." He was watching the sleepy owl still, but then abruptly he burst out laughing.

Dunk joined in till they both were lying on their backs, all but helpless. When the noise died down, they both noticed that they'd waked up the owl. It had walked along its short tree-branch and was leaning against the trunk, staring at them with round black eyes that looked really furious. Dunk cupped his hands to his mouth and yelled out "Suzy, we know you're drunk. Just go back to sleep. We're harmless nuts."

Whatever the owl thought, she shut her eyes again and stayed where she was. It was the tree she had been born in long years ago. She had spent most days of her life sleeping there. She hunted from there through most dark nights. If Ben and Dunk had watched her longer, they might have begun to understand more than they knew about the wide world of animals, trees, rocks, and everything living beyond themselves. They might have begun to see how their worries about Ben's silent elephant or Dunk's reckless father were large and real. But those real worries were ringed on all sides by needy creatures, like this one owl, who have as much right to homes and lives as any two boys in the new spring sunlight.

✢   ✢   ✢

That night the show was almost exactly the same as when Ben had seen it on Thursday. One clown got whacked too hard by another clown, and his scalp started bleeding. The other clowns pretended to be scared of the blood, and all began to run for the exit. The wounded clown stayed calm, though, and bowed to every side of the tent before he left. The lion tried to creep up on the panther, but the animal tamer whipped them back to their stools in the cage.

Dunk liked it all and talked and laughed through every act.

That of course made Ben a little nervous. If Sal appeared with the acrobats again, Dunk would almost certainly stand up and yell and say things about Sal that might spoil the chance to concentrate on her. But Ben kept quiet and went on waiting.

Finally Duffy in his ringmaster suit announced the astonishing Ringoes, Phyllis and Mark. They ran out again to take their first bow, and they kissed in their peculiar way like dolls kissing. Then they climbed to the top of the tent and took their separate trapeze bars.

Dunk said to Ben "Is this going to be dangerous?"

"Yes, you'd better cover your eyes."

Dunk tried that for a second but quickly put his

head back and looked up again. He wanted everything this show had to offer.

Ben almost looked over toward the entrance to see if Sal was already there, but then he thought he should let that be the same kind of surprise it had been on Thursday. When Ben faced the Ringoes, he noticed they weren't smiling nearly as wide as before. He even thought they both looked more than a little scared. Had something gone wrong with them or with Sal?

In another few seconds Phyllis and then Mark started down the wire on their separate bars. They were going fast from the start this time. But they still looked all right—even when they sped up— and yes, by the time the spotlight followed them the whole way down, they were safe on the platform on Sal's broad back. For the first time tonight, they'd earned the name "astonishing."

Ben could feel that his eyes were quickly misting over. He wiped them at once so Dunk didn't see; Ben knew Dunk was braver. Then Ben watched as Sal moved slowly toward the center of the tent. The whole crowd around Ben—Dunk included—were yelling and waving. Ben had to stand up to see, but he stayed very still. He was trying to memorize every one of Sal's features

and moves. He intended to keep them the rest of his life.

Through the next twenty seconds, the act went the way it had on Thursday. But then there were some changes. The first that Ben noticed was the way Sal dropped the flag on the ground when she took her first step into the ring—a few patriotic men in the audience gave loud groans. Duffy was leading Sal and tried to make her take up the flag. She held it a few seconds, dropped it again, and kept on walking. When she got to the center of the ring, Duffy gave the sign for her to make a whole circle, facing everybody briefly. But she stopped in one place and stood completely still. Whether she knew it or not—and how could she?—she was looking straight at the dark bleachers where Ben sat.

Duffy didn't try to force her to turn around. He still hadn't used the stick he carried with the bright brass hook that could tear her ears if she got out of line.

Ben thought "He knows her too well—she might hurt him."

While the clapping and yelling went on, Phyllis and Mark kept waving and blowing kisses to the crowd. But when Sal wouldn't lower herself to the ground, they began to look tense again.

Finally Duffy stepped close to Sal's right ear. His lips were moving and he was talking to her. Nobody could hear him but he kept on whispering.

Sal stayed in place and still didn't move.

Ben could somehow tell that she wasn't privately talking to Duffy or anybody else.

By then most people in the bleachers had sat down and started to wonder if something was wrong. Was this great creature about to go haywire and begin breaking things?

Even Dunk had sat down and was turning pale.

But Ben kept standing for another ten seconds, looking straight at Sal. She was maybe twenty yards away. He couldn't tell whether she saw him or not. So he sat down slowly.

Dunk said "Do you think she's confused or what?"

Ben said "None of my elephant books explain this."

Sal stood where she was another few seconds. Then while the poor scared Ringoes kept bowing, left and right, Sal thrust her trunk out to its full length. It was not her usual salute to the audience—for that, she would have to raise her right leg. This move was aimed at the bleachers straight ahead of her, and it looked to Ben like the kind of searching

she did in her own tent when anybody entered. She was smelling the air apparently. It was her secret business anyhow. Nobody could make her do anything else.

Once she was finished she gave a brand-new salute—her trunk curled tight back against her forehead, and her solemn face came as close to looking glad as it could. Then she was ready to finish the act. She finally crouched down the way she was meant to.

The Ringoes seemed to be grinning sincerely as they jumped to the ground and ran away fast.

Duffy had never showed any fear or even impatience, and Ben could see his lips say the words "Good. Mighty fine, old pal." Then Duffy gave Sal another signal, and she got to her feet again with the grace that only elephants can manage. It looked like a giant building slowly standing up and planning to walk.

Duffy's lips moved again. "Back home now, girl."

Sal turned around calmly and moved toward the outdoor end of the tent. This time the spotlight turned away from her in case she ran.

But though Duffy was trotting to keep up with her, Ben could see that Sal kept up a steady pace and was soon out of sight in the dark. In an instant

she might have been as far off as Asia. Would she ever come back?

Ben thought his eyes might fill up again but no, they didn't. He didn't want to pretend to himself that Sal had found his scent in the crowd and saluted just him. He couldn't imagine that seeing him might have made her act so strangely in the ring.

Dunk tapped on Ben's knee. "She saw you, boy! She *loves* your butt!"

Again Ben couldn't find words to reply. If Sal had truly seen him, and kept on watching him instead of playing her part in the ring, that would be very close to the biggest thing in his life except for his mother's leaving. He had never made anything this fine happen. Good things were stacking up too fast here; something awful might come next. Still, Ben tapped Dunk's knee in return and waited to calm his breathing down so they could watch the final half hour, which again was mainly clowns. It was Dunk's favorite part, but tonight Ben halfway understood why. He had at least as many chances to laugh as Dunk did.

At the end of the show, Ben and Dunk hung back and came out behind the crowd. Dunk

thought Ben was making up his mind whether to go see Sal one last time, so he didn't rush him. Dunk was right.

Once they were out in the chilly dark, Ben knew what he needed to try to do. He saw Duffy standing not far ahead by the lion cage, looking up at the sky. It was almost solid stars.

In the dark Duffy looked more like a bandit or pirate than ever before.

But Ben stopped and said to Dunk carefully "I'm going up there to Duffy now. You can go with me if you want to. I don't know whether he'll think it's a good idea to see Sal, or maybe it's only me that should see her. Remember, she doesn't know you as well and she's probably tired." Ben knew how selfish those words might sound, but as always he was counting on Dunk's loyalty.

And Dunk said "If I'm some kind of big drag on you, then I'll go on back to the bikes and wait. You're the one with the elephant problem, not me." But he didn't laugh; he wasn't making fun.

So Ben said "Come on. We'll see what happens."

Dunk said "I'm your man" and stepped up beside him. The short space between them and Duffy felt endless as they walked uphill.

All that time Duffy stayed looking upward as if he were bathing in warm star shine and it was healthy. As the boys got only six steps away, Duffy looked down, saw them, and said "Four hundred sixty-six billion, five million, nine hundred eight thousand, and twenty-two."

Ben said "If you're saying I owe you that much, you'll be badly disappointed."

Dunk said to Ben "He was counting, Great Wizard of Wazuma."

"Counting what?"

Duffy spread both long arms wide out and looked up again. "I count every star, every night of my life. And tonight's the record. Eighty-four more stars in sight this minute than ever before. God's making new ones every night of His life!"

Dunk said "There's a fixed number of stars, Mr. Duffy. We learned that in school." Dunk knew he might well be wrong about the number, but one thing he truly loved about school was news of the sky, the comets, and planets—astronomy. He hoped to be an astronomer, which was fairly unlikely; but still he kept the ambition alive.

Ben said "This is one *nice* man, Dunk. Beg his pardon." Ben reached across and scrubbed Dunk's scalp with his knuckles, not too hard.

Dunk gave out a loud yell.

The lion, who was nearby, roared so strongly that all their teeth ached.

Duffy put up a hushing finger to his lips. Then he looked just to Ben. "Son, you ready to see her?"

Ben said "Do you think she wants to see me?"

Duffy said "She's been a little weird today, as you saw in her act, but I'm betting yes."

Dunk said "Sure she does. She loves my boy." He reached out and hugged Ben toward him roughly.

Ben took the hug with no complaint.

But Duffy looked to Dunk. "You can come on behind us, son. Keep your noise down, though; or Sal will shut you up." Duffy smashed his right fist into his palm, then put that hand up onto Ben's shoulder and led the way.

Ben wanted to ask Duffy what had gone strange in the act tonight—Sal wasn't sick, was she? But then he decided to wait and try to see for himself.

Off in the distance Patrick—or Otho—was standing alone. He was still in his giant costume, bare-chested, even in the chilly air. As they passed him, he didn't turn at all. He tilted his head back and, like Duffy earlier, he took in the whole sky and so many stars.

Outside Sal's tent Duffy stopped and faced Ben. "Like I said, you saw she was balky in her act."

Ben nodded. "I hope you don't think she's sick."

Duffy said "You almost never know with elephants—not till they've gone too far to bring back." He paused and took his hand off Ben's shoulder. "You be as gentle as you've ever been now. It's late and Sal's tired."

Ben said "Don't worry."

Duffy turned to Dunk. "Son, I'll ask you to wait outside here till we've gone in. I need to see how Sal feels before we bring her people she's barely seen. She's had a lot of sadness in recent months, and it's burdened her mind. I'll let you know as soon as I've checked her."

Dunk didn't seem hurt or disappointed. This was a small change of plans for a boy who'd lived through so many tough things at home—shouting and bruising and even the frequent sight of blood. He sat on the ground by the flap of the tent. "Good luck, Ben. I'll be right here. No hurry; take your time."

The flap was not tied shut; and Duffy stepped inside, bringing Ben behind him. They were both completely quiet.

At first it all seemed dark as the night they'd left outside. But then Ben saw there were two oil

lanterns burning low at the back of the tent.

Between them, and in her usual place, Sal was standing still. There was no hay around her. At the first hint of visitors—or maybe of trouble—her trunk reached out and smelled the air.

By then Ben's eyes had opened enough to notice that Sal's eyes were so wide open he could see the whites. She seemed a little depressed or scared, so he tried to speak toward her. In silence he said *It's your friend, Ben. I wouldn't hurt you in a million years.* He'd already decided that, if he saw her this last time tonight, he wouldn't use the word *Goodbye.* That would be too hard for him and for Sal.

Duffy went up to her, hugged her trunk, and laid his brow against her forehead.

She'd known this man more than half of her life, and he'd never so much as raised his voice to her. So soon her breathing sounded calmer.

Duffy kept his arms around her trunk, but he looked back to Ben. "Come on, son," he said.

When Ben got to Duffy, Duffy took his own arms down and waved Ben closer in to Sal.

For a long moment she didn't move at all. Then she blew out a powerful breath that sounded like sighing. Her trunk turned through the dry sawdust at her feet as if she might find one last piece of hay.

Ben looked up to Duffy to see if things were right.

Duffy was nodding.

So Ben stepped up, one arm's reach from Sal, and tried a few first words aloud. "You were amazing in the show tonight. I was really proud of you. You're going to be fine on your own now—I know."

Sal's silent voice reached him. She said the word *Hope.*

Ben wasn't sure what she meant by that, but he put up his right hand and laid it on her trunk.

She let him press her lightly there. Then her trunk came up and, once more, smelled all through the tangled crown of his head.

When she finished Ben told her *Here's a promise. When I'm grown I'll try hard to find you again— remember that. We're both young enough. We'll spend some time together one day and know each other even better than now.*

Duffy had taken a few steps back and was out of sight.

Ben looked around to find him; but when he saw nothing, he faced Sal again and said *You remember now.*

She said *Remember.* Then she did what Ben had only seen her do once before. She curled her trunk

back up to her forehead and lifted her huge left foot high.

At first Ben thought she was just repeating her salute from the ring. But now she lifted her leg even higher till it formed a wide shelf maybe three feet off the ground. Then her trunk came down.

Ben wasn't sure he understood her meaning. This might be better than he'd expected, and it almost scared him.

When he turned back to Duffy, he was inside the tent flap, waving Dunk in. The two of them came a little way toward Ben and Sal before they stopped in place.

When Duffy saw Sal's leg up in the air, he quietly spoke to Ben. "She's offering you a visit."

Ben's fear had turned to excitement. "What kind of visit?"

Duffy stayed back but said "Climb on her leg there—right back of her knee—and she'll show you the rest."

Ben had seen this happen in books and movies. He'd imagined it happening to him many times but not with Sal. She had seemed so private and alone with herself. He paused a long moment.

As softly as he could possibly manage, Dunk said "Go, boy. This'll last you for life."

Ben wheeled around fast and faced Dunk, standing in the shadows.

Dunk was smiling—this was his good luck and
not just Ben's.

Ben gave both his friends a quick wave as if he
might be leaving for the moon. Then he took a few
steps around to Sal's side.

When she gauged his height, she lowered the leg
some.

And Ben stretched both his arms far forward,
grabbed the far side of Sal's thick leg, and pulled
himself up till he knelt on the shelf she'd made to
help him. Before he was more than two feet off the
ground, her trunk wrapped around him.

First she held him in place on her leg.

And at first Ben liked her grip around him—a
strong grip but not too tight.

Then slowly the trunk came the whole way
around him and lifted him off the leg and thrust him
out in the air straight ahead.

In the first few seconds, Ben thought this
might be one of Sal's acts. Was she holding him
out toward Duffy as some kind of circus stunt?
Or maybe to Dunk? Could she see Dunk standing
there in the dark? Did she know how hard Ben
treated Dunk sometimes, and was she offering

Dunk the chance to punish Ben or pay him back?

Her grip was still just strong enough to hold Ben safely in the air, well off the ground. But then the hundreds of muscles in her trunk began to tighten, one by one.

Ben could feel the extra pressure at once. In silence he told her *Easy, girl. I'm a human, remember.*

But the trunk kept tightening.

Ben was trying his best to stay calm, though soon his lungs were working to breathe against the pressure. If he spoke aloud to ask for help from Duffy or Dunk, he'd use all the air he had left in his body. In silence he tried to speak again. *I'm a young boy, Sal, a lot weaker than you.*

If she heard it she offered nothing back.

He begged her. *Please, lady.*

No word from Sal.

So at that bad moment, Ben looked out and saw Dunk step from the shadows, stand beside Duffy, and whisper a few words.

Duffy waited for what seemed like a slow hour, and then he spoke in his ringmaster's voice. "Set, Sal. Set." Those were the words that should have told Sal to set Ben down.

Sal gave out another breath that ended in a deep long grumble.

Duffy didn't move forward—that could be a mistake—but he tried again. He said what sounded like "Huduganna ilasu."

And scared as he was Ben managed to think "That must be something in Sal's native tongue." He was right; they were words from her part of India—"*Set the boy down.*"

But she raised Ben higher, still straight out before her.

His feet were at least five feet off the ground.

If she slammed him down, it would break him to pieces from his feet to his skull.

Duffy stayed where he was and again said "*Set.* Girl, please *set* him down now. *Set.*"

Ben understood how helpless they were—the three humans here—but all he could think was "Why did she kneel down to me in the show if she meant to kill me now? Or is this some kind of love she can't stop?"

As if he'd heard Ben and knew the true answer, Dunk stepped closer forward.

Duffy said "Back, boy. You don't know what you might cause."

But Dunk came on to where he could reach out and touch the sole of Ben's right shoe. He touched the underside of Sal's trunk and rubbed it very

lightly. Then Dunk took two steps back and spoke to Ben. "Just tell her you're sorry."

Ben quickly wondered what that could mean, but he tried it anyhow. In silence he said *Oh Sal, I'm sorry.*

Everything inside the tent seemed to freeze— the humans and Sal and even the flames in the two oil lanterns. Nobody or nothing moved at all.

And Ben could see everything around him but he couldn't speak. He finally thought "This may be it—I may be *gone.*"

Then Sal let out one more deep breath like a whole rocky hillside rumbling to the valley. Her grip loosened slightly and, easy as blowing a feather from your hand, she pulled Ben back from the empty air and stood him again on the shelf of her leg. When he had his balance and had drawn a deep breath, she slowly nudged him higher on her head till finally he was sitting on her back behind her ears.

Dunk said "All *right!*" and looked around to Duffy.

Duffy had almost knelt to the ground in real relief.

But all Ben's fear had vanished and turned into happiness that grew by the moment. He'd seen other children ride elephants in movies—mostly

brown boys from India or African jungles. They'd laugh as if they were on rocking horses. But this chance meant a good deal more to Ben. He said to himself "She trusts me completely," and then he was happier than he'd ever been. He looked out to Duffy and said "Duffy, thank you."

Duffy said "Ben, it wasn't my idea. I'd have been scared of it—Mr. Grimlet would kill me. Sal's done it on her own."

So Ben leaned forward till his head was almost touching the two great knobs of Sal's skull. He tried to imagine a way to thank her enough for this, but his mind was way too thrilled to think clearly—he'd have the rest of his life to do that. So his chin came down to rest on her head, and he let his joy try to reach her in silence. It was all strong feelings, too strong now for words. He did see one distant thing in his mind— but only in his mind. It was his mother's face, looking almost pleased. If she could have been here, or even heard the news, she'd have smiled outright.

After maybe fifteen seconds Sal's trunk reached upward toward Ben and again smelled his hair.

After that he could tell her the main thing he felt, and he knew the words to use. *I'll remember you every day of my life.* He knew he might live many more years, but he felt entirely sure those words

were the simple truth. Nobody else in all his years would give Ben Barks any more than this.

Ben and Dunk were silent as they walked away toward their bikes in the woods. They were almost into the clumps of dead weeds and thorns when Dunk yelled out "Oh *Lord!*" He stopped in a crouch, looking at Ben and pointing to the right.

Ben could tell Dunk was half joking anyhow but he looked around. Soon he could see the shape of an old man's legs, his wide hips and sloping shoulders. The man's head was tilted back to the moon—there was just a little less of the moon than Ben had noticed a few nights ago. The color of its light was silver—old silver polished but not quite clean. Was everybody outdoors tonight, staring at the sky? Had a spaceship flown past? A dangerous comet? Were angels coming with good or bad news? Or was everything that had happened tonight some welcome dream that Ben shared with Dunk? It might as well have been a dream for all the proof Ben had that it had happened.

But the old man turned around now and faced them. It was Mr. Grimlet, alone out here. It seemed as if he'd aged fifty years in just one evening—his face was so wrinkled and lonesome-looking. At first

he put both arms in the air as if the boys were serious robbers and had stuck him up. Then slowly he recognized Ben and gave a little jump back as if Ben had shot him. "*Oh!*"

Ben said "It's just Ben Barks, sir, and my friend Dunk. We're heading on home."

Dunk pointed to Ben and told Mr. Grimlet "His middle name is *Laughinghouse*. Have you ever heard such a name before? I always think it sounds like a name for the crazy house."

Ben smiled, poked a finger into Dunk's side, and said "Mr. Grimlet, excuse this boy." He was going to say more about Dunk's manners but then he didn't.

Mr. Grimlet came toward them and held out his hand. He shook Dunk's hand first. Then he shook Ben's and asked him "How was it?"

Ben said "What?"

"Your goodbye to Sal."

Ben suddenly thought "He told Sal to lift me; it wasn't her idea." And then he felt as though Sal had no real feelings for him but was just obeying orders from the boss. After that Ben couldn't think of any words to say.

Mr. Grimlet said "I saw her saluting you there in the bleachers. She's never done that before, not that *I've* seen."

Ben was more than relieved. There'd be no need to tell Mr. Grimlet what had happened just now in Sal's own tent—how complicated it was at first and how it eventually got fine. But Ben was worried that Dunk would blurt something wrong. So he put out a hand and covered Dunk's mouth.

Dunk pulled back and spat but didn't try to speak.

Ben said "Yes sir, I waved thanks to her and got a good hug. Thank *you* for everything." Still his great moment was shared with no one but Dunk and Duffy.

Mr. Grimlet said "If you ever want a job when you get grown, boy, you track me down; and I'll hire you *fast*. Old Duffy can't work for many more years. His mind is failing." The boss tapped the side of his skull; it sounded full.

Ben said "Sir, where would I find you, years from now?"

Mr. Grimlet thought a moment, then turned around, searched the sky again, and started toward the tents. As Ben and Dunk were also leaving, the old man spoke just loud enough to hear. "I may be up in the stars by then or under the ground, but keep asking for me wherever you go. I may turn up. I'm too tired to die."

Dunk whispered to Ben "Is he nuts or what?"

In his natural voice Ben said "I like him whatever he is."

Dunk said "*Whatever*—let's get out fast."

Ben took his time as he mostly did.

At the driveway to Dunk's house, Dunk turned in, waved goodbye, and said "Thank you" once more. The house was dark as any haunted house in anybody's nightmare, but Dunk sped toward it.

Ben had stopped and he almost called out "Wait." He wanted to know why Dunk had told him to ask for Sal's pardon. What did Dunk think his friend should be sorry for?

But Dunk was out of sight now.

Ben could ask him the question in school next week if he still needed to. Maybe by then Ben himself would have understood the time when Sal held him in her power, carried him to the verge of death, and then pulled back and gave him her gift.

For now at least Ben also put on speed and raced his way home. When he got there the house was lit up brightly in every window. It looked like an old-time ocean liner, afloat and steaming toward some destination that nobody knew. But Ben knew that these lights might mean bad things—or a sad thing

anyhow. Since Ben's mother died, his father would get a little drunk on some weekends. Then he'd light up the place just to ease his pain and to keep himself cheerful. Ben didn't really dread that, but it did mean he'd probably have to help his father undress and go to bed.

So he parked his bike in the open garage and decided to stop by Hilda's shed and check on her. As he entered her room and paused while his eyes adjusted to her dim light, Ben suddenly thought she might be dead. She'd given him so much trust in the goodness of this whole week. What she said had proved true. Now maybe she'd done all she meant to do and had left them for good. But then Ben could see that Hilda was lying flat on her pillow, looking up toward him.

Her life had dimmed down, but here she still was. Her tail moved slightly. She was choosing to stay.

Ben went over to her, stroked the back of her neck, and talked a good while about his evening and how nobody but she had told him how fine it would be.

Hilda kept on watching him the whole time he talked. Her clear eyes showed that she understood every word of his news, but she never spoke again, and finally she laid her head back down.

At last Ben thanked her and went toward the house and let himself in quietly.

His father's pint of whisky was on the kitchen table, two-thirds full. The room was empty. That might mean his dad wasn't truly drunk but was snoozing upstairs with his clothes still on.

Ben stood in the kitchen, raised his voice a little, and called out "Dad?" Nobody answered and nobody moved in the creaky house. That meant Ben had extra time on his hands, and he thought of another thing he needed to do before turning in. He went to the telephone on the wall and called Robin's number. He still felt a little guilty for taking Dunk and not her to the final show. But then Robin might have envied Ben when Sal picked him up.

As late as it was, Robin answered fast. When she heard his first words, she said "Are you *sick?*"

"Do I sound sick?"

"No but, boy, it's deep in the *night*—where are you?"

Ben said "I'm at home; don't worry. I just wanted to tell you some news."

She said "Your dad's drunk," as if it were a fact.

Ben didn't really know but he said "No he's not."

"You went to the circus, I'll bet."

Ben said "Who told you?"

She waited a little. "I'm younger but I'm not *that* dumb, O High Wazuma. With an elephant in town for just one more night, where else would you be?" She'd learned the name *Wazuma* from Dunk, but this was the first time she'd tried it on Ben.

Ben laughed as quietly as he could manage. "That's why I woke you up—to tell you how it went. See, I figured there wouldn't be anything new; so I didn't ask you again, but—"

Robin broke in. "I'm glad you took Dunk."

"*Good.* You know Dunk never gets to go to things; so I took him, free, with the passes I had. And I was almost right—the show was pretty much the same as Thursday night till down near the end." Ben paused to be sure he should tell her the rest.

"*Hello?* Was there some kind of accident?"

He said "Oh no, it was better than that. But the best part came later. See, once it was over I went into Sal's tent to tell her goodbye—Mr. Duffy, the ringmaster, said I could. At first I was scared that Sal wouldn't know me; but she did and—and this is still amazing—she lifted me up, sat me on her back, and let me lean my head on her head." Again he paused to picture the moment and find the right words. He'd already decided not to mention the

mystery of why Sal had gripped him so tightly and held him so high. It would just keep Robin awake all night, trying to understand Sal's meaning.

Robin said "*Hello?* You're fading out again—are *you* drunk too?"

"Maybe so but I haven't been drinking. For the rest of my life, I'll probably wonder if it truly happened or was just a good dream—Sal picking me up and bearing my weight. That's the reason I've told *you* now. You can always remind me how a strong live elephant trusted me that much."

Robin said "Look, Ben, I'm sleepy but, sure, I'll remind you when we're old and gray." She gave a soft laugh.

And Ben joined her quietly. Then they talked awhile longer about their plans—Ben and his father were going to lunch at Robin's house tomorrow. It would be Sunday and her mother's birthday. Then Ben and Robin would go to a movie downtown in the late afternoon. By the time they'd planned that far ahead, Ben could hear Robin's breath slow down—she was almost snoring. He whispered "Sleep tight." When she didn't answer he thought she was gone. For an instant he felt completely deserted; and in spite of all the long night's pleasure, he feared he'd be this lonesome the rest of his life.

Then Robin spoke up, dazed but clear. "I'm waiting for you, O Fabulous Wazuma."

And they had a last laugh.

After Ben hung the phone up, he walked through the house from room to room, turning off lights and locking doors. He was still so deep in his excellent memories that he almost forgot to check on his father. So he climbed in silence to the top of the stairs, and from there he could hear the usual rasp of his father's breath. There were moments when the breathing would stop, and you might wonder if he'd died or vanished, but then the rasping would start again. Mr. Barks had said he inherited snoring from his own dead father and that, no doubt, Ben would start his snoring any night now.

Ben stopped in the doorway of the first bedroom and waited till his eyes had opened to the dark. He could see his father's clothes, neat on the chair, and his father's body under the covers. When Mr. Barks had drunk a little too much, he was always careful to fold his clothes. But Ben stood there still for a moment to feel the relief of finding him safe. Then he turned to walk down the hall to his own room.

As he moved, though, his father said "Son, are you all right?"

"Yes sir, I just got in from the circus."

His father said "Isn't it late in the night? It feels like it might be four in the morning." For some reason Mr. Barks would never keep a clock in his room.

Ben said "It's about ten-thirty, I guess—maybe closer to eleven."

"Was the show good again?" Mr. Barks rolled over and lay on his back. For a good while he gazed at the ceiling so hard that Ben wondered if he too could somehow see stars.

To bring him back Ben decided to answer him truly. "Dad, the show was not as good as when we saw it together."

"I'm sorry" Mr. Barks said. "That tends to happen in shows—and in life." He laughed a little, turned to face Ben, but then started coughing.

It lasted so long Ben wondered if his father maybe had injured his throat and lungs with the snoring, and Ben was about to go help him sit up.

But then Mr. Barks was breathing better.

So once he was quiet, Ben said "There's some news, though. See, just after the main show ended, big Sal the elephant lifted me right up onto her back. I sat there, high, and looked all around us. It

felt pretty fine. Dunk saw it, he was there, Dunk can tell you it's true."

"Son, I don't need Dunk to tell me. You never lied to me yet, not that I know of."

Ben said "No sir, nothing big anyhow." He knew he'd left out the scary part, and he'd have to warn Dunk not to mention it ever. He also didn't mention how glad he knew his mother would have been, here and now, if she could have stayed.

Mr. Barks said "I hope you're not bruised or cut."

Ben shook his head no. Under his shirt both his sides felt a little sore, but he knew that wouldn't matter at all. So he said "Sal treated me as careful as a child, like she might have had a calf of her own when she was real young."

"Then I'm glad for you, son. You deserved a good break. Go get some rest now."

Before Ben could turn again to leave, his father was back asleep, breathing calmly.

Ben's own room still had moonlight in it, all over the floor and on Ben's bed. He stood in the light till his body felt warm in the silver shine. Then slowly he took off his clothes and smelled them to check for any last traces of Sal. His jeans had a mild clean odor of straw but nothing stronger. As he mostly did, Ben

spread them out on the chair by his bed. Then standing in the midst of the floor, he was instantly tired all over his body. But he thought he might keep this worn pair of jeans forever, to help him recall this excellent night. He said to himself "That might look silly once I'm grown." Well, he knew he could think about that in the morning. For now he wanted to plunge into sleep where he could try to see dream pictures of himself and Sal—Ben high in the air with Sal beneath him, two trusty companions.

He'd intended to say a quick prayer of thanks before he slept. But in less than a minute after his head sank into the pillow, Ben was resting as deeply as if he were diving through a lake of black water. And what came soon to his sleeping mind, instead of prayers or pictures of Sal, were many dream visits from his young mother. He hadn't seen her this clearly in the months since she stayed in the hospital all those hard nights as Ben and his father watched her leave. Now, though, she looked refreshed again and a lot better. She was wearing a dress that Ben remembered—the one she'd worn when they first drew pictures, long years ago.

She asked how he was.

He said "Mother, I'm a good deal better—you seem to be too."

She nodded and asked him to call her by her first name. In life her name had been Gail Barks. Was it still Gail now? Ben thought he'd try it once anyhow, and she could correct him if he was wrong. He said the word "Gail" and then just watched her in the dark of his mind.

At the name she nodded and moved nearer toward him. When she got to just a few steps away, Ben could see that she seemed peaceful finally to be in the far-off place where she'd gone. He could also tell she was curious to know how her son was and where he was headed in the years to come.

She stood down past the foot of his bed—where he could just see her—and she said "Tell me everything you want me to know."

Ben worked hard to give her the answer; but hard as he worked to find clear words, all she needed to know amounted to this—*Tonight I was carried very close to where you are. I got to the edge of what felt like dying, and then I got lifted as high as I've been since I was a young child and you and I played wonderful games that you made up and then let me win. So, see, my spirits have really improved. I can hope to go on and grow up now and maybe live like a trustworthy man with a useful job and a family I can keep.*

Gail Barks smiled but stayed in place, still ready for more.

So again and again Ben told her the cause of this new hope. He told her every small detail of his recent luck with a perfect friend named Sala— Sacred Tree—and his mother seemed thoroughly glad to hear it, over and over, all through the night till she left him at daybreak.

DATE DUE